MIND FOR MURDER

EMILY SWANSON BOOK 2

MALCOLM RICHARDS

StormHouse

Storm House Books

Copyright © 2016, 2019 Malcolm Richards

Large print edition, 2020.

ISBN 978-1-9162104-5-5

Previously published as 'Cruel Minds' in 2016.

**THIS BOOK IS WRITTEN IN
UK ENGLISH.**

PROLOGUE

He ran through the forest, stumbling blindly in the darkness. Rain lashed against his skin. Low hanging branches whistled past his eyes. He didn't know where he was going. But they were coming for him. And if they found him, they would kill him.

Sounds filled his ears as he dashed forward. The machine gun rat-a-tat of rain on leaves; the howl of the wind whipping the trees into a frenzy; the crunch of foliage underfoot. He pushed on, lungs burning, pain throbbing where, just moments ago, fists and boots had pummelled his body.

He risked a glance over his shoulder. White lightning strobed through the canopy, quickly followed by a deafening crack of thunder. He turned back again, tripped over an exposed root and slammed into a tree. His body twisted and spun, hitting the ground hard and punching the air from his lungs. For a moment, he lay there, stunned and struggling for breath. Then, from somewhere behind, he heard the thud of footsteps running straight towards him.

Adrenaline fired through his limbs. Scrambling to his feet, he launched himself forward and got running again. More lightning ripped across the sky, briefly illuminating the forest as if it were daytime.

There was a clearing up ahead. Sitting in its centre was an old shack. He knew he shouldn't go in there. He knew he should keep running. But now he was on the porch and trying the door. Now the pain from the beating he'd endured was consuming his whole body.

The door was unlocked. Shouldering it open, he ducked inside, closed the door again and pressed himself up against the wood. Thunder rolled overhead. Rain attacked the tin roof like a blacksmith hammering on molten metal. Another burst of lightning lit up the room. He was inside a tool shed crammed with shelves. Sharp blades and instruments hung from hooks on the wall.

His heart began to race out of control. A wave of dizziness swept over him. He dropped to his hands and knees, and white-hot fire shot through his broken fingers. He bit down hard on his lip, choking back nausea and a scream. He half crawled, half dragged himself across the dirty floor, until he reached the furthest corner and curled into a ball in the shadows.

He waited. Seconds slipped by, then a minute, his pulse beating in time with the rain. He was beginning to wonder if he was safe here. If they had given up trying to find him.

But he had already been found.

A shadow passed outside the window. The door handle turned and the door swung open, letting in the wind and rain.

The world fell away. He held his breath and tried to make himself small. Boots, heavy and deliberate, stomped across the floor.

He was trapped in the corner like hunted prey. He needed to fight back. To find a weapon and lash out. But his strength was gone. Darkness embraced his body like his mother's arms, when he had once been small and infantile. When he had once been innocent.

Lightning lit up the room. A figure loomed over him, with a blade, curved and cruel-looking, raised up to the ceiling.

"Please," he begged, lifting his shattered fingers in front of his face. "I didn't mean to hurt anyone. It's not my fault!"

The figure stood there, motionless, the blade wavering.

"Please! I'll leave and never come back. You won't ever see me again."

For a second, he thought he was safe. That he would be spared.

Then the blade came down, cutting through the air and deep into his flesh. He screamed as it swung, again and again. Tearing. Slicing. Spilling blood as black as night. Until he was silent. Until he was still. His final, ragged breath floating away on the cold night air.

He became one with darkness.

He became nothing.

CHAPTER 1

Emily Swanson sat on the sofa with her knees pressed together and her arms folded across her stomach, staring at the empty cream walls. The room needed something more. More character. More things. Perhaps a framed painting or a decorative mirror, a potted plant or two in the window. She understood that the blandness was deliberate; nothing to look at meant little chance of distraction. But surely a splash of colour here or there wouldn't hurt.

Attempting a discreet sigh, her gaze moved from the walls to the coffee table, then to the desk in the corner. It was a very tidy desk, she noted, its contents neatly stacked and its surface free of dust. Like the room, it was lacking something. A vase of flowers to brighten it up or an ornamental paperweight.

Movement flickered at the corner of Emily's eye. She turned to stare at the woman who was sitting in the armchair by the window, warm sunlight spilling over her legs. Kirsten Dewar was mid-thirties and smartly dressed, with dark hair and olive skin that contrasted with Emily's blonde ponytail and pale complexion. She had a pleasant face with keen eyes that smiled even when her lips didn't; like now, as she sat with a notepad balanced on her knee and a pen poised over the paper.

This was their sixth meeting in as many weeks. Each session began the same way. After exchanging polite greetings, Kirsten would lead Emily into the room, pour them both a glass of water, and position herself in the armchair. Then she would sit in silence, waiting.

Even now, Emily found those first few minutes excruciating. What was she supposed to say? Was she meant to come with a prepared speech, or did she sit on the couch until her thoughts found their way from her mind to her mouth and spoke for themselves? In their first session together, Emily and Kirsten had sat through twelve minutes of silence, time slowing down with each passing second. Then Emily had embarrassed herself by crying.

The opening silence had thankfully grown shorter with each meeting. At some point soon, Emily assumed it might even vanish altogether. Now, as the fifth minute ticked by, she drew in a long, steady breath and tried to clear her mind of thoughts. Words began to appear, formulating a sentence.

"I slept a whole four hours last night," she said. The knots in her shoulders instantly began to loosen. Her hands remained tucked beneath her thighs.

Kirsten smiled. "Well, that's a lot better than three. Are you feeling better for it?"

"More like I've been hit by a truck. Which is definitely an improvement on being hit by a steamroller."

Kirsten nodded, jotting on her notepad. "Still, it's only been a week since you came off the sleeping pills."

"Ten days to be exact."

"You know if you're not ready, there's no written rule saying you have to stop taking them just yet."

Emily heaved her shoulders. There was a water stain on the bottom left corner of the coffee table. It irritated her, and had done so since her first visit.

"Yes, but one less pill means I don't rattle as much when I walk. Besides, I've started experimenting with valerian root. Next I'll be taking up witchcraft and sorcery."

Kirsten smiled. It was a kind smile, Emily thought. Genuine.

"And how is your sleep when you have it?"

"You mean, am I still having the same nightmare?"

"Are you?"

"A night wouldn't be complete without it."

In the dream, she was tied down to a steel gurney in a stark, white room, and surrounded by surgeons dressed in bloody gowns. Their dead blue eyes stared down at her over their face masks, while in their hands they carried an array of surgical instruments and syringes of neon blue liquid. As needles pricked her skin and scalpels flashed in the overhead light, the voice of her dead mother whispered in her ear. 'Don't worry. It will all be over soon. Then you'll sleep forever.'

Kirsten leaned forward, her smile fading as she rested her pen on the notepad.

"What you went through was incredibly traumatic. Your mind needs time to process it all. Dreams can be an outlet, a way for your unconscious to make sense of it all. I know it may not seem much of a comfort, but it does offer an endgame."

"But I know exactly what happened to me," Emily replied. "I was abducted from my home, put into a coma for three months, then drugged and experimented upon by a maniac. I'd say I've processed it enough."

Kirsten watched her for a moment. "What happened to you won't just disappear overnight. If you break a leg, you can't just get up and walk again. The bone needs time to heal. For that to happen, the leg needs support in the form of a cast and a pair of crutches. Why should your mind be any different?"

"Tell that to Doctor Chelmsford. He believed trauma could be wiped from the mind like dirt from a window. Sometimes I wonder if he was right—do we always need to remember all the bad things that happen to us?"

"Doctor Chelmsford's rather archaic school of thought and deeply unethical means of experimentation are the reasons why he'll be spending the rest of his life behind bars. Doesn't that tell you something?"

"It tells me it's all done with," Emily said. "It's over. Now all I want to do is get on with my life."

"And there's nothing wrong with that. Making plans for the future is part of the healing process." Kirsten picked up her pen and scribbled notes onto her pad. "Tell me, what does getting on with your life look like?"

Emily glanced away, her gaze returning to the stain on the table. Two months had passed since her horrific ordeal at the hands of Doctor Chelmsford. How long would the nightmares last? How long before she could set foot in a hospital, or her GP's office, or even here at the therapy centre, without breaking into a cold sweat?

What did getting on with her life really mean? It meant sleeping through a night unaided. It meant waking up each morning without screaming and having to remind herself that she was safe.

Kirsten was staring at her, waiting for a response.

"I want to have an ordinary day with no bad feelings," Emily said. "I want people to stop asking me how I'm doing every two minutes, as if I'm made of glass and I'm about to break. The truth is I broke a long time ago. If I can be okay with that, why can't everyone else?"

"People care about each other. It's human nature. Don't you think that's a good thing? To have people in your life who are concerned about your welfare?"

Emily bit down on her lower lip and stared through the window at the bland view of rooftops. Sunlight glanced off the windowpanes, making her squint.

"The people in my old life turned against me," she said.

Kirsten continued to scribble down notes, the scratch of pen on paper the only sound in the room.

"Are you worried that's going to happen again with your new friends?"

"I worry about a lot of things, as you know."

"What about the journalists? Are they still calling?"

"The story is old news for now. Chelmsford and the others are awaiting trial. I'm sure the press will come snooping again when that happens." She paused, the muscles in her shoulders knitting together again. "Coming to London was supposed to be about wiping the mirror clean. I had this big idea about becoming a different person. A better person. Someone with confidence and courage. Someone who's not afraid to speak her mind or to stand up for those who can't stand up for themselves. But here I am, still worrying. Still afraid. Like nothing's changed at all. If only my brain came with an off switch."

Kirsten leaned forward. "Emily, you've been through so much this last year, long before what happened with the doctors. Losing your mother, then Phillip Gerard's suicide—those two events alone are enough to send anyone over the edge. But you're sitting here today as a survivor. You're strong. Much stronger than you give yourself credit for."

"I don't feel strong."

"How do you feel?"

"Guilty."

"For being unable to save your mother? For being unable to prevent the suicide of a young boy who had been systematically abused by his father for most of his short life? Tell me, how do you stop cancer, Emily? How do you anticipate someone's behaviour when they can't even anticipate it themselves?"

Emily looked away, tears forming at the corners of her eyes. "I spent my whole life hiding in the shadows. My mother saw to that. I know she couldn't help it. Even before the cancer killed her, she'd been unwell for years; never leaving the house, never letting me have friends, always worrying something bad would happen even on the brightest of days. She trapped me, just like she was trapped inside her own fear. Teaching set me free. It didn't matter I was back in the town I grew up in; every day I got to explore a new world with those children. Even with Phillip . . ." She shook her head, setting a tear free. "I should have saved him. I was his teacher and he turned to me for help. Instead, I behaved like a monster."

"He was taunting you. You were in a deep state of grief. You lost control just for a moment. Emily, we wouldn't be human if we didn't have moments when we're not in control. Phillip Gerard was not in control."

"Phillip Gerard was an eleven-year-old boy. I was an adult who should have known better."

"Even though you'd just lost your mother after giving up months of your life to care for her?"

Silence filled the room. Emily avoided the therapist's gaze and stared at the floor. A brightly coloured rug would surely light up the drabness of the carpet.

"Imagine you had a sister and she was sitting right next to you, right at this moment," Kirsten said. "Imagine she's a teacher, and she tells you that a boy in her class killed himself because she shouted at him. Does that sound palpable to you? Does shouting at someone drive them to take their own life? Or is there a more credible explanation? What would you say to your sister?"

Emily stared at the empty space beside her.

"I'd tell her we all make mistakes," she said in a whisper.

"Yes, we do." Kirsten picked up her pen again. "And we're focusing so much on the loss of life that we're forgetting something hugely important."

Emily looked up. "What's that?"

"That you saved lives."

"Some, I suppose. But some were lost, too. Others, damaged beyond repair."

"And you think that's your fault?" Kirsten frowned. "You saved lives, Emily. You discovered corruption that was so horrendous the perpetrators almost killed you to prevent the truth from getting out. Yet you risked everything to tell the world. Now, justice will be served. The patients those doctors were experimenting on are alive today because you had the courage to intervene. You should be proud of what you've achieved. And you should place the blame firmly in the hands of the guilty."

Emily felt a tingling in her chest. She squeezed her eyes shut, preventing more tears from escaping.

"I'm trying," she said.

Kirsten smiled warmly. "You'll get there. You will. It's just a matter of time and learning to forgive yourself."

Emily opened her eyes again. She returned the therapist's smile. "In that case, it's lucky I have all the time in the world."

CHAPTER 2

The woman stepped from the shadows, a .45 pistol in her hand. She'd been watching them through the window, fires burning in her eyes. See how they smile and laugh, her expression said. See how together they are, how wholesome—a picture-postcard nuclear family society tells us to aim for. And she was aiming for them. They were in her sights.

As she revealed herself, emerging from the shadows and stepping into the well-lit kitchen, the perfect family turned and froze in a frightened tableau. At the head of the table, recognition spread across Jerome Miller's face like cracks in ice. Perspiration beaded his dark reddish brown skin.

"Please," he said, eyes growing wide. "Don't hurt them. They're all I have."

The children started to cry. At the far end of the table, their mother stared at Jerome, then at the woman in the red dress, who now had all the power, who could decimate the family with a squeeze of a trigger.

"You don't have to do this," Jerome said, carefully putting down his fork and raising his hands high above his head. "It's me you want. It's me that's wronged you. Let them live and take me."

Tears slipped from the woman's eyes, but the gun in her hand was steady and unmoving.

"I loved you," she whimpered. "And you loved me. You promised me the world. Now you've taken it all away."

"Please!" Jerome begged. "Put the gun down and let's talk about this!"

The woman in the red dress threw her head back like a lioness and laughed. Her jaw snapped shut. Her face contorted with hate.

She squeezed the trigger twice. Two loud gunshots shattered the air. Jerome flew back, crashing onto the table, knocking dinner plates to the floor. His family stared in shocked silence.

"I'm sorry," whispered the woman in the red dress. She placed the barrel of the gun to her temple and fired. As she fell, the room plunged into darkness.

The silence seemed to last for an hour. Then came the squeak of rollers as large red curtains moved across the stage. No sooner had the curtains closed, they parted again to reveal Jerome, who was now very much alive and standing centre-stage. His wife and children stood on his right, the woman in the red dress on his left. Other bodies swept in from the wings. As the audience rippled with sparse and unforgiving applause, the actors bowed.

Twenty minutes later, the dingy theatre bar was alive with voices and clinking glasses.

"So, what did you think?"

Emily sipped her orange juice as she looked around. Crushed blue velvet covered the walls. Gold-painted cornice, which was cracked and faded, decorated the edges of the nicotine-stained ceiling. A few of the other actors were gathered around tables with friends and family, who had come to see the show and now sat, smiling and nodding emphatically; a clear sign that they had hated every minute.

Jerome tapped his wine glass as he waited for Emily's verdict.

"It was terrible," she said, at last. "Badly written, predictable, not to mention completely misogynistic. But I thought you were very good."

"Thank you. That was very succinct. As an unemployed person, perhaps you should consider writing reviews for the papers."

"Perhaps I will."

Shoulders sinking, Jerome said, "Seriously though, for our opening night there was no one here. If numbers don't pick up tomorrow, we're finished. Then it's back to waiting tables for me."

"Which, to be honest, has more ethical merit than The Devil Wears a Red Dress." Emily twirled the straw in her glass, then looked up to see Jerome's wounded expression. "You're too talented for crap like that. I'm sure another play will come along. Something better."

"Thanks for your positivity." Jerome winced as he gulped his wine. "Jesus, for the amount they charge per glass you'd think they'd invest in something a little classier. Cheap shits." He stared at Emily, who was lost somewhere in the space between them. "What's wrong? I know the show was bad but you've got a face on you like a cat's backside."

"I'm flattered you could tear yourself away from your ego for a moment to notice."

They both smiled, then laughed.

"Touché," Jerome said. "What's up?"

"Bad day at the office."

"Therapy? What did the delectable Doctor Dewar have to say today?"

"That's confidential and you know it."

"Sorry. My lack of boundaries knows no bounds. You know I'm here if you need to talk."

Emily nodded as she stared into her glass. "Thanks. But can we talk about something other than my addled mind?"

"But it's so much fun!" Jerome winked, then reached over to squeeze her hand. "We could talk about my lucrative career path as waiter to the denizens of London. Or the fact your sofa's going to need new springs soon if I don't save enough money for my own place. What a pair we are!"

He laughed. It was such a deep, heartfelt sound that Emily couldn't help but smile.

"You know you can stay with me as long as you want."

Jerome took another sharp sip of wine. "And I appreciate it. But sooner or later, we're both going to want our own space. Heaven help us, maybe we'll both get boyfriends! Besides, not to sound ungrateful, but that sofa is wreaking havoc on my posture."

"Is it weird? Living directly above your old apartment?"

"A little. But mostly because I despise the couple that moved in there. Awful people! I shared the lift with them the other day and they reacted like I was about to pull a knife and snatch their wallets. I'm surprised Harriet hasn't had anything to say about them."

Emily pushed her orange juice away. Laughter exploded from the adjacent table. The noise level in the bar was getting louder by the minute.

"I don't think Harriet's been out of her apartment much. I'm worried about her," she said.

"I know what you mean," Jerome said, nodding in agreement. "She hasn't been the same since her fall."

"It wasn't a fall and you know it."

Emily sighed, feeling the muscles in her chest contract. A group of twenty-somethings spilled through the bar door, their excited chatter adding to the din. She frowned. She wasn't much older than them but sometimes she felt she'd already lived a hundred lives.

Her thoughts returned to today's session with Kirsten, to her desire to move on with her life.

How was she going to do it? She felt trapped; as if the floor was quicksand and she was sinking further and further into a perpetual gloom.

The bar closed in around her. Bodies pressed against each other, forming an impenetrable wall between Emily and the exit. A handsome man called to Jerome, beckoning him to the bar, where a group of cast members had gathered.

"Do you want to meet the guys?" Jerome was staring at her, concern wrinkling his otherwise flawless skin.

Emily shook her head. "There's only so much fun you can have with orange juice. Go have fun. I'll see you at home."

"Are you sure you're all right?"

"Go, before I tell your friends all about how you never wash your underwear."

"Emily Swanson, you're a scurrilous liar."

Concern gave way to a blinding smile. Jerome leaned over, planted a kiss on her forehead, then bounded over to join his friends.

The night was warm and sticky. Londoners still sat on terraces and crowded the pavements outside of bars, making the most of the above average June temperatures. It didn't matter that it was Tuesday and there were jobs to go to in the morning. Emily walked along the Strand, moving away from the towering lions of Trafalgar Square, where tourists still posed for pictures despite the late hour. Soon, she was moving along Fleet Street, once home to the country's national newspapers and named after London's largest underground river.

She still preferred to walk than take the Underground. The idea of being squeezed into one of those trains along with millions of other bodies filled her with sweat-inducing claustrophobia. Besides, walking had helped her to get to know the city well. She had learned which streets were the busiest and which backstreets to take to avoid them. Despite the constant pushing and shoving, she was getting better at manoeuvring through the crowds. But if there were quieter, less stressful routes to get to places, then it seemed ridiculous not to take them. And at least she was getting to places instead of staying cooped up in her apartment, slowly losing her mind.

Taking a left onto Fetter Lane, she journeyed to Holborn Circus, crossed the busy junction, and continued onto Farringdon. It wasn't long before she was back home at The Holmeswood, a Gothic style apartment building hidden among the skyscrapers, where she stood, sipping valerian tea in front of her living room windows on the fourth floor. Below, the street was empty and quiet. Above, the sky was a muddy green—the darkest London was ever going to get.

Thoughts played over in her mind like an orchestra tuning their instruments. She tried to shut them out, but they were relentless; taunting her, pointing accusing fingers. Putting down her cup, Emily fetched sheets and pillows from the hallway closet and made up Jerome's bed on the sofa. He would normally make it himself, but she had a sneaking suspicion that tonight he would require a little assistance. The bed made up, she switched out the living room lights and padded along the hallway to her bedroom.

This was the worst part of the day, and she approached it with quiet dread. Kirsten had told her sleep would be the hardest nut to crack. After being induced into a three-month coma against her will, it was no surprise that her unconscious mind now associated sleep with blind terror. The sleeping pills had helped at first. But drugging herself nightly with more chemicals didn't exactly feel like a cure.

Alongside exploring alternative natural remedies, Kirsten had provided Emily with a CD of relaxation exercises. Slipping it into the player, she hit the play button and sank into an armchair. As calming music began to fill the room, she placed her heels flat on the floor and rested her hands on her lap. Kirsten's velvety voice tickled her ears.

"Close your eyes. Take in a deep, wide breath through your nose. Now, let it out slowly through your mouth. Imagine you are in a calm place. Somewhere you feel safe. A forest or a beach. Take a moment to feel the warm sun on your face and a gentle breeze against your skin . . ."

The bedroom slipped away. Trees grew up in its place. The minty scent of pine needles filled Emily's nose and melodic birdsong whistled in her ears.

"Take a moment to enjoy your surroundings. What do you see? What can you hear? You feel protected in this place. Nothing can harm you. Feeling very relaxed, you lie down..."

The trees turned to ash. White walls closed in around her. Harsh electric light crackled over her head. There was something inside her throat, filling her lungs, choking the life from her body.

Emily sprang out of the chair and switched off the CD. All she wanted was peace and quiet. How was she ever going to achieve that when her mind was constantly filled with chaos?

She wanted a sleeping pill. She wanted it now. It took all her willpower to stay away from the bathroom cabinet. Instead, she forced herself into bed and finished her valerian tea.

When she fell asleep two hours later, the doctors and their surgical instruments were waiting to greet her like old friends.

CHAPTER 3

"You know what you need, don't you?"

Emily tensed her shoulders. When Harriet Golding began with that question, she invariably followed it with 'children' or 'a man.'

"What you need is a holiday," the elderly woman said, as she pushed a cup and saucer towards her guest with a trembling hand. They were sitting in her cramped living room, surrounded by piles of books and shelves of ornaments.

Surprised, Emily thought of the last time she had taken a holiday. It had been seven years ago, when she'd brought her mother to

Somerset for a long weekend, and they'd stayed at a beautiful old guesthouse with a view of the River Sheppey. What should have been a relaxing break had quickly descended into twelve nerve-wrenching hours. Convinced that her house would burn down while she was away, Emily's mother had grown increasingly agitated. When she'd erupted into full-blown panic, Emily had packed up the car and driven them back home, the weekend over before it had even begun.

A holiday might be the answer, she thought. A few days away somewhere quiet, far from the noise and pollution of the city. Far from people.

"You know, that's the first good idea I've heard all week," Emily said. "And thank you for not trying to marry me off for once."

Harriet's cracked laughter was interrupted by a cacophony of coughs and splutters. Emily put down her cup and placed a hand on her neighbour's arm.

"Don't you go worrying yourself. I'm tough as old boots, me," Harriet said, waving Emily away, before spooning more sugar into her tea.

Emily stared at her, unconvinced. Her neighbour's health had been deteriorating the past two months, leaving her gaunt and tired-looking, with constantly trembling hands. The night she had been attacked by the doctors' men was taking its toll. Watching her friend grow frailer each day left a horrible ache in Emily's chest.

"You're looking at me funny," Harriet said, using a handkerchief to wipe spittle from the corner of her mouth. "I hope you're not sitting there blaming yourself again. I've told you a million times, the only ones to be pointing fingers at are the thugs who thought it was fine to throw an old woman down the stairs."

Emily stared at the carpet. "But it would never have happened if I hadn't given you—"

"I don't want to hear another word. The trouble with you, Emily Swanson, is you're always giving yourself a hard time. I'm still here, aren't I? And as long as there's still tea in the pot I ain't planning on going anywhere soon. Got it?"

Emily leaned forward and squeezed Harriet's hand. "You're a good friend," she said, smiling weakly. Despite Harriet's words, the guilty weight in her chest remained. She stared at the towers of books filling the room. "Where's that son of yours?"

Harriet snorted. "Andrew? I sent him for a walk. You know what he said to me this morning? That I should go into one of them retirement homes for old folk! I won't dirty the air with what I suggested he do in return. My own son, trying to get rid of me! What a travesty! When my time comes, I'll go quietly in the privacy of my own bed, thank you very much. If Andrew doesn't like it, he can take his bloody books and find his own place to live."

"I'm sure he's just concerned about your health."

"I tell you what that boy should be concerned with—finding himself a nice wife, that's what."

Emily tried to stifle her smile. At the age of fifty-two, Andrew hadn't been a boy for quite some time.

"Speaking of concerns," Harriet said, slurping her tea, "is Jerome still sleeping on your sofa?"

Emily nodded.

"People will talk, you know."

"Let them. Besides, I'm sure people have far more scandalous tales to gossip about than a friend sleeping on my sofa."

"All the same, you'd think he'd have found a place to live now you're back with us again. I hope he's not taking advantage of you."

Emily bit down on her lip, refraining from asking Harriet to mind her own business. "I'm sure Jerome will find his own place just as soon as he can afford to. Until that happens, he can stay as long as he likes. Anyway, it makes me feel safer having someone around."

Harriet narrowed her eyes. "I've said it before and I'll say it again—it's a pity he's fancy or you two would be perfect for each other. Still, you don't want him sleeping on your sofa for too long. What if that fiancé of yours shows up one day wanting to woo you back?"

Emily stiffened. Perhaps she would tell Harriet to mind her own business, after all. Not that it would do any good.

"I haven't spoken to Lewis in a year," she said through tight lips. "And if he did show up, the only thing he'd be wooing is the door in his face."

Cackling, Harriet set her cup and saucer down with a clatter. "You definitely need a holiday!"

———

By the time Emily returned to her apartment, her mind was clogged with unwanted memories. She found Jerome at the table, nursing a mug of coffee.

"How's the hangover?" she asked him.

"Like a pickaxe to the head. Where've you been?"

Emily slumped into the chair next to him. "Across the hall. Harriet is still convinced we'd make couple of the year. If only you weren't fancy."

"Fancy? That's a new one. Well, let the woman have her dream, I say. You have to feel sorry for her—she has more chance of us getting together than someone ever taking Andrew off her hands."

Emily prised the mug from his fingers and took a sip of coffee. She liked the way Jerome made it: syrupy and bittersweet.

"I think that's the last thing Harriet wants. She'd be all alone. Anyway, maybe Andrew's happy being single. There's more to life than getting married, you know."

"I think we're both living testaments to that." Jerome rubbed his tired eyes then returned his gaze to Emily. "Someone's got a bee in their bonnet. Why the angry face?"

"Harriet brought up Lewis again. I wish I'd never told her about him."

"She just wants to see you happy."

"By marrying the man who walked out on me after my mother died? Who chose to save his career rather than his relationship after everything happened with Phillip?"

"The man's a prick, and if I ever have the displeasure of meeting him, I shall tell him so, too." Jerome stole back his coffee. "Harriet's just being Harriet. She has an opinion about everything, but she doesn't mean any harm."

"Doesn't mean I have to like it, though." Emily sank lower in the chair. She could feel the start of a headache. Judging by the pressure already building at the base of her skull, it was going to be a humdinger. She glanced at Jerome, who'd picked up his phone and was flicking through emails.

"What are you doing this weekend?" she asked.

"Acting my heart out. Sunday's a day off, though. How come?"

"I was thinking about getting away for a few days."

Jerome glanced up from the screen. "You mean like a minibreak? Emily Swanson, you're becoming so London! I'm impressed. Did you want me to come with you?"

Emily shrugged a shoulder.

"So, Harriet was right. You're in love with me."

"The only person in love with you is you." She wrestled the coffee mug out of Jerome's hands again and brought it to her lips.

"A break would do you good, you know," Jerome said. "Recharge the batteries, reset that crazy brain of yours..."

"Less of the crazy, please."

"I'm just saying you've been through the wringer lately." He shifted his gaze for a second. "You're looking tired, too. I know you're still having trouble sleeping."

Emily stared at him, heat prickling her skin, then looked away. If Jerome had heard her screaming herself awake at night, he'd been keeping quiet about it. She shouldn't have been surprised, really. The walls of the apartment might be thick, but they weren't exactly soundproof.

"So where would you go on this minibreak?" Jerome asked, holding out a hand. Emily gave him back the mug, which was now empty.

"I don't know. Somewhere quiet and leafy with no crowds."

"Sounds terrifying." He frowned, then his face slowly lit up with an idea. "How about going on a weekend retreat? A friend of mine goes twice a year. He swears by it, says it helps put his life into perspective. You could work on your meditation or try out some yoga. Give your mind a spring clean."

A weekend dedicated to clearing her mind certainly sounded appealing. Emily had only just begun experimenting with meditation and was struggling to get the hang of it; perhaps a weekend of learning the correct techniques would help her decide if she should continue with it or try something new. But what if a weekend spent exploring the dark recesses of her mind accidentally freed all those nefarious thoughts she'd been keeping locked up in cages?

Or what if you're overthinking things, as usual?

She liked the idea of a retreat. Spending a weekend at a place designed for relaxation could only be a good thing. And surely they weren't all focused on meditation.

"You know, that's not a bad idea," she said.

Jerome shrugged and held up his hands. "What can I say? I've never had a bad idea in my life."

CHAPTER 4

Saturday came, bringing clear skies and warm spring sunshine. Emily headed out of London in a steady stream of traffic. It was the first time she'd driven a car since selling her beloved VW Beetle, which had been a gift to herself after graduating from university. When she'd moved to the city last year, owning a vehicle had felt superfluous.

The hire car, a three-door Peugeot hatchback, was easy enough to manoeuvre. It was the other drivers who were the problem. Negotiating London streets was like competing in an off-road rally where laws had no meaning. Cars pushed in front of her. They tailgated to make her speed up. Horns blasted at her to get a move on, even before traffic lights had switched from amber to green. Her anxiety levels rocketing, Emily sucked in a deep breath. Up ahead, a gridlock of traffic filled the road.

"Bloody weekend drivers." Reclining in the passenger seat, Jerome glanced up from his phone screen and emitted a glum sigh as the car ground to a halt. "What time are we meant to be at this place?"

"Last night," Emily said.

"You didn't have to wait for me, you know. You could have gone on your own."

Having to endure Jerome's current mood was beginning to make Emily wish that she had.

"What's this place called, anyway?"

Emily sighed. "For the fourth time, Meadow Pines."

"Well, I hope Meadow Pines has an internet connection."

"I thought the point of a retreat was to get away from all that. Peace and quiet. Back to nature and all its beauty."

"For normal people, yes. But now I'm facing a hellish life of waiting tables yet again, I need to keep my car to the stage floor."

"About that . . ."

"You don't need to say another word." Jerome tugged the seatbelt away from his neck, then returned to staring at his phone screen.

"I was just going to say I'm sorry," Emily said.

Two days ago, the cast of The Devil Wears a Red Dress had learned that Friday's performance would be their last. Scathing reviews, social media backlash, and pitiful audience numbers had left the theatre with little choice but to shut the play down. Emily had managed to book Jerome the one remaining place at Meadow Pines, the countryside retreat they were now travelling to. It had meant missing out on the opening evening, but despite Jerome's foul mood, she was glad to have a familiar face coming along.

Eventually breaking free from the exodus of traffic, Emily navigated the car onto the A3 and headed in the direction of southern Hampshire. Jerome switched on the radio, blasting rock music from the speakers. Ninety minutes later, they were crossing over the River Test and heading into the New Forest National Park: 218 square miles of unenclosed pastureland, heathland, and forests.

Jerome stared at the sweeping landscape of meadows. He'd abandoned his phone a few miles back, complaining there was no signal.

"I hate the countryside," he muttered.

Emily eased her foot down on the brake pedal. Ahead of them, a young pony with dappled hide stood at the roadside, grazing on grass.

"Look at that!" she said, smiling.

Jerome shrugged a shoulder. "Shouldn't it be in a field or something?"

Further along, a chestnut mare and her young foal stood in the centre of the road, unconcerned by the vehicle and its passengers.

"They're New Forest ponies," Emily said, enthralled by the gentle beasts. "They've lived here freely for thousands of years. In fact, that's why there's so much heathland— because of all the grazing."

"Great. Try not to hit them on the way around."

Giving Jerome a sideways glance, Emily rolled the car forward and drove in a wide arc around the ponies.

"There are all sorts of wild animals roaming around," she continued. "Deer, donkeys, even cattle. In fact, the New Forest has a very interesting history."

As heathland disappeared and thick forest grew up on either side of the winding road, Jerome muttered under his breath and sank further into his seat. Emily cleared her throat, eager to share her findings from her internet research.

"The forest was established in 1079 by William the Conqueror as a reserve for the royal hunt. What the tourist board doesn't tell you is that he destroyed over twenty small villages and farmsteads in the process, making their inhabitants homeless."

"Nice guy."

"Yes, well, some believe King William was punished by the forest for such cruel behaviour. Cursed you might say." Emily's voice had taken on an overly dramatic tone, remnants of her teaching career. "Both of William's sons lost their lives while hunting within those trees. First Prince Richard, who died after inhaling a pestilent air. Then Prince Rufus, who was killed by a misdirected arrow.

No sooner had William mourned his sons, tragedy struck again. His grandson, Henry, was pursuing deer through the forest when he was suddenly torn from his steed. The huntsmen found him hanging above the ground, choked to death by tree branches; quite literally slain by the forest."

Emily smiled to herself. The children had always enjoyed her gruesome tales from the annals of history, particularly if they had involved beheadings or burnings at the stake.

"You can take the teacher out of the school but you can't take the school out of the teacher," Jerome said, glancing up at the tree canopies that whipped by overhead.

A twinge of anxiety broke through Emily's excitement. She didn't want to think about school or being a teacher. That part of her life was over and she had no business revisiting it. As they drove deeper into the forest, she refocused her attention on the surrounding greenery. Living in London had its merits, but she still missed the unpolluted air of the countryside. The pace of life was so different, too. While London was in constant motion, a great machine in which its millions of inhabitants were the cogs that kept it moving, the countryside was governed by nothing and no one. It was alive; a living, breathing entity that had existed long before people and was likely to continue existing long after they'd faded into the ether.

The trees began to fall back, replaced by grassland and roadside cottages with thatched roofs. Minutes later, they came upon the ancient village of Lyndhurst, which had stood for at least a thousand years and was known as the New Forest's capital. The high street was busy, scores of tourists ambling along the pavements and snapping pictures of the Tudor and medieval architecture. Others were busy taking photographs of the village's other visitors: a small herd of cattle trotting along the side of the road, snout to tail.

Emily drove on, leaving the sights of Lyndhurst dwindling in the rear-view mirror. In the passenger seat, Jerome shook his head. They passed more cottages, then the tiny village of Emery Down. The road narrowed into a single lane. Trees grew up again, immersing the car and its passengers in a shadowy expanse of greens and browns.

"Do they at least have a TV at this place?" Jerome asked. They were the first words he'd spoken in fifteen minutes.

A car was approaching from the opposite direction. Emily shrugged as she slowed down, then pulled over to let the vehicle pass. "You didn't have to come along. I just thought it would be nice. Something to take your mind off the play shutting down."

"I know and I'm grateful. But even if I didn't want to come, you can't be left alone. Look what happened to you the last time."

"I've been a grown woman for some time now. I don't need a chaperone, thank you very much."

The forest grew thicker, the light darker. The coolness of the shade prickled Emily's skin, distracting her from the irritation burning in her chest like indigestion. By the time she turned off the road minutes later, the irritation had given way to determination. She was going to have a relaxing weekend, even if it killed her. Although his current expression said otherwise, she was sure Jerome would, too; just as soon as he'd rid himself of his hangover.

Pulling into a small stretch of gravel that served as a car park, Emily wedged the Peugeot in between two other vehicles and turned off the engine. In front of them was a large, flat meadow where families of fallow deer, many of them with unusual white coats, grazed on feed left by local park keepers. Jerome stared up at the large sign by the car park entrance.

"Bolderwood Deer Sanctuary? If I knew we were going hunting, I would have brought my trapper hat."

To the left of the parked vehicles, clusters of visitors stood watching on a purpose-built viewing platform. One young boy leaned over the railings, shouting and jeering at the placid-looking creatures while his family clicked away on their phones and cameras. All around the deer sanctuary, the ancient oak trees of Bolderwood rolled out as far as the eye could see.

"This doesn't much look like a retreat to me," Jerome said.

"It's our meeting point. Meadow Pines is a little tricky to get to by car, so we're getting picked up."

"Exactly where are you taking me?"

Smiling, Emily pushed open the driver door. "Come on, grumpy. Let's grab our bags."

Stepping onto the gravel, she took in a breath and let it out steadily. The air was heavy with forest smells. The sun was warm on her skin. Any anxiety she'd been feeling was brushed away. She watched Jerome shut the car door, then adjust his sunglasses. He looked around, lips curling in disapproval.

"It's not even a proper car park," he complained, kicking at the loose gravel.

"Toto, we're not in London anymore."

"You may jest, but at least London feels safe. Anything could happen out here."

"Safe? Have you seen the latest crime statistics?"

"I bet they don't include being eaten alive by a herd of ravenous ponies."

As they pulled out their backpacks from the boot of the car, Emily's gaze wandered over to the deer. They were beautiful; their white coats giving them a mystical, ethereal appeal.

She couldn't understand why Jerome found the natural world so unnerving.

A loud grumble of an engine unsettled the animals. A few of the young looked up, ears twitching, snouts sniffing the air, as a mud-encrusted Land Rover turned off the road and pulled onto the gravel. Emily and Jerome watched the driver turn off the engine and climb out. She was a pale-skinned young woman, perhaps in her early twenties, with wavy red hair that she wore tied behind her back. She opened the file in her hands, pulled out a card, and held it up. Written in black ink were the words: Emily Swanson & Jerome Miller.

"Be nice," Emily whispered.

Jerome nudged her in the ribs as they walked towards the Land Rover.

"Hi, I'm Marcia Hardy. I'm the assistant manager at Meadow Pines," the young woman said, as she returned the name card to her folder. She shook Emily's hand, then hesitated slightly before shaking Jerome's. "You came from London?"

"That's right," Emily said.

"One of our other guests came from there as well. I've never visited, but I'd like to."

Marcia shifted from one foot to the other. Her gaze flitted from Jerome to the ground, then back again.

"You're better off here in the peace and quiet," Emily said. "And peace and quiet are exactly what I'm here for. Did we miss much yesterday evening?"

"In terms of activities, not really. Pamela will explain more about that. You did miss the welcome dinner last night, but you still have plenty of time to get to know the other guests. If you choose to, that is."

She stared at Jerome again.

"Who's Pamela?" he asked.

"Pamela owns Meadow Pines. She's also my mother. Well, if you'd like to put your bags in the back, I'll drive you to the house. It's a few miles into the woods and a bit of a bumpy ride down an old dirt track. You might want to hold on to something."

"We just leave the car here?" Jerome said, casting a suspicious eye over the tourists on the viewing platform. "What if someone steals it?"

"Our guests leave their vehicles here all the time. We've never had any trouble. No one ever comes out this way at night and during the day it's just tourists."

Peeling her gaze from Jerome's face, Marcia turned and opened the rear door of the Land Rover.

"I think you have a fan," Emily whispered, nudging him in the arm.

Jerome narrowed his eyes. "Oh my God, he's not white! Run for the hills!"

Both smiling, they threw in their bags, then climbed into the backseat of the Land Rover.

"Here we go," Marcia said. Starting the engine, she drove the vehicle out of the parking area and headed north.

———

They'd been on the road for two minutes when the forest suddenly disappeared. Heathland speckled with grazing ponies filled the view. Spinning the wheel, Marcia took a sharp left. The Land Rover skidded, almost turning a hundred and eighty degrees. In the backseat, Jerome slammed into Emily's side. The smooth asphalt road came to an end, replaced by a narrow gravel track that was barely wide enough to contain the Land Rover.

"Sorry about that," Marcia called from the front. "It's going to be a bit of a rough ride from here."

The vehicle's passengers bounced up and down as its wheels ran in and out of large potholes. Emily couldn't hide her amusement as Jerome held onto the passenger door, the barrel of red wine he'd imbibed the night before now threatening to resurface.

The road, if it could be called that, plunged back into the forest. Marcia shifted gears and threaded the steering wheel between her hands. The Land Rover slid off the gravel and into the trees. Soon they were weaving between towering trunks, following a muddy track.

"Have either of you visited a retreat before?" Marcia asked as she expertly steered the vehicle around a large fallen branch.

Emily shook her head. "It's our first time."

She was suddenly thrown forward as the vehicle headed down a stony incline. All around them the forest stirred.

"Well, Meadow Pines isn't your typical retreat," Marcia said, when they were on flat ground again.

"What do you mean?"

"Pamela will explain when we get there."

"How many other guests are staying?"

"We have a full house, so including the both of you and one other latecomer, that makes nine."

A flurry of birds whipped past the front of the Land Rover, arching up to the branches. The deeper the vehicle moved into the forest, the less light there was. It was like being underwater, Emily thought. Of all the retreats she'd researched, Meadow Pines had been one of the remotest. It wasn't easy getting away from people in a country as small as Great Britain. Sometimes, she wished she lived somewhere like America, where it would be easy to travel to places so remote you could go weeks without seeing another face. Short of scouring the country for a cave to dwell in, hiding out in the heart of the New Forest seemed like the most viable alternative.

Now, as they drove closer to their destination, Emily wondered about the other guests. Seven wasn't a huge number to contend with, but they would all be staying under one roof. It would only take one of them to recognise her from the newspapers and then any chance of a peaceful weekend would be snatched away.

As if reading her mind, Marcia said, "It's a big house with plenty of room, so people manage to stay out of each other's hair. Plus we have forty acres of private land for you to explore. It's mostly forest, but there are plenty of walking trails and we also have our own lake. Do either of you like to garden?"

Tightening his grip on the passenger door, Jerome glared at Emily.

"I used to, before moving to London," she said.

"Well, we grow all of our own vegetables at Meadow Pines, so we always appreciate any help out in the field. In fact, we're getting pretty self-sufficient. If Pamela had her way we'd be living fully off the grid, but we can't afford the initial expense of providing our own power sources. At least, not yet."

Emily watched the trees whistle past while the Land Rover continued its journey. "It sounds beautiful."

A few minutes later, just as Jerome's nausea was reaching uncontainable levels, Marcia brought the Land Rover to a halt but kept the engine running. A locked field gate blocked the way. Fishing out a bunch of keys from her jacket pocket, Marica selected one and handed it to Emily.

"Would you mind?"

Emily hopped out of the Land Rover and moved up to the gate, making quick work of the padlock. Swinging the gate open, she waved the Land Rover through, then secured the padlock once more. It seemed strange to have a locked gate this far out in the forest, but she supposed every property required boundaries. Even weekend retreats that aimed to break boundaries down.

"Thanks," Marcia called as Emily climbed back inside and handed her the keys.

The Land Rover got going again, taking them deeper into the trees. Emily glanced at Jerome, who was silent and frowning, his gaze fixed on the back of the driver seat. A few minutes later, the track opened on a wide, grassy clearing and the Land Rover ground to a halt.

"We have to walk from here," Marcia said, switching off the engine. "It's not far."

Climbing out, Emily and Jerome heaved their bags onto their shoulders and followed their guide across the clearing.

"How are you enjoying yourself so far?" Emily whispered.

Jerome shot her a sideways glance. "I hate you."

Through the undergrowth, they saw another path trailing off into the distance.

"This way," Marcia said.

They hiked along the dusty path that had been worn into the ground over time by hundreds of pairs of feet, all making the same journey. As they walked, Emily looked up at the jade-coloured canopy. Sunlight pierced through the leaves and shone in dusty spotlights on the forest floor. Insects buzzed and birds sang. She smiled. For the first time in months, the knotted muscles in her shoulders began to loosen. Next to her, Jerome glanced around with wide, anxious eyes.

The path grew narrower. Trees leaned in on both sides. Then as the path turned, the forest fell away and the trio emerged into bright sunlight.

"Welcome to Meadow Pines," Marcia said.

Before them was a meadow of tall grass and wildflowers. A grand, red-brick manor house surrounded by a low stone wall stood on the far side. Emily slid to a halt, admiring its sloping roof, pipe-like chimney stacks, and elegant latticed windows. Purple and white blooms of Clematis grew on trellises, covering the lower half of the house and drooping over the arched doorway.

To the right of the building was a large vegetable patch filled with rows of young potato plants, baby carrots and lettuces, and staked vines of beans. An old greenhouse sat just behind, glass panes and metal framework speckled with lichen. Tomato vines grew inside, their leaves pressing against the glass.

"It's incredible!" Emily gasped. It was as if their journey through the woods had led them a hundred years back through the passages of time.

Marcia smiled. "It's quite something isn't it? The house is Edwardian, built in 1905 as a hunting lodge by some lord or other. It stood empty for the longest time. Pamela acquired it ten years ago. She's worked hard to transform what was essentially a place built for violence into a place of great peace."

They were crossing the meadow now, Emily carefully placing her feet to avoid crushing the flowers. She risked a glance over her shoulder to see that Jerome was lagging behind, his face pulled into a scowl as he struggled with his bag. She had yet to tell him exactly what kind of a retreat they were about to enter, and now she wondered how badly he would react.

"I read that Meadow Pines used to be a meditation retreat," she said, turning back to Marcia, who nodded.

"We used to run a ten-day Vipassanā silent retreat. It's kind of the grandmother of mindfulness. But where mindfulness is about relieving stress and anxiety, Vipassanā is about liberation. Setting yourself free."

"From what?"

"From the self. From attachment."

Emily dropped her voice to a whisper. "And why change the retreat to what it is now?"

"Well," Marcia said, staring up at the house. "If you want to stay in business, you need to move with the times."

Emily followed her gaze. The front door had opened and now a tall, middle-aged woman with short silver hair was stepping out. She moved towards them in fluid strides, her cotton trousers and sleeveless blouse accentuating her toned limbs and perfect posture.

"Welcome friends," she said, smiling warmly as she extended a hand. "I'm Pamela Hardy and this is Meadow Pines. You must be Emily and Jerome."

"Pleased to meet you," Emily said, while Jerome muttered a half-hearted hello.

Pamela came to a standstill beside Marcia. The likeness between mother and daughter was strong. "I don't believe we've seen you here before, have we?"

Emily shook her head. "It's my first time. At any kind of retreat, actually."

"Well, in some ways that gives you an advantage. We run things a little differently around here, so you won't waste valuable time making comparisons." Pamela turned to face the house. "Let's get you all signed in, shall we? Then we can give you the grand tour."

Spinning on her heels with the grace of a dancer, she started back towards the open door, with Marcia trailing silently behind.

Emily shot a glance at Jerome, who was still frowning.

"Come on," she said.

They followed their hosts through the garden, where white rose bushes grew in tiny islands dotted around a well-kept lawn. As Emily stopped to admire them, she remembered the garden that she had lovingly tended back when her life had been so quiet that it had bordered on obsolete. Those memories felt foreign to her now, as if they had escaped from someone else's mind and found their way into her own.

Entering the house, she stepped inside a large foyer with a high ceiling and panelled walls. The temperature was noticeably cooler, and Emily paused to enjoy the tingling sensation on her skin. Pamela was on the move again, pushing a door open on the right and welcoming them into a small room that served as an office.

Taking a seat at her desk, she propped a pair of glasses on the end of her nose, then logged on to a prehistoric looking desktop computer.

"This won't take long," she said, indicating for her guests to sit. "Marcia, could you go and speak to Ben and Sylvia? There was an issue about this morning's breakfast. Perhaps you could try to smooth things over?"

Her expression souring, Marcia shifted her weight from one leg to the other. "Where are they now?"

Pamela shrugged. "There aren't too many hiding places around here. I'm sure you'll find them."

Marcia hovered in the doorway for a moment longer, staring intently at her mother. Then without saying another word, she turned and headed back to the foyer.

"Here we are," Pamela said, pulling two sets of forms from the printer and placing them side by side on the desk. "If you could read through these documents and sign at the bottom. It's nothing to be concerned about. Just the usual terms and conditions, disclaimers, that sort of thing."

"Disclaimers?" Jerome said, arching an eyebrow.

Pamela smiled. "Honestly, it sounds more dramatic than it is. It's an agreement, that's all. Just to make sure we're all on the same page and everything's above board."

Picking up a pen, Jerome cast a lazy eye over the forms, then added his signature in the required boxes. Pamela smiled as she waited for Emily to finish reading every word. That was something she'd picked up from Lewis. Always read the small print. Otherwise you could be signing your life away.

She suddenly found herself thinking about the day Lewis had proposed to her. It had been Christmas Day. His parents and Emily's mother had met for the first time. Lewis had insisted Emily pull the last Christmas cracker with him. He'd tucked an engagement ring inside, and when Emily had pulled the cracker, the ring had shot across the room and knocked over a wine glass. What a lovely surprise that had been. Everyone had been overjoyed. Even Emily's mother had been unable to suppress a smile.

"Emily?" Pamela smiled at her from across the desk, her gaze drifting down to the papers in Emily's hand.

"Sorry." Picking up a pen, Emily signed her name on each page, then handed over the documents.

"Wonderful. Now, if you could please hand over your car keys and any mobile or electronic devices, then I can show you to your rooms."

Jerome's mouth fell open an inch.
"Excuse me?"

"I trust you read our literature before deciding to stay with us? This is a digital detox retreat. Which means we don't allow any technology at Meadow Pines."

Jerome slowly turned and glared at Emily, who fixed her gaze on the table. "My friend here invited me along at the last minute. It must have slipped her mind to mention that small but crucial detail."

"Well, let me explain," Pamela said, as she pulled out two large envelopes from the desk drawer and placed them on top. "Here at Meadow Pines, it is our belief that living in an age of digital technology does more harm than good. Devices that are meant to connect us all, in fact, have the opposite effect. And they're dangerously addictive. When was the last time you had a conversation that wasn't interrupted by a text message or social media update, or by a furtive glance to make sure you weren't missing out on the latest viral video?"

She paused, staring at her guests. It was clear this wasn't the first time she had delivered the speech, yet Emily could sense her passion hadn't wavered.

"Here at Meadow Pines, we ask you to surrender your digital devices so that you give yourselves permission to look up. To reconnect with the natural world, your fellow human beings, and yourself. This computer," she continued, nodding at the monitor, "is the only one we have on site. This telephone is the only landline. In an ideal world, I wouldn't have them at all. But unfortunately in this modern world, we're unable to make a living without them. It's an ironic but sad truth."

"What about the car keys? Why would you need them?" Emily asked.

"A simple trick to remove the temptation to quit before the weekend's over. You'd be surprised how quickly people can fall to pieces without technology."

Jerome pulled his phone from his pocket and cradled it in his hand. "So, no Wi-Fi?"

"I'm afraid not. Even without Wi-Fi there's no service all the way out here."

"But what will we do instead?" he asked, his voice climbing higher.

"Write, draw, paint, walk, reflect—all those simple and wonderful acts that have been left on the wayside by the digital age. We want you to make Meadow Pines your own space. To do with it what you will. It's how we differ from most retreats; we don't run a timetable of events. The only structured activity we deliver is late morning yoga, and even that's completely voluntary. Although I will add that even if you're a novice, yoga is a great way to help channel your focus and to release any pent-up stress."

Emily took out her phone and car keys and placed them on the desk.

"And your wristwatch, please," Pamela said. "We want you to be completely free, and that includes free from time. You won't find any clocks at Meadow Pines. Instead, we use a simple electronic bell system to announce mealtimes and yoga sessions."

Unbuckling the watch, Emily handed it over. Then Pamela held out the second envelope to Jerome. He stared hesitantly at its open mouth. Emily gave him a nudge, but his fingers had become fused to the phone casing.

"What about security?" he asked.

"All items are individually sealed and labelled in envelopes. Then they're locked in the cabinet behind me." Pamela offered him a reassuring smile. She was good at that, Emily noted. "Your belongings will be safe, Jerome. After all, we're in the middle of the New Forest, and a good handful of miles away from the nearest signs of life."

Shoulders heaving, Jerome expelled an unsteady breath, then let his phone slip from his fingers. He watched it slide to the bottom of the envelope.

"All done," Pamela said with a grin. "And you're still alive."

Jerome narrowed his eyes. "For now."

For reasons Emily couldn't explain, she felt a sudden nervous flutter inside her chest.

CHAPTER 5

Now technology-free, Emily and Jerome were led out of the office and up a grand oak staircase, where original paintings of the New Forest and the manor house hung on the walls. Reaching the top floor, they followed Pamela down a long corridor with oak doors on both sides and small chandeliers hanging from the ceiling.

"Our visitors' sleeping quarters," Pamela said. "As Marcia may have told you, we have a full house this weekend. Emily, you're in Room Eight, just there on the end. And Jerome, you're opposite in Room Nine."

Pamela opened the door to Emily's room. The interior was a simple affair, small and square, with turquoise painted walls, and furnished with a single bed, a chest of drawers and an old wardrobe. Sunlight filtered through a latticed window, making patterns dance on the floorboards.

Emily dumped her bag on the bed and moved over to the window. The view was of the garden and the meadow, capped by a vista of treetops and crystalline blue sky.

"It's perfect," she said.

"Well, I'll leave you to get settled in," Pamela said. "Dinner will be in a few hours. You'll hear the bell when it's ready. The menu is strictly vegetarian. Our chef, Sam, is a wonderful cook, and all the vegetables he uses are grown right here. If you have any more questions, you can find me in the office, or if you happen to see Marcia around, she'll be happy to help."

Jerome frowned, confused. "What about the grand tour?"

"That was it. As you're already learning, we like to keep things as simple as possible. The quicker our guests are left to themselves, the more time they have to reconnect with the world. Besides, it's always more fun to discover rather than be shown, don't you think?" Smiling, Pamela turned to leave. "Oh, just one more thing. While we actively encourage our guests to connect with each other, we do ask that you refrain from work talk or using the space as a networking opportunity. And while this is by no means a silent retreat, please be aware that some people may be more open to conversation than others."

Giving them one last smile, Pamela turned and headed back downstairs. Once they were alone, Emily risked a quick glimpse at Jerome.

"What do you think?" she asked.

Jerome snorted, then shook his head. "I think I'm going to kill you! What kind of insane asylum have you brought me to?"

Emily shrugged. "It's a retreat, not a five-star hotel. What were you expecting?"

"Not to have my phone confiscated for one thing. And not to be sleeping in a prison cell for another."

"You haven't even seen your room yet."

Dragging him by the arm, Emily crossed the corridor and entered the opposite room. It was a similar set up as her own, but even smaller. The window looked out on a distant and barren hill that rose over the forest like the hump of a great whale. A lone tree grew at the top of the hill, its dead branches reaching to the sky like the arms of a dying man.

"Beautiful," Jerome said.

"Correct me if I'm wrong, but wasn't it your idea for me to go on a retreat?"

Letting out a deep sigh, Jerome slipped his hand into his pocket, remembered his phone was gone, then threw himself down on the bed.

"I feel like I've lost an arm! What the hell are we supposed to do for two days?"

"You heard the woman—walk, paint, reflect." Emily glanced away and shrugged. "Anyway, now that you're here and there's no escape, you may as well try to get into the swing of things."

"You get into the swing of things," Jerome said, kicking his shoes off. "I'm going to sleep."

"Well, I'm going to unpack, then I'm going to take a walk and see what Meadow Pines has to offer. Are you sure I can't tempt you?"

Jerome responded with a wide-eyed glare.

"Suit yourself." Emily backed out of the room and shut the door.

"While you're on your travels, see if you can find something to eat that doesn't involve mung beans," Jerome called out. "And try not to make friends with the other guests—they're probably all cult members."

Sighing, Emily returned to her room and spent the next couple of minutes unpacking her clothes. When she was done, she sat on the edge of the bed. A small wave of anxiety crested in her stomach. She had always been awkward at meeting new people, wishing she could bypass all those same introductory questions. What's your name? Where are you from? What do you do? All normal questions with normal answers—if you weren't Emily Swanson. It wasn't that she disliked people. It was the attention that made her uncomfortable. People wanted to know things about her, and they would take those things and make judgements. Especially if they'd read about her in the newspapers. What if the guests of Meadow Pines recognised her? What if they asked questions?

She had the sudden and inescapable feeling that she'd inadvertently trapped herself like a caged bird.

Drawing in a deep breath, Emily shook her arms and hands, expelling the paranoia. After taking a minute to centre herself, she stood up, left the room, and quietly made her way downstairs.

———

The first place to explore was the house. Conscious of the silence, Emily tiptoed through the foyer like a child sneaking out of her room after bedtime. It certainly was a grand old building, she thought, staring up at the high ceiling. She made a mental note to find out more about its history.

The first room she came to had been turned into an art studio. Mixed-media creations formed by the hands of past visitors were tacked to the walls and ceiling. Poster paints, oils and watercolours sat in rows on work surfaces, while other craft materials were stacked in trays. The stillness of the room instantly reminded Emily of her old classroom after the children had left for the day. She hung in the doorway, memories stirring, then pulled herself away.

The next open door revealed a carpeted room littered with large cushions. A small altar sat at the far end, while the smoky scent of sandalwood hung heavy in the air along with an overwhelming sense of calm.

Moving to the rear of the house, Emily came to the dining hall. This was where she imagined Lords and Ladies of the Hunt would have feasted all those years ago. In the centre of the room, beneath a large chandelier, two galley-style dining tables were pushed together, end to end.

A loud clatter of dropped pans shattered the quiet, startling Emily and dragging her gaze to a set of swing doors on the other side of the room. A male voice released a string of expletives before silence resumed once more.

Deciding to explore outside, Emily headed back to the foyer, passing by the closed door of Pamela's office. Entering the walled garden, she welcomed warm sunlight on her face. The day was still bright, the sky a deep, relentless blue. Cupping a hand over her eyes, she smiled as she watched the wildflowers of the meadow dance in the breeze. Her gaze shifted from right to left, resting on the small field of vegetables.

Marcia Hardy was stooped over, busy pulling up baby carrots and placing them into a wooden wheelbarrow. Helping her was a woman with deep brown skin who Emily guessed to be in her late forties. She wore a loose cotton tunic over cotton trousers. A colourful kitenge headscarf was wrapped around her long dreadlocks. Sensing eyes upon her, the woman looked up and waved. Emily raised a nervous hand in the air.

Leaving the women behind, she strolled through the meadow, moving in a wide circle until she had passed the house and reached the forest's edge. Skirting the treeline, she noticed a path winding its way between the trunks. Butterflies flitted in the air. Laughter echoed over the meadow. Emily looked back at the distant figures of the working women. Her eyes came to rest on the house. Meadow Pines really was a beautiful place.

Stepping onto the path, Emily entered the woodland. As she walked, she practised her breathing exercise. In for four, hold for seven, out for eight. As she exhaled, she felt the knots of tension in her neck and shoulders unravel a little more. They had been building for months, years even. It made sense that it would take time and patience to unpick them all. But here at Meadow Pines, surrounded by nature, Emily suddenly felt as if she had all the time in the world.

To be away from all the noise and chaos of the city, even if for a few days, felt like a blessing. Here, encouraged by the tranquil quiet, she could allow her mind to rest and to think positive thoughts. She wasn't sure about participating in yoga classes or meditation, but for now, simply being here, embraced by the forest, was all the mindfulness she needed.

Which was why, when a short, sharp scream rang out through the trees, Emily felt a twinge of annoyance, before her instinct to panic kicked in.

Hurrying along the twisting path, she hoisted herself over a fallen tree trunk. A young woman with shoulder-length dark hair, and dressed in sweatpants and a T-shirt, stood in the centre of the path, her head swinging wildly from side to side. She was very thin, Emily noted, her skin as white as paper against the tree bark.

"Are you all right?" she called out.

The woman spun on her heels, a startled cry escaping her throat. "There was a snake," she said, her eyes returning to scour the ground. "I think it was an adder. The only poisonous snake in the whole country and it just happens to live right here!"

Taking a step back, Emily searched the scrub for signs of the adder's distinctive zig-zag markings.

"No one's died from an adder bite in over twenty years," she said. "In most cases, people are bitten when they've come across one in their path and tried to move it out of the way."

"Why would anyone do that?"

"Ignorance, I suppose. If you leave adders alone, they'll do the same to you."

The woman gave the foliage one final, frightened look, then moved towards Emily.

"Do you work for the zoo or something?"

Emily smiled. "No. Living in the countryside, it's just something you pick up."

"Oh, you're from around here?"

She hesitated, her defences building a wall around her. She stared at the young woman, whose face was kind, her eyes wide and childlike. Emily shook her head, pushing away her paranoia. If she wanted to move on, she needed to start trusting people.

"Actually, I grew up in Cornwall," she said, studying the woman's face for any trace that she'd been recognised. "But I live in London now."

"London? Why did you want to move there? All that noise and pollution."

"A change of scene, I guess." It wasn't a lie exactly.

"I've never been to Cornwall. Or to London for that matter. I never go anywhere. My name's Melody, by the way." The woman held out a bony hand. "Melody Jackson."

"Emily Swanson. I just arrived. I was exploring."

"Do you mind if I tag along?"

"Be my guest."

The two women walked along the path, eyes occasionally darting to the sides.

"Is this your first time at Meadow Pines?"

Emily nodded. "How about you?"

Melody brushed her hair out of her eyes. Her movements were quick and nimble, as if her limbs were racing ahead of her body. "Oh, I've been here lots of times. I don't live too far away, so it's easy for me to get to. Meadow Pines is my little escape from it all. My island. What made you decide to come here?"

The path opened on a small glade, where sunlight dappled the forest floor. Foxgloves grew in patches, their bell-shaped, purple flowers hanging from long tapering spikes.

"My friend thought it would be good for me," Emily said, glancing away. "Life has been a little . . . hectic lately."

"That's why I keep coming back," Melody sang. She crouched down and plucked a foxglove from the ground.

"I wouldn't do that," Emily warned. "They're poisonous. They'll give you a rash."

"Really?" Melody dropped the plucked flower to the ground and rubbed her fingers against her sweatpants.

The women cut through the clearing and picked up the path again. Soon, they heard the babble of running water. A stream lay up ahead. Steppingstones ran from bank to bank. Following Melody, Emily hopped from one to the other, smiling to herself at long ago childhood memories, until she had reached the other side.

"Have you met everyone else?" Melody asked, stooping to brush a wet leaf from her shoe.

"Not yet."

"I haven't spoken to everyone, but most of the guests seem nice." Emily noted the stress in Melody's voice when she said: 'most of them'. "There's Daniel, who is a social worker. He's from Italy but now he lives in London, just like you. He's very handsome." She giggled like a schoolgirl, but then her smile faded. "Then there's Ben and Sylvia. They're business types from Manchester."

"What are they like?" Emily asked.

Melody shrugged, stared off into the trees. "Not particularly friendly. All they've done since they've been here is complain. The food's not good enough. The water's not hot enough. You should have seen the fuss Ben made when he found out they'd have to sleep in separate rooms! But that's Pamela's policy—whether you're in a relationship or not—being here is as much about reconnecting with yourself as it is about reconnecting with the people around you."

The path disappeared beneath a brush of gorse and hawthorn. Emily came to a halt, her eyes darting between the trunks as she tried to find it again.

"It's getting so overgrown," Melody said, beckoning Emily with a hand. Once they were back on the path and moving again, she continued with her description of the other guests.

"So next, there's Helen. She's a journalist for Modern Living—the magazine for the new woman. That's what she calls it, anyway."

Emily stopped still. Her heart skipped a beat. "A journalist?"

"She's here writing a feature about alternative weekend getaways," Melody said, giving her a strange look. "But Pamela has given her strict instructions not to interview the other guests. After all, modern living is exactly what we're here to get away from!"

They got moving again, Emily trailing slightly behind. The mention of a journalist being here at Meadow Pines had instantly dampened her mood. Even if this Helen would not be conducting interviews, a little digging could quickly reveal Emily's past.

Relax, she told herself. There's no internet access here, no phones. Even if the journalist did happen to recognise her from the newspapers, there was little she could do about it right now.

But what about after?

Melody was still talking. ". . . apparently she's some sort of artist. The bohemian type, I suppose you might say."

"Sorry, who is?"

"Janelle. The lady with the headscarf. She's very nice, although I'm already sensing tension between her and Sylvia."

"Really? What makes you think that?"

"Well—and I don't like to speak ill of people—but Sylvia seems to be a little bit racist."

"I see."

"She hasn't said anything, of course. But it's more the way she looks at Janelle. I could be wrong, but it's a shame, don't you think? You'd hope in this day and age that we could all just get along."

"It's a nice idea," Emily said.

"Anyway, that leaves us with Oscar. And I'm afraid I can't tell you anything about him. Pamela said he's stuck in traffic. He's wasting a lot of money—half the weekend will be gone by the time he gets here."

The path came to an end, bringing them to the northeast corner of the meadow. "There are lots of other paths to walk," Melody said. "I can show you a longer one, if you like. It goes to my favourite spot—the lake. It's beautiful there. Most people tend to stick around the house, but why would you do that when you have the great outdoors all around you?"

Emily smiled. She liked Melody—despite her nervous disposition and unstoppable chatter, she was friendly and approachable. And although she'd clearly made it her business to get to know the modus operandi of the other guests, she seemed content to enjoy Emily's company without asking prying questions. For now.

"Shall I take you there? To the lake?" she asked.

"Perhaps later," Emily replied. "I should check on my friend."

"Yes, I saw you arrive together. Is he your boyfriend?"

Emily laughed. "No, Jerome is a good friend. Although I'm sure he doesn't think the same about me right now. I sort of persuaded him to come along—he hates it here already."

"What is there to hate?"

"A lack of concrete."

"It's nice to have a friend," Melody said, staring into the distance. "Derek is my best friend. I always look forward to giving him a cuddle when I get home from work."

"Your husband?"

"My cat, silly. I'm going to keep walking for a bit. It's very nice to meet you, Emily. See you at dinner."

Emily said goodbye as she watched Melody disappear back into the forest. Now that she was alone, she turned and stared across the meadow. Unease cloyed at her stomach as she thought about the journalist Melody had mentioned.

"It's fine," she told herself. You're safe. Just as long as she doesn't find out who you are.

But that was the thing about journalists, Emily thought, as she dragged her feet back towards the house—finding out who people were was what they did best.

CHAPTER 6

Jerome was not in his room. A quick search of the house found him sitting on a swing chair on the back porch, and deep in conversation with an attractive man with short, black hair, an olive complexion, and a short growth of stubble. Emily watched them for a moment before the thud of the closing door alerted them to her presence.

"I was beginning to think you'd made a break for it," Emily said, the faintest of smiles on her lips as Jerome glanced in her direction.

"Hello, I'm Daniel," the man said in a distinctive Italian accent. He got up and offered Emily his hand.

"Emily. Nice to meet you." She smiled politely as Jerome hopped off the swing seat and joined them. "I see you decided to leave your room."

"You two know each other?" Daniel asked.

"Oh yes, Emily was the one who dragged me along on this godforsaken trip," Jerome replied. "But now that you've kindly given me a little tour, I'll admit that perhaps I've been a little too quick to judge. The view is quite something, isn't it?"

"Yes, it is," Emily replied, noting that Jerome's gaze was fixed on Daniel rather than the surrounding landscape. "I've just been for a walk in the forest. It's beautiful."

"This is your first time here?" Daniel's dark eyes reflected Emily's features.

She nodded.

"Mine, too. I'm hoping a few days out of the city will help reset my stress levels. It's been a very long time since I took a break."

"Being a social worker must be exhausting."

Daniel's mouth hung open in surprise.

"I was just speaking with Melody," Emily blurted, her face blushing. "She seems to know a lot about the other guests."

"Ah, that will teach me to break the rules and talk about work. Imagine if Pamela found out. I'm sure I would be forced to do a walk of shame all the way back to my bike."

"A motorbike?" Jerome asked, his eyes brightening.

"I'm not a fan of cars." Daniel turned to Emily. "But yes, being a social worker brings a lot of stress. We get a bad reputation, but all these government cuts aren't making it easy for anyone. People have no money, no job, their debts are spiralling out of control. And although we don't have the funding or the resources to deal with them all, the papers say that when a parent hurts their child, it's our fault we weren't there to prevent it." He paused, his eyebrows knitting together. The brightness Emily had first seen momentarily darkened. "But there I go talking about work again. I'm sorry."

"I think what you do is very brave," Emily said. Her thoughts flew back to Phillip. A social worker had been involved with his family until his parents had convinced the system that all was well again. It wasn't long after that Phillip had shown up to school, unwashed and in last week's uniform, with a lead-like dullness in his eyes.

"I don't get all this digital detox crap," Jerome suddenly said. "My phone is my stress relief, so why take it away from me? Besides, what if I get a call for an audition? I could be missing out on a career-making role."

"I think not being glued to your phone for a couple of days will be good for you," Emily said.

Daniel rubbed a hand against his stubble. "I have to agree. Don't get me wrong, I love technology—look at all the things we can do now that thirty years ago were just science fiction. I can pick up my phone and make a video call to my parents who are twelve hundred miles away in Palermo. If I have a question, I jump on the internet and there's my answer in less than a second. It's breathtaking. But the downside is that it's addictive. Where will we be in even five years? I'm afraid we'll have become as emotionless as the technology we're plugged into."

"I know plenty of people who were like that long before social media came along," Jerome said.

Emily gripped the porch railings as she watched a pair of birds hop from one treetop to the next. Above the house, the sun shimmered in golden waves. Voices floated on the air, drifting in from the front of the house. Emily cocked her head and heard snippets of Pamela's welcome speech.

"Looks like the final guest has arrived," Daniel said. "Perhaps we should say hello."

Jerome nodded in agreement.

"I think I might take a nap," Emily said. The knot of anxiety in her chest would not loosen.

Jerome cocked his head. He waited for Daniel to step off the porch, then he said, "But you never nap. You can't."

"There's a first time for everything. Who knows, by the end of the weekend you might be looking at a whole new me."

———

Lying on the bed with her eyes closed, Emily imagined Kirsten Dewar's soothing voice filling her ears.

Imagine you are in a calm place. Somewhere you feel safe. A forest, or a beach.

In her mind, she was lying on soft sand next to a glistening ocean. The tide rolled in, then ebbed away. The drag of the water was a soothing whisper, the warm breeze a gentle hand stroking her face.

You feel protected in this place. Nothing can harm you.

Emily felt the tension in her body seep into the mattress. A fog drifted into her mind, disorienting her thoughts, swallowing them whole. She was sinking into the black depths of sleep.

Voices called her name. Faces swam before her like spirits of the dead. Hands pulled at her. The darkness cleared and she found herself at the Ever After Care Foundation, in Doctor Williams' attic of horrors. Pain-stricken faces stared up from hospital beds, their eyes pleading with her to tear out the needles and the cannulas, to end the suffering and let them go quietly into the night. In the last bed she saw herself; withered and gnawed and writhing in pain. Picking up a pillow, she placed it over the face of her other self, pressing down with all her strength. The body on the bed kicked and thrashed. Then it was still. Emily lifted the pillow. And saw her mother's cold, dead eyes staring up at her.

Emily sat up with a jolt, blinking the nightmare away. Perspiration beaded her brow. Her chest heaved up and down.

How long had she been asleep? It felt like only moments since she shut her eyes, but now there were long shadows spilling over the floorboards.

Turning to the window, she saw the sun sinking towards the treetops. She stared at her wrist, at the white outline where her watch was usually strapped. Anxiety kicked and bucked in her stomach.

Rising on unsteady feet, she moved to the dresser and took out her toiletry bag. Her fingers trembled. Her chest was tight, making it hard to breathe.

Soon she would feel a numbness at the top of her head and in her extremities. Then paralysing terror would come in pulsating waves, dragging her to the floor, where she would curl her body into a foetal position and sob until the terror subsided.

It might last for minutes. Maybe an hour. She could let it happen, let it consume her, strip her of control.

Or she could try to stop it in its tracks.

Unzipping the toiletry bag, Emily removed a foil blister pack and pushed out a pill. She moved to swallow it, then hesitated, staring at the tiny compound of chemicals pinched between finger and thumb. How many more pills would she need to take before she felt safe again? Before she woke without her own screams ringing in her ears?

She was hyperventilating now. Squeezing her eyes shut, she cupped the pill and attempted the breathing exercise that had saved her again and again.

In for four, hold for seven, out for eight. She chanted the mantra in her head, the words spilling over each other, then untangling like wool. She pictured the wide, sandy beach, a flat, crystalline ocean. The sun beating down from a cobalt sky. In for four, hold for seven, out for eight. On the ocean was a white yacht, its sails fluttering lazily on the whisper of a breeze.

In for four. Hold for seven. Out for eight.

Lungs opened. Breathing slowed. Limbs softened. Emily unclenched her fist. Angry, crescent-shaped grooves were carved into the flesh of her palm.

She stared at the pill in her hand, a sense of achievement melting away the panic.

From somewhere in the house, the deep tone of a bell echoed. Then a voice snapped her focus back to the room.

"Dinner time, sleepyhead. You've been out of it for hours." Jerome stood in the doorway, bouncing up and down on his heels. "You've missed out on a ton of drama! Remember that couple Pamela mentioned earlier—Ben and Sylvia—the ones who'd complained about breakfast? Well, they're completely monstrous. They've just blown up about the lack of structure to the weekend. You know, why are they paying to do nothing in the middle of nowhere when they could be doing nothing at home for free? I mean, they have a point, but hello, do your research. Plus, they've broken half of the rules, sounding off about work, bragging about how much money they make. Also, I think they're kind of racist."

Emily stared at him blankly.

"Pamela had them in her office for twenty minutes," Jerome continued. "So much for her zen-like qualities. Oh, and I've met the final guest, Oscar. Not the friendliest person in the world. In fact, on a scale of rudeness, he's London rude. Your friend Melody tried to be all welcoming and he completely blanked her." Jerome sucked in a large gulp of air. "This place is great!"

Emily pulled herself to the edge of the bed. "How long was I asleep?"

She felt Jerome watching her as she struggled to get off the bed. As he reached out a steadying hand, his eyes moved to the medication lying on the dresser.

"Panic attack?"

Emily nodded.

"How bad this time?"

"I'm fine."

"Do you need a few minutes?"

She got to her feet. "Seriously, I'm fine."

Jerome hovered next to her, hands dug into his pockets, eyes examining her with the attention of a doctor. "In that case, let's go see what non-carnivorous delights await us."

CHAPTER 7

Quiet chatter rippled through the dining hall. Emily's gaze moved from guest to guest as she attempted to put names to faces. Pamela was seated at the head of the table, with Marcia on her left. Sitting opposite each other in the next two seats, discontent hanging over them like a black cloud of flies, were a man and woman in their late thirties. Ben and Sylvia, she assumed. On Ben's right, Daniel was engaged in conversation with the young woman seated across from him. This had to be Helen. Emily stared warily at the journalist, noticing how her smile failed to reach her eyes.

On Helen's left, a stern-faced man in his mid-forties was hunched over the table, steely blue eyes scowling at the empty seat opposite. Beads of perspiration glinted on his bald head. Was this Oscar? As if sensing he was being watched, he turned his head and glared at Emily. She quickly looked away.

"Good job I like a challenge," Jerome whispered. Giving her a wry wink, he headed to the table and sat on the chair opposite Oscar.

"Great to meet you, I'm Jerome," he said, extending his hand across the table. Oscar stared at him. His hands remained on his lap.

"You know, if you stand there much longer you'll turn into a statue." The woman in the headscarf smiled at Emily. She nodded at the empty chair beside her. "I promise not to bite."

Emily sat down.

"I'm Janelle Magoro. Should we even be doing surnames here? It sounds so formal."

Janelle had a kind face. Her eyes lit up like stars when she smiled. Emily introduced herself, then glanced over at Jerome, who had already abandoned his attempts at conversation with Oscar and was now talking with Daniel and Helen.

"Are you okay, Emily? Is this your first time at a retreat?" Janelle patted her on the forearm. Why was everyone obsessed with that question? "You look like a first-timer. These places seem odd at first. A little out there, I suppose you could say. But once you've been to a few you get to know the drill. Slipping into the right headspace becomes much easier."

"Have you been to many retreats?" Emily asked. Janelle's hand remained on her forearm. She stared at it, feeling its weight.

"Oh, I've done the rounds. Yoga retreats, artist retreats, women's, monastic . . . it's good to take time and re-centre yourself, don't you think? These days, time has become our most precious commodity. The older I get, the less

I want to spend my time trying to catch up. Coming to places like Meadow Pines helps to remind me life should always be set at one's own pace. Don't you agree?"

Janelle raised her eyebrows, waiting for Emily to share her pearls of wisdom about the tribulations of modern living.

Emily shrugged. "It's very peaceful here."

"And a wonderful space to create in. Although some of their art resources leave a lot to be desired."

Emily stared at the empty seat on her left. Melody was the only guest missing from the table. She was about to ask Janelle if she had seen her when the kitchen doors swung open.

A sinewy young man with sandy hair, grey eyes, and a mass of wiry facial hair wheeled out a trolley filled with steaming pots of food. Marcia jumped up and began handing out plates, while the man placed the pots in the centre of the table. There were dishes of lentils and beans, sticky rice, and a vegetable stew. The blend of aromas was dizzying, causing a wave of excited chatter around the table.

Standing up, Pamela raised a quietening hand.

"I hope everyone has found some fulfilment on their first full day at Meadow Pines," she said. "Often, the first day is the most challenging—a rude awakening to how hectic our lives have become, how dependent on technology we now are, feeding from it like babies at their mothers' breasts. It's on this first day that we feel the sting of withdrawal. But tomorrow, we realise the illusion—that the milk is sour and empty of nutrients."

Jerome leaned back in his chair, catching Emily's eye. He bit down on his lip to suppress a smile.

"Tomorrow, we open our minds. We acknowledge our worries and fears, the anxieties that nibble at us every day, and then we release ourselves from them so that we may instead reconnect with the self."

Pamela paused, allowing a moment for the guests to absorb her words. A clack of shoes on floorboards disturbed the quiet. Melody hurried into the room and dropped into the seat next to Emily.

"Sorry I'm late," she mumbled.

Something was wrong. The friendly, happy woman Emily had met earlier that day was now sullen and nervy, her eyes bloodshot, the skin around them red and irritated.

"Are you all right?" Emily mouthed.

Melody nodded and stared at the table.

"Here at Meadow Pines we eat in silence," Pamela said, refocusing her guests' attention and earning a look of disgust from Jerome. "Let's use this time to enjoy and reflect. But first let us give thanks to Sam for cooking this wonderful feast of vegetables harvested from our very own garden!"

Murmured thank yous went around the table as Sam set down the final dish and sat in the empty seat beside Pamela. As everyone silently ate, Emily looked around the table. Ben and Sylvia ran forks through their meals as if they'd been laced with poison. Melody picked at her food, pushing it around the plate without attempting to eat. Emily was worried by the drastic change in her mood.

Jerome wasn't worried about anything. She watched as he shovelled food into his mouth as if dinner had become a competitive sport.

Emily wasn't the only one watching the room. Across the table, Helen's eyes moved from face to face. As she worked her way around, Emily quickly dropped her gaze to her plate. By the time she looked up again, Helen had finished observing her fellow guests and was now busy eating.

But now Emily felt someone else's eyes upon her. Turning her head, she saw Oscar staring directly at her. Something changed in his expression.

Was it recognition? Surely she was being paranoid.

Emily glanced away. When she looked back again, Oscar was still staring.

———

As soon as dinner was over, the table began to empty. Daniel and Helen volunteered to wash the dishes. Ben and Sylvia returned upstairs. As they left the room, Emily heard them complaining about the bland food and the ridiculous philosophy of silent eating. While Janelle moved up a few seats to talk to Pamela and Marcia, Melody stood up and wandered out into the hall, shuffling in zigzags like a lost child.

"How are you?" Jerome asked, leaning across the empty seat.

"Better." Emily watched Melody disappear through the door. Across the table, Oscar was on his feet and brushing crumbs from his shirt.

"Excuse me," he said. His voice was deep and hollow, like words falling into a bottomless pit. "I don't mean to stare, it's just that you look so familiar to me. Have we met?"

Ignoring the palpitations in her chest, Emily shook her head. "No, I don't think we have."

His eyes pierced through her as he straightened his shirt collar. "It's so strange. I'm usually very good with faces and I'm almost certain I've seen yours before. My name is Oscar."

She hesitated, the silence all too telling. "Emily."

"Emily just has one of those faces," Jerome said, redirecting Oscar's attention. "People always think they've met her before."

Oscar's smile wavered. "And you are?"

"Jerome Miller, actor and best friend."

For a moment, Oscar's gaze shifted to the three women deep in conversation at the far end of the table.

"Perhaps you're right," he said. "Tell me, Emily, have you been to Meadow Pines before?"

Emily shook her head.

"I see. Well, if you'll excuse me."

He pushed his chair under the table. Without acknowledging either of them again, he left the room. A cloying wave of anxiety racked Emily's body.

"What was that all about?" Jerome said, moving to the seat next to her.

"It's the bloody newspapers," Emily whispered. "I just can't get away from it!"

"You don't know that. Besides, you do have one of those faces."

Emily's eyes narrowed. "And what is that supposed to mean?"

"Nothing. I'm being funny." He placed his hand over hers. "Look, don't worry about it. Even if he does recognise you, so what? It doesn't mean he'll bring it up, and it doesn't mean you have to talk about it if he does."

"The whole point of coming here was to get away from it all. Honestly, you'd think being in the middle of nowhere for the weekend might have achieved that. But between that journalist and now this, there's no chance of me getting some peace and quiet, is there?"

Slouching in her chair, Emily folded her arms across her chest. She felt anxiety turn to frustration, frustration to annoyance.

"That journalist hasn't even spoken a word to you," Jerome said. "If you want peace and quiet, all you have to do is shut your door or go for a walk. It's as simple as that."

Emily shook her head. Shutting her door might shut out the people, but it didn't shut out her mind.

"Perhaps I'll go for a walk now before it gets dark," she said.

"That's the spirit! You want some company?"

"Why don't you go do the dishes with Daniel? I'm sure he'd only be too pleased to receive your helping hands."

"I don't know what you're talking about, Emily Swanson," Jerome said, feigning embarrassment. "Besides, he has Helen on drying duty."

"Even more reason to get in there. Make sure she isn't snooping around, asking questions."

"My dear, Emily," Jerome said in a mock, upper-class accent, "believe it or not, there are billions of people in this world who aren't even aware of your existence."

Emily blew out a long stream of air. "It's not them I'm worried about."

CHAPTER 8

Melody was in the garden, staring forlornly at the rose beds. Emily placed a hand on the young woman's shoulder and felt her muscles tighten.

"Are you all right?" she asked. "You looked upset at dinner."

Melody smiled, then a long sigh escaped her lips. "I'm fine."

"I think I might go for a walk. It's a nice evening and I'd love to see the lake. Shame I don't know the way . . ."

Melody swung her shoulders from side to side. "You're kind," she said, peering up at the dusky sky. "But we better hurry or we'll lose the light."

"Lead the way."

Emily had taken three steps when she stopped in her tracks. She could feel eyes boring into her back. Turning to face the house, her breath caught in her throat. Oscar was standing in the open doorway. He was watching her, his thin smile growing sharp edges in the shadows. Emily stared back at him, her skin prickling. He nodded in her direction.

"Emily? Are you coming?"

Emily turned, taking in Melody's questioning gaze and the meadow beyond. When she peered back at the house, Oscar was already gone.

———

The evening was warm and heady, the sun-baked earth dry beneath their feet. Above the canopies, the sky was ablaze with molten fire.

"This way," Melody said, leading Emily north across the meadow.

They entered the forest side by side. It didn't take Melody long to find the path that led to the lake. As they walked, they listened to the sounds that evening brought in the forest. Birds sang out from branches. Crickets chirruped in the undergrowth. Nocturnal creatures stirred from their daytime slumber. The path twisted and curled around countless tree trunks, then changed trajectory as the ground began to slope. Minutes later, the trees parted and Emily saw the tranquil waters of the lake.

"Come on," Melody said, at last. She led Emily along the lake's edge until they came to a wooden jetty, where a small rowboat was moored to the end, gently bobbing up and down. The jetty was old and rickety-looking, and for a moment, Emily felt reluctant to follow Melody onto it.

"It's fine, really. See?" Melody sprang on her feet, hopscotching like a child between the planks until she reached the end.

Emily tested the jetty with her foot. Satisfied she would not go plummeting into the lake, she moved along the planks until she stood next to Melody. They sat down, swinging their legs over the water. It was a small lake, bordered by beech, oak and pine trees. Some were bent over like crooked old men, their lowest branches touching the surface. A flurry of wings flew over the water as birds splashed and fished. Emily watched a large heron swoop down, using its impressive wingspan and long legs to control its descent.

"I can see why this is your favourite place," she said.

Melody continued to swing her feet.

"Sometimes I daydream that I live in a beautiful log cabin right by this lake. Every morning I open the shutters and the sun streams in. It's always warm. I walk to the end of the jetty, take off my clothes, and I get in. The water's cool against my skin. I swim for hours. And I catch fish, which I cook on a campfire for me and Derek. Later in the day, we go for a long walk in the forest, and when evening comes, we sit on the jetty like we are now, watching the sunset. Every day is the same, but it doesn't matter because every day is beautiful."

Emily closed her eyes, picturing Melody's daydream. Sadness overwhelmed her. She looked at her companion. Tears glistened on Melody's skin like drops of sunset.

"What is it?" Emily asked. "What's wrong?"

Melody giggled but it was a pitiful sound. She was quiet for a long time, staring into the water. The sun had reached the treetops. It would be dark soon, making their journey through the forest and back to the house difficult.

"Sometimes I think I must be the loneliest person in the world," Melody said. More tears ran down her face. "Sometimes I think the only thing keeping me here is Derek."

Emily took Melody's hand, feeling her pain infect her like a disease. Thoughts of her mother, of Phillip Gerard, swam in her mind.

"Loneliness is the cruellest thing I can think of," she said.

Melody squeezed her fingers. "There are far crueller things than loneliness."

Pulling a tissue from her pocket, Emily handed it to her.

"Has something happened?" she asked.

Melody dabbed away her tears then methodically began to fold the tissue over and over into neat squares, as she stared over the lake.

"Melody? You can tell me. I'm a good listener."

"It's nothing," she said, smiling and shaking her head. She was still avoiding Emily's gaze. "Look at me—what a show! I'm so sorry. You didn't come to Meadow Pines to hear someone you barely know prattle on about their problems. This is supposed to be a place of peace, for goodness sake, and here I am muddying the waters with self-pity."

"You don't need to apologise." Emily offered her a smile. "I may be a stranger at Meadow Pines, but isn't that what this weekend is supposed to be about—reconnecting with each other regardless of whether we're strangers or friends?"

"I suppose you're right."

The sound of snapping twigs crackled in Emily's ears. She turned, peering over her shoulder at the treeline.

Melody stood. She had heard it, too.

Quiet fell over the lake.

"Probably a deer," Melody said.

"Isn't this place enclosed?"

The sound came again—the unmistakable crunch of a branch underfoot. Only this time, it was closer.

Emily got to her feet, scanning the forest. The light was fading like a sputtering candle flame, the shadows drawing longer. More snaps and cracks echoed over the water. Someone or something was moving at a deliberate pace, heading away from the lake.

"Come on," Emily said, unease coiling in the pit of her stomach. "Let's get back to the house."

They waited a few minutes until they were certain that whatever—or whoever—had been watching them was long gone. By the time they'd made it out of the forest and back to the house, dusk had settled over Meadow Pines like a blanket.

"I feel silly," Melody whispered as Emily said goodnight. The other guests had already returned to their rooms and the upstairs hall was silent.

"You don't need to," Emily replied, reaching out to touch Melody's arm. "Everybody has moments of feeling lost. I'm sure you'll wake up tomorrow and feel as right as rain. In a place as lovely as Meadow Pines you don't have a choice."

Melody surprised her with a rib-crunching hug. "You're funny. Goodnight, Emily."

"Goodnight."

Melody disappeared inside her room and shut the door. Emily stood for a second before she turned and tiptoed along the corridor.

Jerome was sitting on his bed, wearing only his underwear as he stared sullenly at the wall.

"What are you doing?" Emily asked him, her head poking around the door. She'd been hoping for some of Jerome's cheer to lift her mood. Her conversation with Melody had left her feeling miserable, her head filled with memories of her mother.

It had been just over a year since her death, and although Emily had started to get a handle on the pain, burying it deep beneath flesh and sinew, it was still very much present.

But it wasn't just those painful memories that were bothering her. The sounds she and Melody had heard—had someone been watching them?

Jerome looked up. "I feel bad, Em. Maybe coming to a retreat wasn't the best suggestion."

"What do you mean?" She moved into the room and sat down beside him.

"Maybe Ben and Sylvia have a point—there's nothing to do in this place. Nothing to fill the silence. Which means there's nothing to stop all those bad thoughts from swimming to the surface."

Emily frowned. "Are you talking about me or are you talking about yourself?"

"A little of both," Jerome said. He reached up and plucked a leaf from Emily's hair. "After you left, I helped Daniel and Helen to clear up. We talked for a while—Helen's not all that bad, by the way—and then they both went off to their rooms. I sat out on the porch for a while. One minute, I was trying to assimilate myself into nature, trying to get down with this whole retreat thing, the next I was thinking about when I was fourteen years old and getting my head kicked in every day at school for being queer. I don't want to think about that stuff. It's in the past and it's too depressing to bring up again."

"It's good to reflect sometimes. To see how far you've come," Emily offered.

"I can reflect very well by looking in the bathroom mirror, thank you." Jerome shook his head, let out a heavy sigh. "I've changed my mind again—I don't like this place, Em. I don't like the way it messes with my head.

And the people are weird. And I want my phone back."

"I think you need to ignore that overactive imagination of yours and get some sleep," Emily said. It was unsettling to see Jerome so morose. In fact, thinking back, she wasn't sure if she'd ever seen him so miserable. Angry, yes. Scared, yes. But never sad. "Look, maybe we've both got off on the wrong foot with Meadow Pines. Perhaps we should both be a little more patient and see what tomorrow brings. Things always look better in the morning."

Jerome narrowed his eyes as he wrapped an arm around her shoulder. "Well, if I don't feel enlightened by lunchtime I want my money back."

———

Twenty minutes later, Emily was ready for bed. Leaving the window open, she switched off the light and climbed under the sheets. The mattress was thin and lumpy, making her pine for her comfortable bed at home.

Nocturnal forest sounds crept in through the open window. Owls hooted. Tree branches rustled. Bats fluttered over the meadow.

In the black sky, countless stars glittered. It had been a long time since Emily had experienced the true darkness of the countryside.

In the blackness of her room, she took in a deep breath through her nose, held it, and then let it slowly escape from her mouth. Her body was tired, but her mind still buzzed with the day's events. Instinctively, she thought about taking a sleeping pill. Then remembering sleeping pills were no longer part of her nightly ritual, she turned on her side and tried to tune out the night-time sounds.

A memory came to her. She was a young girl, tucked up in bed in her childhood home, her mother's gentle voice floating up through the floorboards as she sang along to an old Tammy Wynette record.

Emily's mind became calmer. Thoughts settled down. Her eyelids grew heavy. Outside, the owls ceased hooting. The breeze dispersed.

As she was about to fall into the arms of sleep, she heard voices. At first, she thought they were coming from outside the window. But as her mind snapped awake again, she realised the voices were coming through the wall.

There were two voices: male and female. The woman sounded angry; her words hushed yet aggressive, firing out like muted gunfire. The man's voice rumbled through the wall, deep and low.

Emily sat up, trying to make out their words.

The woman's voice came back again, a little louder and a little angrier. She was cut off by the man, whose tone was now sharp and threatening. For a long time, the only sound was Emily's breathing.

Then the woman spoke again, her tone sharp and final. Hurried footsteps moved across the floor. A door opened and closed.

Emily listened as someone moved along the corridor outside, their footfalls growing softer and softer, until they were swallowed by the quiet.

Resting her head on the pillow, she stared into the darkness, wondering who and what she'd just heard.

CHAPTER 9

She had slept badly, tossing and turning in the throes of recurring nightmares. Dawn had broken some time ago, and now early morning sunshine filtered in through the window. Tired and restless, Emily hauled herself out of bed and dropped to the floor, where she spent the next thirty minutes stretching her limbs. Although her body had recovered from the trauma it had endured at the hands of Doctor Chelmsford, she continued the daily exercise regime that had been set by her physiotherapist with military-like rigour.

When she was satisfied that her muscles were sufficiently loose, she sprang to her feet, took her antidepressant with a drink of water, grabbed her toiletry bag, and headed to the bathroom. After a hot shower, Emily dressed into loose-fitting clothes, combed the knots out of her wet hair, then stood in front of the window for another fifteen minutes. Not knowing the time was disorienting. But it was strangely freeing. Her usual morning routine included working out exactly how many hours and minutes of sleep she hadn't had, then calculating the time she'd need to go to bed to make up for it.

Not that she'd ever caught up.

Now, although she knew her sleep had been patchy at best, there was nothing she could do about it except to acknowledge the fact and move on.

Five more minutes passed. Emily grew restless. She'd heard no electronic bells, which meant it was still early. Perhaps she would go for a walk to clear her mind before breakfast. Then she'd consider joining the yoga class. After all, she couldn't avoid Helen and Oscar forever. People were inquisitive and judgemental—it was human nature—but did it really matter what strangers thought of her, anyway?

What really mattered were the opinions of the people closest to her. The people that cared about her.

Feeling a twinge of renewed determination, Emily took in a breath to centre herself then left the room.

Silence greeted her. She thought about knocking on Jerome's door, but picturing his bleary-eyed, irritated face changed her mind.

Moving along the corridor, she thought about the altercation she'd heard coming through the wall last night. She stared at the door next to hers, realising she had no idea who occupied the room. It made sense that it was either Ben or Sylvia; they were the only couple currently in residence at Meadow Pines. And at dinner last night, they'd both been in terrible moods. Perhaps Emily had heard a lovers' quarrel.

Drifting along the corridor, her mind wandered back to a time when she'd shared her home with Lewis. She batted the thought away, confused at why she was thinking about him so much lately.

Was she missing companionship? Jerome certainly kept her in good company, but as wonderful as it was, friendship lacked the intimacy that a relationship brought.

Was it intimacy that she was missing, then? That interminable closeness of togetherness?

Annoyed that she was suddenly feeling so needy, Emily hurried along the landing and made her way downstairs. She'd never bought into the idea of needing to be with someone to feel complete. She believed happiness had to be achieved within the self, and that any intimate relationship should enhance, not validate her existence.

But with Lewis she had fallen too much, too soon. When he'd proposed, she'd said yes without a moment's deliberation. And when he'd walked out on her, leaving her with the press swarming at the bottom of the garden, she'd been the first to blame herself.

Now, a year on, a different story was unfolding. If Lewis had truly loved her, he wouldn't have left her that day, slipping through the back door, the end of their relationship contained in his hastily scrawled note left on the kitchen table.

A sudden rush of anger heated Emily's insides. She reached the foot of the stairs and marched across the foyer, wondering if she would be able to let someone get as close again. Perhaps she wouldn't. Perhaps that was just fine.

Deciding to walk off the dark mood that had settled on her shoulders, Emily passed the closed door of Pamela's office and headed out to the garden. The sky was a clear blue, peppered with wisps of clouds. A light breeze soothed her hot skin.

Shaking any last thoughts of Lewis from her head, Emily pushed open the garden gate. In the northwest corner of the meadow, two figures were moving in her direction. Sam the chef and Marcia Hardy. They walked side by side, deep in conversation, oblivious to Emily's presence. As they moved closer, she watched their arms swing loosely by their sides, their hands occasionally touching. Fingers grazed each other, then intertwined.

They were almost at the gate before they looked up and noticed Emily. Hands quickly unclasped. The space between their bodies widened.

"Good morning," Marcia said, a polite smile on her lips. Her eyes darted sideways to where Sam stood, before flicking back to Emily. "You're up early."

"It's a bad habit," Emily said.

An awkward silence filled the gap between them.

"Breakfast won't be ready for another hour yet," Sam muttered. He stared at the ground, his face fraught with concentration.

"That's fine. I thought I might take a long walk. Clear out the sleep." Emily looked past Marcia and Sam, retracing their route. "You don't live here at the house?"

Soft pink blossoms spread across Marcia's cheeks. "I do. Sam lives over in Lyndhurst."

Suddenly feeling like an ageing chaperone, Emily uncrossed her arms and stuck her hands in her pockets.

Marcia looked up at the house.

"Will you be joining the yoga class later?" she asked. Her face was now a deep shade of scarlet.

"Perhaps. I've never done it before."

"Well, there's a first time for everything. Personally, I like to run. I usually do a lap or two while Pamela takes care of the yoga."

Emily stared at the young couple, the space between them thickening like cement.

"Well, we're running a little late so we best get in," Marcia said. "Sam needs to get breakfast under way and I should see if Pamela needs any help. Enjoy your walk."

Emily watched with mild amusement as Marcia hurried through the garden, then stopped to scowl at Sam, who seemed happy to take his time. Young love, she thought.

Above her, the sun was already heating up. Shutting the garden gate, she set out across the meadow. By the time she reached the treeline, beads of perspiration were dampening the back of her neck. It was going to be another hot June day, no doubt about it.

The forest was thankfully much cooler. At first, Emily walked aimlessly, following paths that either brought her back to the meadow or became so buried in the undergrowth that she was forced to turn back. Some of the paths were signposted, while others were left anonymous, as if the forest had secrets to hide. Eventually, she came upon the signposted trail that would bring her to the lake.

Soon, she was sitting on the edge of the jetty, admiring dark green waters and breathing in the minty scent of nearby pines. Slowly, her mind began to clear of thoughts, settling down until it was as smooth and tranquil as the lake's surface.

Emily sat perfectly still, watching a family of swans glide away from the bank. Remembering the noises that she and Melody had heard last night, she glanced over her shoulder at the trees behind. In the daylight, it seemed silly to think someone had been watching them. After all, the forest was filled with all kinds of wildlife, large and small.

As Emily returned to watching the many birds occupying the water, she found herself thinking about Melody's lake house daydream. Last night, it had filled her with sadness—it was the loneliness of it all, she supposed—but now, as she pictured herself in Melody's place, she felt a deep yearning to return to the countryside.

London life certainly had its merits—you could eat food from any country in the world, enjoy a wealth of vibrant and diverse cultures, visit hundreds of theatres, museums and galleries, and admire centuries-old architecture—but the pandemonium of millions of people living in one place was sometimes unbearable.

Emily was getting used to it, slowly. But there were days when she wanted nothing more than to head out into a field or a wood, where she was completely alone and free to sit in silence for hours.

After Phillip's death, she had wanted to disappear. London had allowed her to do just that. It was like a vast ocean; she needed only to dive beneath its surface to never be seen again. But now that time had passed and Emily had undergone yet more life-changing events, she was feeling the need to resurface.

A large splash pulled her from her thoughts. The heron from last night had returned. She watched it glide along the lake, then dip its long beak beneath the water in search of breakfast.

Suddenly aware of aches and pains in her lower spine, Emily got to her feet. How long had she been sitting there, wrapped in blankets of thought? An hour? Perhaps more? Without clocks or watches, time had become as slippery as the fish the heron now battled with.

Not quite ready to return to the house, Emily left the jetty and strolled along the edge of the lake. Spying a new trail, she followed it through the forest. As she walked, her eyes wandered over wildflowers and moss-covered trees. The trail coiled and bucked, writhing between the tree trunks. Minutes later, the trail merged with a small clearing.

Emily slid to a halt.

A towering oak tree with a wide trunk stood at the edge of the clearing. It was clearly very old; perhaps as old as the forest.

But it wasn't the tree itself that had caught Emily's attention. A symbol was carved into the bark. Four long arrows pointed north, east, south, and west, while four shorter arrows were carved at symmetrical angles in between.

At first, Emily thought it was a compass. Then as she cocked her head, she decided it looked more like a star.

Something else caught her eye.

Below the carving, a length of rope was tied around the tree trunk like a belt. Curious, Emily moved around the tree and stepped into the clearing. Sunlight shone through the leaves and dappled the ground. Dust and plant seeds floated in the rays.

Emily's eyes followed the rope, moving away from the trunk and up to the branches. She caught her breath. Her heart smashed against her chest.

The sound of running footsteps filled her ears.

Dressed in a tracksuit and panting lightly, Marcia Hardy jogged into the clearing.

Her eyes followed Emily's horrified gaze.

When she saw what was in the branches, her face contorted with terror and she let out a piercing scream.

CHAPTER 10

The dull clang of the electronic bell resounded through the house and the garden, and out towards the trees, startling birds from branches. Jerome was already up, showered, and dressed in loose clothing. He'd slept well —surprisingly well, he thought, considering the mood he'd been in—and now that he was finally hangover-free and feeling refreshed, it seemed like a good idea to keep the positive energy flowing by getting some exercise. But first, there was breakfast to attend to.

After all his complaining about a distinct lack of meat on the menu, last night's dinner had been exceptional. He hoped breakfast would be just as delicious.

Leaving his room, Jerome pressed his ear against Emily's door. It was quiet in there, which he assumed meant she was already up and somewhere downstairs. These days, the only time Emily might sleep in was if she got sick. Being induced into a three-month coma against your will would do that to you, Jerome supposed.

As he cleared the stairs and strolled to the dining hall, he wondered if Daniel would be taking part in the yoga class. Last night, he'd seemed a little hesitant—yoga was new to him and he was reluctant to take his first class surrounded by the more experienced. Jerome had put him at ease by announcing that he was also a beginner. It was a white lie, of course—he'd been taking yoga classes for over a year, until his diminishing income had forced him to quit—but it had earned him points and a smile from Daniel.

Stopping in front of a wall mirror, Jerome checked his appearance, rubbed his palms over his cropped hair, then entered the dining hall.

The room was empty.

Bowls, half-filled with gloopy leftover porridge, still sat on the table—which meant that the bell he'd just heard was signalling the start of the yoga class, not breakfast.

Just how long had he slept?

Unable to contain his disappointment at missing out on a meal, Jerome grabbed an apple from the fruit bowl. By the time he'd reached the garden, the apple was a distant memory.

Pamela Hardy and most of the guests were sitting on yoga mats on the front lawn.

Emily was not among them.

Daniel was sitting in between Helen and Janelle, shifting awkwardly on his haunches. Seeing Jerome, he straightened up and flashed him a smile that caught the morning sunlight.

"Nice to see you, Jerome," Pamela called, holding up a hand. "I trust you slept well?"

Jerome nodded as he stooped to pick up a yoga mat from a small pile on the lawn. "Like the dead."

Dressed in matching designer tracksuits, their expressions more suited to a funeral than a yoga class, Ben and Sylvia turned to glare at him.

"Good morning," Jerome said, giving them his widest smile. He moved to the back of the group and placed his mat directly behind Daniel.

"So, you decided to brave it?" he said, grinning.

Daniel nodded. "And now I'm worried I'm going to make a complete fool of myself."

"I'm sure you'll do just fine. And don't worry, I've got your back."

Next to Daniel, Helen rolled her eyes.

"Where's Emily?" Janelle asked. "Is she not joining us?"

"That's a good question."

Jerome looked up at Emily's bedroom window. The curtains were open.

Perhaps she was hiding away from everyone. After all, she did like to spend an inordinate amount of time on her own. And last night, she'd been worrying that her past was about to resurface like a drowned corpse.

A burst of colour distracted him from his thoughts. Dressed in a flamingo pink leotard, Melody scurried out of the house.

"Sorry! Sorry everyone!" she called. She swept up a yoga mat, then headed straight for Jerome. "I slept straight through the bell."

"Both bells," Jerome winked, as she sat down next to him.

Melody responded with a sheepish grin and a giggle.

"Well, unless anyone else is joining us, we should begin," Pamela said, straightening her spine. "If you'd like to bring your hands together in front of you and close your eyes, I think we'll begin with an Intention."

The guests did as they were instructed. Pamela drew in a breath. Before she could speak, a blood-curdling scream rang out from the forest and echoed over the meadow.

Jerome's eyes snapped open. He twisted his head towards the trees. A second scream quickly followed

"Emily!" he cried.

He was up and racing in the direction of the forest before the others had got to their feet.

CHAPTER 11

The man was hanging from the tree, a thick rope pulled tightly around his neck. Bloodshot eyes stared over the clearing like two red mirrors. His tongue, which was black and bloated, protruded from blue lips. He swayed slightly in the breeze, the rope rubbing against the branch.

At first, Emily didn't recognise him. But then as voices and hurried footsteps approached, she realised who he was.

Jerome was the first to arrive. He burst into the clearing, panting and sweating, his expression turning from confusion to horror.

The others arrived moments later. A chorus of shocked gasps and cries filled the air.

It was Janelle who spoke his name. "My God, is that Oscar?"

"Yes." Emily was having a hard time peeling her eyes from his horribly swollen face.

Panic swept through the group. At the centre of it all, Pamela stared in open-mouthed silence.

"Are you all right?" Jerome had moved up beside Emily and was now rubbing her shoulder.

Emily shook her head. "I was just walking and . . ."

Taking her by the arm, he pulled her away from beneath Oscar's feet. Emily turned and numbly observed the rest of the group, who were in various stages of shock and upset. Marcia had stopped screaming and was now sobbing into Pamela's shoulder. Standing on her own, Melody swayed from side to side, her skin turning to ash.

"We should call the police," Pamela said above the moans and whimpers. No one disagreed. "Marcia, would you go ahead and make the call? Melody, would you mind going with her?"

Marcia was rooted to the ground, her face streaked with sweat and tears. Melody tugged gently on her arm, pulling her away from her mother's side.

The rest of the group watched as the two women left the clearing, half-running in the direction of the house.

"Should we cut him down?" Janelle had moved up next to Helen, whose back was pressed up against a tree.

"We can't," Emily said. "The police won't want us tampering with any evidence."

"She's right." Helen nodded, and their eyes met for a moment.

Janelle clamped her arms around her ribs. "We can't just leave him like that."

"I'm afraid we have no choice." Pamela's voice was unusually curt, her skin slick and pale. "There's no sense in standing here upsetting ourselves even further. Let's all return to the house. I'll have Sam make some camomile tea."

Near the edge of the clearing, Sylvia looked up at Oscar's body, shuddered with revulsion, then pulled on Ben's arm. As Ben trailed behind, he slowly shook his head—not in pity, Emily observed, but in disgust.

She watched as Daniel and Helen followed behind. Her brow creasing, Janelle opened her mouth to say something, then quickly shut it again and caught up with the others.

Emily was motionless. Memories of Phillip Gerard raced through her mind. An uneasy, displaced feeling gripped her body, as if the world had suddenly tipped ninety degrees.

"Let's go," Jerome whispered.

As they followed Pamela out of the clearing, Emily looked over her shoulder. Instead of Oscar, she saw Phillip, his young body dwarfed by the oak tree.

By the time they'd made it out of the forest, her mind was racing. She thought about her encounter with Oscar after last night's dinner. He'd shown no outward signs of depression or of intention to commit suicide.

His behaviour had been odd, though. The way he'd kept staring at Emily had been unnerving. And when he'd asked her if she'd visited Meadow Pines before, there had been definite intention behind his words. What did it matter to him if this was Emily's first or fiftieth visit to the retreat?

"I wonder why he did it," she thought aloud. "And why here? Why go to the trouble of coming to Meadow Pines?"

The others had regrouped and were halfway across the meadow. Emily could see them deep in conversation, probably asking the same questions.

"Who knows what motivates a person to go to such extremes," Pamela said. With her head down, she strode forward, closing the gap between her and the rest of the group.

"I wonder if he had a family," Jerome said. "Can you imagine what they're about to go through if he does?"

Something was happening up ahead.

The group had come to a standstill at the garden wall. Emily watched Ben stab a finger at Daniel's chest, then Daniel throw his hands in the air. Both men's faces twisted with anger.

Sensing trouble, the others took a step back.

"What's going on?" Emily wondered.

Then all hell broke loose.

Ben swung a fist and struck Daniel on the chin. Daniel stumbled back, slamming into the garden wall. He quickly regained his balance, then flew at Ben, taking his legs out. They both hit the ground and rolled.

Emily and Jerome stared at each other in disbelief. Then they were racing across the meadow.

CHAPTER 12

Pamela had almost reached the group when Marcia and Melody appeared at the front door. They were quickly followed by Sam, who threw himself into the brawl. Sylvia shrieked and the other women shouted at the men to stop. Emily and Jerome arrived in time to see Sam stumble back, his arms clamped tightly across Ben's chest as he dragged him from the brawl.

"Get the hell off me!" Ben's fists swung wildly, but Sam's hands were like iron grips.

On the ground, Daniel rolled over onto his hands and knees.

"This is a place of peace! How dare you show such disrespect!" Pamela's voice was like thunder rolling over the house. Sam released his grip on Ben, who slumped to the grass, puffing and panting. "What is going on here?"

"Why don't you ask this racist piece of shit?"

Daniel glowered at Ben, before spitting blood onto the grass. Eyes fell on Ben. Beside him, Sylvia wrapped her arms around her ribcage.

"Ben was only voicing his opinion," she said, eyeing the group. "He has every right—it's a free country, you know! You shouldn't have made him angry."

"Ben was saying some not very nice things about Oscar. He thinks he's selfish," Janelle explained. "Like the rest of us, Daniel took offence."

"Anybody who's going to do something like that hasn't got a thought for anyone else. They don't give a shit about the pain it will cause," Ben said, climbing to his feet. His lower lip was purple and already swelling.

"I hardly think when someone decides to take their own life they're thinking rationally enough to act selfishly or unselfishly," Janelle replied. "And fighting like children about it isn't helping anyone. All you've done is make a terrible situation that much worse."

"I agree. Violence helps no one," Pamela said. Her eyes moved from the crowd to Marcia and Melody, who were huddled together in the doorway. "What did the police say?"

"About what?" Sam asked. "What have I missed?"

Abandoning the discretion he'd displayed earlier, he moved up to Marcia and slung a comforting arm around her shoulder.

"Oscar is dead. He hanged himself," Pamela said through tight lips. "The police, Marcia— are they on their way?"

Fresh tears spilled down Marcia's face. "I can't get hold of them."

"Surely someone must be manning the station."

"No, that's not what I mean. The phone isn't working. There's no dial tone."

"But I took a booking just this morning." Confused, Pamela shook her head. "Fine, well there's no use trying a mobile phone—we'll have to get hold of them online."

There was a long pause before Marcia spoke again, and it was obvious to Emily that she was gearing up to deliver more bad news.

"We can't. Someone's broken into the office. The laptop's gone, along with everything else. Phones, tablets, even the car keys—it's all been stolen."

"What are you talking about?" Pamela looked from one shocked face to the other, then back at her daughter.

Emily shot a worried glance at Jerome.

"Fucking wonderful!" Ben said, his fat lip making him lisp. "A suicide and a robbery!"

Still kneeling on the ground, Daniel continued to glare.

"It's true," Melody sobbed. She shot a look at Emily, her eyes wide and frightened.

Deep lines grew like fissures across Pamela's brow. Shaking her head in disbelief, she pushed open the garden gate and marched into the house, with the others quickly following behind.

CHAPTER 13

Standing at the back of the office, Emily strained to see between the bodies. She caught a glimpse of the cabinet where Pamela had secured the guests' belongings. The door was now hanging from just one hinge.

"You know what this means, don't you?" Sylvia said, her voice trembling between anger and hysteria. "We're bloody stuck here! Who had access to this office? Don't you keep it locked?"

Nervous voices filled the room, followed by suspicious glances. Emily's mind raced. First, Oscar's death, now a robbery—what exactly was happening here? She glanced at Jerome, who was standing next to her with his shoulders hunched and his hands dug into pockets, watching the confusion through troubled eyes.

For a moment, Pamela was stunned. When she spoke, her words tripped over themselves. "No, I—I don't usually keep the office locked. We're in the middle of the forest . . . no one comes out this way."

"So, you're saying it's one of us?" Sylvia replied, turning to the other guests. "Go on, which one of you was it?"

"Now just a minute, let's not go accusing anybody of anything just yet," Janelle said. She stood at the back of the room, arms wrapped around her ribs.

"Not accuse anybody of anything?" Ben said, his eyes almost bulging from their sockets. "Are we all just imagining that empty cabinet over there? I handed nearly a grand's worth of equipment over to these jokers. Now it's gone. Who's going to compensate me for that?"

"Don't worry, you'll be compensated," Pamela said, and Emily could hear the strain in her voice. "Marcia, please tell me you still have the Land Rover keys?"

"I left them in the living room," she replied. She'd been silent since they'd entered the office, staying close to Sam. "I'll go check they're still there."

"Please hurry."

Pushing her way out of the crowded room, Marcia darted into the foyer and headed towards the Hardys' living quarters.

With one less body sucking up the air in the office, Emily found it a little easier to breathe. She thought about her items that had been stolen. She didn't care about the phone; no one called her, anyway. The wristwatch could also be replaced. But without the car keys, she and Jerome were going to have a hard time getting back to London.

While they waited for Marcia to return, Pamela addressed the group. "I'm not sure what's going on here," she said, "but it seems our only option is to take the Land Rover and drive down to Lyndhurst. The rest of us will just have to wait until help arrives."

"We're not staying here like prisoners." Sylvia shook her head and shot a sideways glance at Ben. "Are we?"

"I'm afraid we don't have much choice," Pamela said. "Marcia will take the Land Rover. She will drive to Lyndhurst. There's a police station there. Sergeant Wells will take care of everything."

At that moment, Marcia hurried back into the room, the keys to the Land Rover jangling in her hand. "I found them."

The relief in Pamela's voice was undeniable. "Right, as this office is now a crime scene, I suggest the rest of us vacate it as quickly as possible. We should all return to our rooms and wait for Marcia to come back with the police. Sam, perhaps you wouldn't mind making something to eat for about an hour's time?"

"Of course." Sam moved through the group until he was standing beside Marcia again.

"Perfect. I'll sound the bell when it's ready."

"We should organise a search party," Ben said. "If someone here's done this then there's a good chance they've stashed everything inside the house. We just have to find it."

"The only people who will be searching my house are Sergeant Wells and his constable. Besides, I think Oscar takes precedence over some petty theft, don't you?" Pamela marched to the door and held it open. "Shall we?"

Ben was first in line, with Sylvia inches behind. He stopped in front of Pamela, glaring at her. "This is disgusting treatment. I don't like being told what to do like I'm some little boy."

Behind him, Sam's voice came low and threatening. "No one's telling you to do anything, my friend. It's a polite suggestion."

Ben whirled around. "Oh, I'm not your friend, and I'll do as I please. This place is a fucking joke, and I'll make sure everyone knows about it."

His angry gaze shifted to Daniel. Then with Sylvia hanging off his arm, he strode through the doorway and headed for the stairs.

The group was silent and still, the shock of Oscar's death and the robbery hanging heavy in the air. One by one, they made their way back to their rooms. As Emily reached the stairs, she turned to see Pamela lock the office door and pocket the keys. Sam and Marcia shared a lingering look, then Marcia joined her mother and they went out to the garden.

Emily reached the top of the stairs in time to see Helen disappear into her room. Jerome was standing with Melody, Janelle, and Daniel.

"You look pretty beat up," he said to Daniel. "You need some ice for that?"

"I'll live." Daniel winced as he ran fingers over his bruised jaw. "I guess some people just can't help being assholes no matter how bad the situation."

The sound of raised voices and stomping feet came from Room Four. Sylvia appeared in the doorway, stared at them with angry eyes, then darted across the hall and into the opposite room.

"I don't like this," Janelle said. "I don't like that Oscar is still hanging there. It feels wrong just to leave him like that."

"Did anyone speak to him?" Daniel asked. "Who was the last person to see him?"

"I saw him at dinner," Jerome said. The others agreed.

Emily thought about seeing Oscar not long after dinner, when she'd caught him staring at her from the foyer. She glanced at Melody, who was pale and trembling, and her mind raced back to the lake, to the noises that they'd heard.

"I think I'll get some rest while we wait," Daniel said. He glanced at Jerome, gave him a pained smile, then disappeared into Room Seven.

"Me, too. I need some quiet time to let it all sink in." Janelle returned to her room, leaving the three of them stood in the corridor, silence closing around them like a clamshell.

"How are you doing?" Emily reached out and touched Melody's shoulder.

Melody's eyes glistened. "I've never known anyone who killed themselves before. It's just horrible."

"Yes, it is. But the police will be here soon. Hopefully, they'll be quick with their questions and then we can all go home. Do you want some company while we wait?"

"If you don't mind, I think I need to lie down. I don't feel well."

Troubled, Emily watched Melody return to her room at the end of the corridor, then stared at Jerome.

"So much for a relaxing weekend," he muttered. Together, they walked to Emily's room, where Jerome threw himself down on the bed. "It's like a bad joke or something. Welcome to Meadow Pines, where you can rest in peace—permanently!"

Emily didn't laugh. Instead, she moved to the window and looked out across the meadow. She could see Marcia in the northwest corner, heading for the path that would take her to the Land Rover. She watched her disappear, then paced to the centre of the room, chewing on her lower lip. Her gaze moved to the wall.

"What are you doing?"

"It wasn't Ben and Sylvia," she said. "That's Oscar's room."

Jerome sat up, watching her. "As usual, I have no idea what you're talking about."

"Last night, I was lying in bed trying to get to sleep when I heard voices coming through the wall. A man and a woman arguing. I'd assumed it was Ben and Sylvia."

"God, they're detestable," Jerome said, his nose wrinkling. "And what a massive racist. Did you hear what he called Daniel? I'm surprised he didn't want us sitting at separate dinner tables."

"They're not the most pleasant of people. But if it wasn't them I heard arguing, then who was it?"

Jerome shrugged his shoulders, got to his feet, and moved to the window. "Janelle's right, you know. It's weird to think Oscar's still out there, dangling from a rope. Did you see his face? How am I ever going to get that image out of my head?"

"It had to be one of the other women here at Meadow Pines."

"What did?"

"I hear an argument coming from Oscar's room. The next morning, he's dead." Emily moved away from the wall and paced the floor. "Why would he come here to do it? I mean, he must have specifically chosen Meadow Pines, which means it must have had some sort of significance to him."

"Maybe he wanted somewhere scenic to end it all?"

"And what about the robbery?" She frowned, deep lines creasing her brow. "Something's not adding up here."

Jerome stared at her, his eyes narrowing. "Oh, no. Don't you dare think about it! You've already got yourself into enough trouble this year without courting any more. The police will be here soon. So why don't you do yourself a favour and stay out of it."

"But don't you think something weird is going on?"

"Emily, don't . . ."

"But the timing of it all—it can't just be coincidence."

"Maybe, maybe not. I don't know, and I don't want to. In fact, the only thing I want to think about right now is how the hell we're getting home. I suggest you do the same."

Annoyed, Emily slumped down on the bed. "Why isn't the landline working?"

"Why are we still having this conversation?"

"Last night when Melody and I were at the lake, we heard something. I think someone was watching us."

"In fact, I think I'll just go to my room." Muttering under his breath, Jerome headed for the door.

Emily felt a surge of annoyance. She turned and glared in Jerome's direction. "You know, you're being ridiculous."

"I'm being ridiculous?" Jerome had frozen in the doorway. Now he turned and jabbed a finger at Emily. "The last time you got involved in something that wasn't your business, you ended up getting kidnapped and held in a mental hospital for three months."

"It wasn't a mental hospital. It was a rehab centre."

"You know what I mean! You just can't help yourself, can you? It's not your business, Emily. You're not the police, and you're not a P.I. Why can't you just be like everybody else? Why can't you just be normal?"

The words pierced her skin like needles. Emily sat on the bed, skin flushing scarlet. Jerome turned to leave. Then turned back.

"Last time, you almost died," he said. "You'd do well to remember that."

The door slammed shut behind him.

CHAPTER 14

Resentment boiled in Emily's stomach. Jerome was right, of course. After her treatment at the hands of Doctor Chelmsford, she was lucky to be alive and to have her mind intact. Unpleasant memories returned to her—hands holding her down; needles piercing her skin; bodies, starved and withered, decaying on beds.

She shook the images from her mind. But Jerome's words remained. 'Why can't you just be normal?' Emily had lived her entire life being normal, right up until her mother had grown sick, until Phillip had thrown himself from the school roof. All normal had ever done was pull a naïve veil over her eyes, blinding her to how cruel life could be. No wonder she had broken so easily—normal had made her weak.

Angry tears stung Emily's eyes as more unwanted memories forced their way into her mind. She spied her toiletry bag on the dresser. One pill would smother the memories in a blanket of numbness. The trouble was they'd still be there, waiting to torment her again once the chemicals had worn off.

Sitting down on the bed, Emily leaned back and allowed the coolness of the wall to seep into her skin. One day, she would be free of those conflicting feelings, she told herself. One day, all those terrible thoughts would leave her in peace. She just hoped that day would come soon.

Closing her eyes, she focused on her breathing, trying to empty her mind. Her thoughts were always so untamed, like stampeding wild horses. She tried to rein them in, to acknowledge each thought, then let it go. Minutes passed, but her mind would not release her.

What had happened to Oscar to drive him to suicide? Why had he chosen to die here? The questions presented themselves, over and over. Had Oscar randomly picked Meadow Pines as the place to end his life? Or did Meadow Pines have another significance?

Emily sat up, another question making itself known. "Had Oscar been here before?"

A noise that sounded like furniture scraping over floorboards interrupted her thoughts. Emily caught her breath. The noise had come from inside Oscar's room.

Hopping off the bed, she crossed the floor and pressed her ear against the wall. Silence greeted her. Was she losing her mind now? She was beginning to worry it was true when the sounds came again.

On the other side of the wall, things were being moved and replaced, opened and closed. Tip-toeing across the floorboards, she opened the door and crept into the hallway. She hovered for a moment, hearing only silence. Moving closer, she pressed her ear to Oscar's door. Someone was in there, moving about.

Without hesitation, Emily pushed open the door and peered inside. The woman had her back to her, and she was leaning over the bed, delving through the contents of what was presumably Oscar's suitcase.

"What are you doing?"

Startled by Emily's voice, the woman immediately pulled out her hands and spun around to face the door.

"Jesus, you scared me!" Helen said, sounding more irritated than startled. She glanced down at the suitcase, then back at Emily. "Come inside and close the door."

Emily moved into the room, shutting the door behind her.

"You shouldn't be in here," she said.

"Neither should you." Helen eyed her suspiciously.

Emily stared at the mess the journalist had made. "What are you looking for?"

"Evidence."

"Of what?"

"I'm not sure yet." Helen returned to the suitcase and continued rifling through its contents. She spoke as she worked. "Don't you think it's strange that this guy kills himself at the exact same time there's a robbery?"

Emily nodded emphatically. "And then the landline goes down."

"Exactly."

Helen pulled out a shirt, shook it, and threw it to one side. Emily continued to watch the journalist work, a confusing mix of disapproval and curiosity clouding her judgement.

"The police will be here soon," she said, coming to her senses. "I'm not sure you should be going through Oscar's belongings."

"Can't help it. Journalistic instinct." Helen threw everything back inside the suitcase, tossed it to one side, then moved over to the wardrobe. "You're Emily, right? We didn't get a chance to talk yet."

"Yes." Emily nodded, an uncomfortable feeling crawling up the back of her neck. "You're a journalist? Who do you write for?"

"Modern Living magazine. Do you read it?"

"No."

Reaching into the wardrobe, Helen stuffed her hands inside the pockets of Oscar's jacket. "You're not missing much. I was supposed to be writing a review of this place for a feature on UK getaways, but now we have a dead body and a robbery on our hands, Modern Living can suck it up—this story's getting me into the nationals."

"A suicide isn't exactly front-page news."

"No, but with the right angle I could make page four."

"And what would be the right angle?"

"I'll tell you when I find it."

Emily folded her arms, watching Helen's every move. For a moment, she caught herself admiring the journalist's bravado. Ambition was never a bad thing, she supposed. But the way Helen was sifting through a dead man's belongings without a second thought quickly turned that admiration into unease.

"The last journalist I knew who went chasing a story is still missing," Emily said.

"Really? Who was that?"

Emily thought about Reina Tammerworth. She had been investigating the mysterious death of her sister, Carmilla, who had died while under the care of Doctor Chelmsford. Reina had vanished a week after Alina Engel. The police suspected that Alina's husband,

Karl Henry, had murdered her. But with Karl currently in a prison cell, refusing to answer any questions while he awaited trial, the chances of recovering her body were becoming remote.

"Just someone," Emily said.

Helen closed the wardrobe door. "Well, 'just someone' should have been more careful. Here, help me with this."

She lifted the bottom end of the mattress with one hand and felt underneath with the other. Emily stayed by the door.

"Do you think it was someone here that took the phones?" she asked, watching Helen struggle.

"Let's look at the possibilities," the journalist said. "One, a member of staff did it."

"But there are only three of them. Two of which would run the risk of destroying their business if they were caught."

"True, but who was the only person missing when we found Oscar's body?"

"Sam, the chef. But he and Marcia are clearly in a relationship. It doesn't make sense that he'd risk losing her and his job."

Helen dropped the mattress and looked up. "Good thinking. We could make a journalist out of you yet, Emily. So, if the staff didn't do it, then that leaves us with option two—that one of the guests is responsible."

Emily thought about it. "Pamela keeps the office unlocked. That cabinet didn't look so hard to break into. But where would they hide their haul without the rest of us finding it? And if it is one of the guests, then why are they still hanging around?"

"All good points, but option two remains viable. What about option three—that we have an intruder in our midst?"

It was the option Emily liked the least—a stranger stalking through the forest and breaking into the house was the kind of mental image that led to terrible nightmares. "Well, we're in the middle of nowhere," she said, attempting to dispel the theory. "The nearest town has to be at least five or six miles away by road. But you have to get to the road first. Plus, it's a bit of a stretch to think someone might happen to be wandering through the depths of the New Forest on the off-chance of scoring some valuables."

"Unless they already know this place exists," Helen said, slipping her hands underneath Oscar's pillows. "Which would mean the suspect would have to be local."

"It's a possibility, I suppose. But all three options are ignoring something."

"Don't you mean ignoring someone?" A rather dead someone." Helen replaced the pillows, then shook her head, her eyes still roaming the room. "People who commit suicide leave notes. Where's Oscar's?"

Emily stared at the floor. Phillip hadn't left a note. But Phillip had been eleven years old and his suicide had been a spontaneous action.

"Perhaps it's on his body," she said. "Folded in his pocket or something." Emily thought of him still hanging there, then shuddered as she pushed the image from her head.

"Perhaps you're right. But we can't know for sure while he's still hanging there."

"I guess we'll have to wait until the police take him down."

Helen brushed hair from her eyes and looked around at the mess she'd created. "What do you think, Emily? Oscar's death, the robbery . . . coincidence or connected?"

Emily thought about the argument she'd heard last night through the wall. She debated whether to tell Helen about it, but quickly decided to keep the information to herself. Regardless of her own curiosity, she wasn't about to trust a journalist. Besides, Helen was as much a suspect as anyone else.

Emily heaved her shoulders. "How would I know?"

She waited for Helen to tidy Oscar's room, then followed her out to the corridor. No sooner had they closed the door behind them, the dull clang of the lunch bell resounded through the house. Lifting a finger to her lips, Helen winked at Emily, then made her way downstairs.

Jerome's door was the first to open.

"Someone's hungry," he said, spying Emily. His smile faded. "Listen, I didn't mean to snap at you before. It's just—well, you're still recovering. The last thing you need right now is to get mixed up in more trouble."

Emily stared at him.

"I just want you to be okay, that's all."

"I'm fine," she said, her voice hard and cold. Doors opened. The other guests emerged from their rooms, eyeing each other as they headed for the stairs. Emily glanced at Jerome and guilt welled in her chest. "Look, I know you're worried about me and I appreciate it. I really do. But I can take care of myself."

Jerome nodded, but he wouldn't meet her gaze. "I worry, that's all. I don't want you to get hurt."

Deciding now was not the best time to tell Jerome about her encounter with Helen, Emily hooked her arm in his.

"You're a good friend," she told him. Together, they made their way down to the dining hall.

CHAPTER 15

The others were already sitting down, waiting as Sam dished up hot lentil soup. In an apparent bid to keep the peace, Janelle had wedged herself between Ben and Daniel. Helen sat opposite them. She looked up as Emily entered the room, catching her eye.

The emptiness of Oscar's seat pervaded the room like an uninvited dinner guest. Emily slipped into the adjacent chair, letting Jerome sit next to Daniel. Helen passed a bowl of soup to Emily, who took it without saying a word. At the end of the table, some colour had returned to Melody's complexion. She leaned in towards Emily.

"Are you all right? You look funny."

Emily gave her a weak smile. "I'm fine. Just a little spooked."

Marcia still wasn't here. She wondered how long it had been since she'd set off for Lyndhurst. The absence of time was beginning to feel more like a trap than a release.

Once everyone had bowls of soup in front of them, Pamela stood up. "I think we all agree our present circumstances are deeply upsetting," she said. "Nevertheless, I'd like to ask everyone here to take a moment to think of Oscar's family. They no doubt have an extremely difficult time ahead of them, so for a few minutes, let's try to focus on sending positive thoughts and—"

"Why aren't the police here yet?" Helen was staring at Pamela intently, her eyebrows raised. "I mean, how long does it take to drive to Lyndhurst. Ten, fifteen minutes?"

All eyes turned towards Pamela.

"We're not easy to get to," she said. "You've experienced that for yourself. The police station is small, manned by just a handful of officers. It may take them some time to get organised."

"Hicksville," muttered Sylvia, not quite under her breath.

Helen persisted. "Still, it has to have been over an hour, hasn't it? Does anyone actually know what time it is?"

Murmurs travelled along the table.

"She has a point," Janelle said, her usual warmth waning. "Even if the emergency services are busy organising themselves, wouldn't Marcia have headed back to let us know what's going on? She knows we have no means of communication."

"That's right," Ben said. His lip had grown even fatter, like a ripe plum. "Where is she? And what is the time? I've had enough of this digital detox bullshit. You have a computer in your office. Computers tell the time."

Pamela looked around the table. She hesitated before sliding a hand inside her pocket and pulling out a wristwatch.

"It's a little after two-thirty."

Sylvia's eyes narrowed. "And where did you get that from?"

"It stays in my pocket. We need to have a way to time meals and the yoga sessions. Look, might I suggest that we eat the lunch Sam has kindly prepared for us and give Marcia a little more time. This isn't the city. Things can take a little longer. Besides, I think it's best we keep ourselves—"

"What about the computer?" Sylvia interrupted. "Can't we just jump online and get help that way?"

"No phone line means no internet," Sam explained.

"Has anyone tried the phone again?" Helen said. "Perhaps there's some sort of fault that can be fixed. Like a disconnected wire or something."

Frustration crept into Pamela's voice. "Of course we've tried. You're more than welcome to check for yourself. The junction box is on the outside wall to the left of the porch."

Helen was on her feet and moving out of the room before Pamela could say another word.

"And what about compensation?" Ben pushed his bowl of soup away and folded his arms. "Not just for the things we've had stolen, but for this whole waste of a weekend."

Emily watched Pamela's calm demeanour fracturing like a broken eggshell. She wasn't envious of her having to manage the chaos.

"As I clearly mentioned before, everyone will be compensated," Pamela said.

Sylvia waved a hand in the air. "And what about getting out of here? Have you thought about that?"

"We'll have to deal with transport once Sergeant Wells has arrived. I'm sure there's a simple solution. If your vehicle is insured perhaps you can get replacement keys."

"Perhaps isn't going to get me home, is it?" Sylvia snapped. She glared at Pamela, then shot a sideways glance at Ben.

"This will all be over very soon," Pamela said, exhaustion creeping into her voice. "I'm sure by the time we've finished eating, Marcia will be back with news."

"Or on her way to the nearest pawn shop," Ben snorted.

Spent, Pamela sat down. Quiet descended over the table. Emily stared into her soup. She had no appetite. In fact, except for Jerome, no one had lifted a spoon. Pamela was probably right, she thought—rural police forces lacked both the resources and manpower that city constabularies possessed. It was understandable that it would take longer to organise themselves, but the knowledge did nothing to quell the doubt in Emily's mind.

When Helen burst into the room moments later, that doubt quickly turned to panic.

"Get up! Get up, now!" she breathed, skidding to a halt on the flagstone floor. "You need to see this with your own eyes!"

CHAPTER 16

Emily followed the others past the Hardys' living quarters, through the back door, and out to the porch, concerned chatter growing louder with every step.

Helen raced ahead, pointing to a metal box attached to the exterior wall. The group crowded around, bustling against each other as they strained to see. A gap opened and Emily squeezed into it. She now had a clear view of the box, and the severed wiring inside.

"Whoever broke into the cabinet must have cut the line to stop us from getting help,"

Helen said. "Or to at least buy them more time to make a break for it."

Daniel waded through the bodies until he stood beside Emily. "Wouldn't that suggest the thief is an outsider? And that he's now long gone with our belongings."

"Not necessarily. Perhaps the thief is right here, waiting for the right moment to grab their stash and run," Helen said, causing each person in the group to turn and eye the others.

"Well if it's one of us, we need to find out who," Janelle said, her calm demeanour all but gone. "I have places to be on Monday. I can't be stuck here, waiting for a replacement car key."

Strained voices filled the air. Helen held up a hand. "The question is, how do we go about uncovering the thief's identity?"

"That's easy," Ben said, pushing his way to the front, with Sylvia close behind. "We do what I said—we conduct a search of everyone's rooms."

"Absolutely not." Heads turned towards Pamela, who had moved away from the group in a clear attempt to re-establish her position as leader. Her eyes moved from face to face. "I understand your concern and I sympathise with you all, but I will not have you ransacking my house like Vikings. When Sergeant Wells gets here, whoever stole your belongings will answer to him."

"But when will he get here?" Helen said. Heads swivelled in her direction. "The police should have been here ages ago. Meanwhile, a thief is about to get away with our belongings, and poor Oscar is still out there hanging from a tree."

A chorus of agreement rang through the group. Emily felt a hand squeeze her arm and she looked up to see Jerome's worried face peering down at her.

"I don't like this," he whispered. "It's getting out of control."

Emily could only agree. Tensions were already running high, but now, with the discovery of the sabotaged phone line and the idea that a thief was hiding among them, the group was quickly sinking into paranoia. How long would it be before a mob mentality took hold?

"We form a search party and go room to room," Ben said. "If no one has anything to hide, there'll be nothing to find. At least that way we'll know who we can trust."

"Good idea," Helen said. "But everyone needs to agree."

"And if we don't?" Daniel said.

"Well, I guess Sergeant Wells will know who to call on first when he arrives."

"You can't do this," Pamela said, thrusting a hand on her hip. "It's unethical and I won't allow it."

Helen smiled. "What if we have everyone's permission? You all want to get out of here, right? The quicker we find the thief, the quicker we find our car keys. Let's have a show of hands."

Ben, Sylvia, and Helen raised their hands. They were quickly followed by Janelle.

"What about the rest of you?" Helen stared at Jerome. "Do you give permission for your room to be searched?"

"Only if you promise to make my bed while you're in there," he said. "Maybe fluff up the pillows?"

"How about you, Emily?"

She didn't like the idea of strangers rifling through her belongings, but Emily had a sinking feeling that it was going to happen with or without her permission. And she didn't want to give Helen an excuse to start asking questions that would lead to her name appearing in newspapers again.

Reluctantly, Emily nodded.

Helen turned to Melody. "You've been very quiet. What about you—can we search your room?"

"No." Melody's body seemed to shrink in on itself like a punctured balloon.

"No? Why not?"

"It's my private space. I don't want you going in there."

"It'll be all over in two minutes," Sylvia said, taking a step towards her. "If you have nothing to hide, then there's nothing to worry about."

Melody shook her head. Her lower lip began to tremble. "No! It's my room, my space. You're not allowed to violate it."

"I think perhaps Melody and I will sign up for that search party," Jerome said, moving up beside her. "Someone needs to make sure everything's above board."

"I'll join you." Daniel shot a challenging glare at Ben.

Helen gazed at Pamela, a slight smile etched on her face. "The more the merrier. We'll only search the guest rooms. For now."

Before Pamela could reply, the group began to disperse.

"Are you coming?" Jerome waited for Emily, who shook her head and dug her hands into her pockets.

A tight, anxious knot was twisting her stomach. She had no interest in rummaging through people's personal belongings, and now that Jerome would be there to oversee the search, she knew it would be conducted with both sensitivity and military-like precision.

"Make sure they behave themselves," she told him, then watched him disappear inside the house.

Now, only Pamela and Sam were left behind. Both were silent and unmoving.

"A few stolen phones and people are up in arms," Emily said, the air around her feeling thick with trouble. "A stranger hangs himself and no one wants to know."

Pamela nodded, slowly and deliberately. "You've just summed up everything that's wrong with modern society."

CHAPTER 17

They began with Jerome's room. To everyone's surprise, Helen had elected not to join the search. Instead, she had set herself up in the art room to work on the outline for her news story.

"I hope you're going to leave that bed as neat as you found it," Jerome said, as he stood in the doorway, watching Ben and Sylvia take apart his room. "If there's one thing I can't stand it's creased sheets."

"We need to check your bags," Ben said.

"Be my guest."

Out in the corridor, Melody was growing increasingly agitated, hovering from one foot to the other, and swinging her arms from side to side.

Finding nothing, Ben and Sylvia left the room. Seconds later, Helen's door opened and Daniel and Janelle emerged.

"It's clean," Janelle said. She stared across the corridor at Oscar's door. "Should we take a look?"

"Maybe a quick one, but don't touch anything," Jerome replied. Brushing past Melody, he followed Ben and Sylvia into Emily's room. Being here without Emily felt like an invasion of her privacy, especially when strangers whom he disliked with increasing intensity were rifling through her belongings. But seeing as how Ben and Sylvia were conducting their search with about as much subtlety as a police raid on a drug den, he had little choice but to watch them with hawk-like attention. While Ben pulled back bedsheets and pillows, Sylvia picked up Emily's toiletry bag.

"You don't need to look in there," Jerome said, raising a hand.

"Why not?"

"Because there's such a thing as discretion—something that's clearly an alien concept to you."

He marched up to her. Ben stepped in between, blocking his path. Smiling, Sylvia unzipped the bag and pulled out strips of medication.

"Okay, now you're crossing a line." Pushing past Ben, Jerome snatched the pills away. "This has nothing to do with what you're looking for."

"What's wrong with her?" Sylvia asked.

"Nothing. You don't know her. You've no right to be making judgements." Jerome returned the toiletry bag to the dresser. "I think we're done in here."

Janelle's and Daniel's rooms were next, followed by Sylvia's and Ben's. Each pair searched the others while Jerome stood in the hall, keeping a watchful eye. Hovering beside him, Melody moved on to chewing her fingernails.

"Well, I guess you're both off the hook," Jerome said to Ben and Sylvia, once their rooms had been searched from top to bottom. "To be honest, my money was on the pair of you."

"Us?" Ben's face soured to a dangerous shade of purple. "We can more than afford to get what we want without resorting to stealing!"

There was now just one guest room remaining.

"I said no." Melody stood between the search party and the door. Lines creased her forehead as she swayed back and forth, her eyes not quite meeting theirs.

"What is your problem?" Sylvia said, thrusting a hand on her hip. "We've all been through it and not one of us complained."

Ben reached a hand towards Melody, who flinched and stepped back. "We'll be quick," he said. "It'll be over before you know it."

"I said no!"

Jerome moved up beside Melody. "We agreed outside that people needed to give their consent to have their room searched. Melody hasn't given it, which means you'll just have to wait for the police."

"Where are the police?" Sylvia had moved closer to Melody. "We could be waiting all day."

Ben sidled up next to her. "That's right. And if someone is saying no to us, then I'd say that was a pretty solid indicator they have something to hide."

"Guess what? You're not the cops!" Jerome was fast losing his patience with these people. He glanced at Daniel for backup.

"He's right." Daniel nodded in agreement. "Melody doesn't want us in her room. We have to respect that."

Next to him, Janelle's eyes were filled with conflict.

"Okay fine, we're not the police," Ben said, ignoring Daniel and squaring up to Jerome, until there were just inches between them. "But neither are you. So, if we want to search that room, who are you to stop us?"

Anger coursed through Jerome's veins. He leaned in until his eyes were level with Ben's. "First of all, there's this thing called personal space," he said, his voice firm and steady. "Second of all, who do you think you people are? Melody has said no. It's been a while since I used a dictionary, but I'm pretty sure that means you'd do well to get the hell out of my face."

Ben took a slow step back. "We'll see about that," he said.

Before anyone could react, Sylvia slipped to the side and barged past Melody. She threw open the bedroom door and stepped inside.

"Stop!" Melody shrieked, running into the middle of the room. "Please, stop!"

Ben followed her in, a sly smirk twisting his lips. Daniel and Janelle stood helplessly watching from outside.

"You assholes!" Jerome wanted to take the couple's heads and smash them together, to throw them down the stairs, one after the other. Instead, he stood and watched as they took Melody's room apart.

"We have to do what needs to be done," Sylvia said, catching his eye. She picked through the garments hanging in the wardrobe as if browsing through a clothing store and seeing nothing she liked. Then she moved to the dresser, where a framed photograph sat on top.

"Is this your cat?" Sylvia laughed as she held it up.

Melody wept and dug nails into her thighs, watching as Ben moved onto the bed and began stripping it down to the mattress. As he held up a pillow, his eyes lit up. Realisation rippling across his face, he reached inside the pillowslip.

"Look what I found!" His voice was filled with triumph as he pulled something out and showed it to the group.

Out in the corridor, Janelle's mouth hung open, while Daniel stared in stunned silence.

Melody shrieked and pulled at her hair. "I told you not to come in here! I told you!"

Behind her, Jerome turned away and slowly hung his head.

CHAPTER 18

The day was heating up. Tiny beads of perspiration lined Emily's brow as she sat on the porch seat and watched birds flit over the treetops. Pamela and Sam had returned indoors a few minutes ago, and now that she was alone, she took a moment to absorb the stillness.

She understood why people were upset—discovering Oscar's body and then learning they'd been robbed hadn't exactly done much for the equilibrium of the group—but all of that fighting and shouting and pointing of fingers had left Emily shaken.

But it wasn't just the dissension among the guests of Meadow Pines that had unsettled her. It was Oscar. There was something about his suicide that felt . . . off.

From somewhere above, she heard voices, doors opening and closing, and she hoped Jerome was managing to keep the search party under control. He could certainly give Helen a run for her money—years of serving hard-nosed Londoners had taught him a thing or two when it came to pushy characters—but she was worried about how he would handle Ben. Daniel had already taken a beating from the man—although they'd both come out of it worse for wear—but Jerome wasn't a fighter.

Yes, he could talk his way out of situations and he could act the tough guy when he wanted to, but if it came down to an actual fight, Emily wasn't confident he'd walk away unscathed. She was glad he wasn't alone up there with them.

Growing restless, she crossed the porch and went inside, slowing down as she passed the

Hardy's living quarters. It was quiet in there. Perhaps Pamela was meditating, or perhaps she was pacing up and down, wondering where her daughter had got to, and worrying about the future of her business. Suicide and theft weren't exactly great selling points. And if Helen's story made the national newspapers, Meadow Pines could suffer a terrible blow to its reputation—if not an irreparable one.

Soup bowls still sat untouched on the dining hall tables. Picking up a jug of water, Emily filled a glass and drank it down. It was cold and refreshing, and for a few moments, pulled her away from her busy mind. When she'd had her fill, she paced towards the kitchen doors. It was quiet in there, too.

Leaving the dining hall, Emily wandered along, passing by the meditation room and the art room. She could hear the search party moving about upstairs. Voices grew louder. Bodies spilled from rooms. Then Melody's hysterical voice pierced the air, quickly followed by Jerome's angry tones.

Emily hurried to the foot of the stairs and looked up. An argument had broken out. She heard people shouting, accusing each other. Melody was sobbing.

"Shit." She turned to head back to the Hardys' living quarters, but then Pamela appeared in the hall, eyes dark and troubled. She looked exhausted, as if she hadn't slept for days. She flashed Emily a questioning glance, then hurried upstairs.

Emily followed, reaching the top of the steps in time to see Pamela pushing her way into Melody's already crowded room.

"Look what I found!" Ben shouted. "It was stashed inside Melody's pillow."

Emily hung back in the corridor. She heard Melody crying, but she couldn't see her through all the bodies.

"I'm not a thief, Pamela! Please believe me, it's not what you think!"

Sylvia's voice was sharp and acerbic. "Then how do you explain this? I knew that Goody Two-shoes act was a load of crap!"

When Jerome spoke next, Emily was shocked to hear him so angry. "We agreed we'd only search the rooms of those people who gave consent. These two idiots practically pulled out pitchforks and burning torches and forced their way into Melody's room. You should be ashamed of yourselves!"

"Well, lucky that we did," Ben snapped. "Because see what we found. Now she needs to tell us where she's stashed the rest of it."

Emily moved up to the doorway. Through the gaps, she stole glimpses of Melody, who was sitting on the bed, hair draped over her face as she wept. Ben stood over her, holding the source of all the drama—a black touchscreen tablet.

Taking it from him, Pamela regarded the tablet as if it was a bloody knife. "Melody? What do you have to say about this?"

Braying sobs escaped Melody's mouth. "I didn't steal anything, I swear! It's mine. I brought it with me. I didn't want to hand it in. I'm sorry, Pamela!"

A wave of muttered voices surged through the room. Pamela let out a heavy sigh. When she spoke again, her words were quiet and considered, heavy with disappointment. "No mobile phones. No technology. You've been here enough times to know the rules, Melody! You deliberately hid this from me?"

"I'm sorry! I just wanted to have it close to me, so I didn't miss Derek."

Emily edged closer. Janelle and Daniel were blocking the doorway, their backs turned to her. She could see the top of Jerome's head in the far left corner. Helen wasn't here.

Clasping the tablet to her chest, Pamela turned to address the group. "As disappointing as Melody's behaviour is to me, I can assure you she's no thief," she said. "I remember her handing in her phone when she checked in yesterday, but she most certainly did not hand in this tablet."

Ben laughed and shook his head. "Oh, come on! Don't you know when you're being played?"

"This isn't proof of anything except that Melody deliberately broke the rules of Meadow Pines," Pamela replied coolly.

On the bed, Melody wept into her hands.

Ben continued to argue, but Emily was no longer listening. She tapped Janelle on the shoulder.

"Where's Helen?" she asked.

"She's downstairs working on her story." Janelle turned back as Pamela handed the tablet to Melody.

"You're giving it back to her?" Ben was incredulous.

Pamela avoided his gaze. "I'd say the weekend was over, wouldn't you?"

Something wasn't right. Backing away from Melody's room, Emily headed for the stairs, a frown creasing her brow. After Helen had cajoled the group into searching the rooms, it made no sense that she would be sat downstairs, missing out on the drama.

But Helen wasn't downstairs.

Checking each room, Emily found them all empty. She paused in the foyer, a growing unease clawing at her stomach. Then realisation hit her. If Helen wasn't in the house, it could only mean one thing. Helen was somewhere outside—and Emily had a horrible feeling she knew exactly where to find her.

CHAPTER 19

A gentle breeze teased the rose petals as Emily hurried through the garden and pushed open the gate. Shielding her eyes from the sun, she turned her head, scanning the vegetable field and the meadow. What was Helen up to? Had she arranged the room search as a distraction? So that she could slip away unnoticed?

Emily circled the house, stopping to check the back porch then moving around the side to peer through the kitchen windows. The room was empty. Which meant Sam was missing, too.

Suspicion mounting, Emily made her way to the edge of the forest. She thought back over the last couple of hours, to when she had found Helen searching Oscar's room. She'd been looking for evidence, she'd said. Evidence that would help boost her story and get her into the national newspapers.

But Helen hadn't found anything useful. She hadn't—

Emily spun around. "Of course."

Returning to the front of the house, she slipped through the garden gate and headed across the meadow.

Helen had been looking for a suicide note. Emily had suggested it could be somewhere on Oscar's body.

She started to run, clearing the meadow and dashing into the cool shade of the forest. It took a few minutes to find the right path, but then Emily was hurrying along it, ducking under branches and weaving through the undergrowth. As she reached the clearing, breathless and with her clothes clinging to her skin, she came to an abrupt stop.

Oscar was no longer hanging from the tree. Now he was laid out on a sheet of tarpaulin, the rope still trailing from his distended neck, and his lifeless, bloodshot eyes staring upward. Helen was leaning over him, her face twisted with revulsion. Sam stood to one side, watching her, an axe slung over his shoulder.

"What have you done?" Emily's horrified voice shattered the silence. Helen immediately tensed, straightening her body. Sam dropped the axe to his side. They both shot glances at each other.

Emily tore her gaze from Oscar and glared at Helen. "I knew you couldn't be trusted."

Helen smiled, rolled her eyes.

"Not that I have to explain myself to you," she said, "but I was talking to Sam while everyone was upstairs, and we agreed how awful it was that poor Oscar was still hanging out here with no sign of the police . . ."

She shifted her gaze to Sam, her eyes round and doe-like.

Sam nodded. "It wasn't right to leave him up there like that."

"Which is why Sam cut him down," Helen quickly added.

Emily moved closer. This was not the first body she'd seen. She had witnessed her mother's last breath snatched away by cancer. She had seen Phillip Gerard's crumpled form in the playground. She had seen the dead and dying victims of Doctor Williams, hidden away in the attic of the Ever After Care Foundation. After seeing so much death, she'd presumed being this close to another lifeless body would be easier to stomach, but the same familiar surge of nausea churned her insides.

Oscar barely looked human. His body was bloated, his skin horribly discoloured, his ears and nostrils caked in dried blood. His fat, black tongue sat on his chin like an overfed leech.

Emily looked away, instead focusing her disgust on Helen. "You didn't find anything of worth in Oscar's room, so you thought you'd just cut him down and go through his pockets?"

Helen's smile was wide and innocent. "As I said, I didn't cut Oscar down. Sam did. And I haven't touched him."

"But you were about to."

Helen instinctively glanced at Oscar's body. Emily followed her gaze. Something was poking out of the dead man's shirt pocket.

"You were right," Helen breathed as she crouched down.

Sam stepped forward. "What is it?"

"You do realise that you're now tampering with police evidence?" Emily warned. Part of her wanted to turn around and head back to the house, to have nothing more to do with Helen's underhand, manipulative ways. As for Sam, he was an idiot. How easy had it been to dupe him with fluttering eyelashes and sympathetic words? Emily flashed him an angry look.

Helen reached towards Oscar's pocket, then drew back, uncertainty passing over her face. Perhaps there was an essence of conscience in there after all, Emily thought.

"We'll just say it fell out." Helen shrugged, then plucked the object from Oscar's pocket.

Perhaps not.

Helen stood up, turning it over her in her hands.

"What is it?" Sam repeated.

Shaking her head, Helen said, "It's not a suicide note. It's a picture."

It was a passport photograph, the kind taken in a photo booth at a shopping mall. The man in the picture was white and looked to be in his early twenties. He was clean shaven, with dark, wiry hair and deep brown eyes. A small but visible scar was etched into his skin, just above his left eyebrow. His expression was blank, as if any trace of emotion had been erased by the camera flash; as if, like Oscar, he'd already expelled his final breath.

Helen held the picture up to Emily, who refused to take it. "I wonder who he is. His son perhaps?"

"Oscar doesn't look old enough to have a child that age." Emily glanced down at the body on the tarpaulin. Flies were already gathering on his face.

"You should put that back where you found it," Sam said. "Then let's cover him up. The insects are getting to him."

"You recognise him?" Helen asked, holding up the picture. Sam shook his head. She flipped the photograph over. There was nothing written there, no clue as to who the man was.

"Maybe we should take it back, show it to the others."

Emily stared at the man's empty face, memorising every detail. "Your fingerprints are on it," she said. "Sam's right, you should put it back before you get anyone else into trouble."

Wiping the photograph against her vest, Helen crouched down, then slipped it back inside Oscar's pocket. She backed away as Sam came forward and folded the edges of the tarpaulin over the body. A collective sigh of relief shifted through the clearing. Now, it was just like staring at a roll of carpet.

"I guess we should go back to the house and face the music," Helen said, rubbing her palms against her stomach. "No doubt Nancy Drew here will be dying to tell Pamela what we've done."

Emily wasn't listening. She stared up at the old oak tree. Oscar had hanged himself from its lowest branch, but the lowest branch was at least fifteen feet from the ground. He would have needed to stand on something, then kick it away.

Emily scanned the clearing. There was nothing. She moved closer, examining the trunk for easy footholds, places to grab.

Helen followed her, watching as she rubbed fingers along the back of the oak tree. "What are you doing?"

Emily examined the carving she'd discovered earlier that day. It was old; at least, old enough for its edges to have been worn smooth by the weather.

"Is that a compass?" Helen asked, getting uncomfortably close.

Emily shrugged. "I thought it was a star."

She stared up at the tree branches and dense canopy, then down at the ground. A posy of dead flowers, their petals brown and withered, lay rotting at the base of the tree.

"We should get back," Sam said.

As they left the clearing, Emily couldn't shake the feeling that the circumstances surrounding Oscar's death were not as straightforward as they seemed. By the time they'd crossed the meadow, she was wondering if it was even a suicide.

CHAPTER 20

Jerome and Daniel were waiting on the front step when Emily returned to the house with Helen and Sam trailing just behind. By the look on Jerome's face, Emily already knew she had some explaining to do. She met the men in the garden.

"Marcia?" she asked.

Jerome shook his head. "Pamela's playing it cool, but I think she's starting to worry."

"Where is she now?"

"I'm not sure. Somewhere inside."

"And the others?"

"Ben and Sylvia are sulking in their rooms. Janelle's with Melody. That girl can certainly cry. Where've you been? I saw you sneaking off downstairs."

Emily took in a breath. "Helen and Sam cut Oscar down."

Jerome's eyes almost burst out of his head. "What did you just say to me? Emily Swanson, you better tell me straight you had nothing to do with that!"

"I didn't," she said, turning to see Helen and Sam enter the garden. Sam still had the axe in his hand. "I realised what she was up to and I went after her to try and stop it. I got there too late."

"You know you can play the innocent in front of your friend there, but I didn't see you running away when we found that photo." Helen moved up until she was by Emily's side. "And come to think of it, you didn't run away when we were in Oscar's room, either."

Jerome stared at Helen, then at Emily.

Helen smiled. "Oh, she didn't mention that?"

Anger ignited Emily's insides. What was it with journalists? "I heard noises through the wall. I went to see what it was," she explained, her jaw clenching. "Helen was searching through Oscar's things, apparently looking for leads for her story."

"Well, that's one way of putting it, I suppose," Helen shrugged. "But the fact remains, things aren't what they seem here and I intend to find out exactly what's going on, with or without any of your help."

"Is that so?" The voice startled them.

Emily turned to see Pamela standing in the doorway, arms folded across her chest. Her eyes, cold and angry, were fixed on Sam.

"My living room," she said. "Now."

———

Emily and Jerome sat on the back porch, facing away from each other as they stared into the trees. As the minutes ticked by, the air grew thick and hot, until Emily felt as though she was inhaling molasses. Restless and irritable, she got up and moved over to the railings. She glared angrily at the forest. Then she shot a glance at Jerome.

"So, we're not even going to talk about this?" she said. "You're just going to ignore me?"

Jerome pursed his lips and arched an eyebrow. He was silent for another minute. Then he said, "I don't understand you. After the conversation we had—after everything you've been through—you still had to go and get yourself involved."

Emily turned on him. "You're not my keeper, Jerome. You don't get to tell me what to do."

"You're right, I'm not your keeper. I'm your friend. I care about what happens to you." He stared off into the trees, the veins at his temples throbbing. "I've watched you go through hell this year and come out the other side. A little screwed up, yes. But you came out alive. I just don't understand why you would put yourself in the firing line for more trouble. Are you a masochist? Is that it? Or are you still punishing yourself for what happened to Phillip?"

A flare of anger burst inside Emily's head. "This has nothing to do with Phillip! I heard someone moving around in Oscar's room and I went to see who it was. I didn't touch anything. I didn't get involved. When I realised what Helen was going to do with Oscar—what she manipulated Sam into doing—my first instinct was to stop her." She stabbed a finger in Jerome's direction. "I don't need to explain my actions to you or to anyone."

"You know what, Emily Swanson? Sometimes you're a real asshat!"

Jerome stood up and stormed towards the back door. He stopped. When he turned around again, his steely gaze was swamped with hurt. "You know, maybe you should try letting people give a shit about you sometimes," he said. "Maybe you wouldn't feel so alone. God knows, you might even start giving a shit about them, too."

"I tried that already," Emily said, the words shooting from her mouth. "Look where it got me."

They stood in silence, anger and hurt clashing in the space between them. Jerome was frozen with his head bowed and his hands hanging by his sides, like a scolded child. Guilt pressed down on Emily's chest.

"Something's not right here," she said. The guilt spread from her chest up to her throat. "You saw the tree Oscar hanged himself from —that branch was too high for him to have reached it without standing on something."

Jerome scuffed the floor with his shoe. He looked up, then back down at his feet. "So, he climbed the tree then jumped."

"How do you climb fifteen feet up a tree trunk with nothing to hold on to?" Emily said, their fight already being pushed to the recesses of her mind. "Last night, I heard Oscar arguing with a woman in his room. This morning he's dead. When they cut him down, they found a photo of a man in his shirt pocket. White, dark-haired, a few years younger than us. It has to mean something."

Jerome was quiet for a long time, staring past Emily and into the forest. He rubbed his face with his hands. "I just want to go home."

"We can't," Emily said. "Not until we've been given the all clear by the police."

"It's been hours. Where are they? Where the hell is Marcia?"

"That's the million-dollar question." Emily moved up beside him, her feet testing the ground like a soldier in a minefield. "We're stuck here for the time being, Jerome. There's nothing we can do about it."

"So, you're activating detective mode just to kill some time?"

"I'm not activating any kind of mode. But I am going to go and check on Pamela. Just to see if she's all right. She must be worried about Marcia. Plus, her business is going to take a hit when this gets into the papers. I'm sure our journalist friend will see to that."

Jerome folded his arms across his chest. "And while you're in there playing Good Samaritan, I don't suppose you'll be casually dropping the odd inquisitive question about a certain photograph you've just uncovered?"

Emily reached out a hand, then drew it back. "I'll be five minutes."

"Speaking of our journalist friend," said Jerome, holding the door open. "I'd be very careful to avoid answering any of her questions. She clearly doesn't give a rat's ass about who she hurts to get her story."

Emily nodded. "Let her ask. As Martha Graham once said, what people in the world think of you is really none of your business."

The words felt strange on her tongue. A few hours ago, she'd been worried about how the others would react if they found out about her past. But in comparison to Oscar's death, what she had or had not done now felt inconsequential.

"I thought RuPaul said that," Jerome said.

"Philistine." Emily stopped in the doorway. "You're wrong about something else, too."

"What's that?"

"I do care about you. I care very much."

CHAPTER 21

Leaving Jerome on the porch, Emily ducked inside the dimly-lit corridor and took a moment to adjust to the coolness of the house. The Hardys' living quarters were up ahead. Emily hovered outside. It was quiet, so she knocked on the door. Pamela answered a few seconds later, looking weary and lost.

"I wanted to check in, see how you were doing," Emily said.

Pamela tried to smile as she invited her inside. The door opened on the living room. Colourful woven mats covered the floorboards. Abstract paintings hung on burnt orange walls. A trace of sandalwood hung in the air like a memory.

Sam stood, hunched up in the corner. His eyes briefly met Emily's and she saw anger burning in them.

"Thank you, Sam. That will be all," Pamela said, her tone clipped. It was clear the reprimand she'd delivered had been severe. Head bowed, Sam gave Emily one final look before he strode across the floor, brushing past Pamela as if she were invisible.

When they were alone, Pamela ushered Emily to a small couch before sinking into an armchair next to a bookcase filled with spiritual teachings and theology studies.

On the other side of the room, a fat Chinese-style Buddha with a round belly and wide smile sat on an altar. Sculptures of Hindu gods and goddesses dominated a shelf above—Ganesh, the Deva of Intellect and Wisdom, whose father, Shiva, lopped off his head and replaced it with an elephant's; Parvati, mother of Ganesh and goddess of love, fertility, and devotion; Kali, the dark mother, four-armed goddess of creation, preservation, and destruction.

"In answer to your question," Pamela said, leaning back on the chair, "this hasn't been one of my better days. But for the sake of maintaining order within the group, let's just pretend I'm fine. How are you? I'm sure this isn't the weekend you had in mind when you signed up."

"I'm sure it's not the weekend you had in mind either," Emily said. "Still no word from Marcia?"

Pamela's eyes found the window. Her face paled. "She's always so reliable. I don't understand it."

"There could be any number of reasons why she isn't back. Perhaps she's had car trouble. Perhaps, like you said, the police are being slow at getting their act together. It must be difficult not to worry, though—especially with everything that's happened."

Pamela took a moment to adjust her position and smooth out the creases in her clothing. "Marcia and I, we don't always see eye to eye," she said, a weary smile on her lips. "When she was a teenager, she was very wilful. To be honest, I often wonder if I did the right thing moving her out here at such an impressionable age. She was cut off from society, home-schooled, with no real friends to speak of. But ten years on, she's still here. That must mean something, don't you think? That she doesn't hate being here as much as she used to say she did. Or, at the very least, she finally warmed to its merits."

"Perhaps we should send someone else to Lyndhurst, even if it means walking," Emily said. She searched the room with her eyes. There was no clock on the wall, no television, no stereo equipment; no indication that they were living in the twenty-first century.

"Perhaps." Getting up, Pamela moved to the window. Outside, the forest swayed in the breeze. "When we first came to Meadow Pines there was so much work to do. The house had been empty for years. All the woodwork was rotten, all the windows smashed in. Animals had made it their home. Marcia and I worked day and night, putting every last drop of energy into transforming what was essentially a ruin into what you see today."

She was quiet for a moment, lost in memories. Then her shoulders sagged. "Meadow Pines was supposed to be my oasis. A sanctuary from the toils of modern living, where the outside world remained on the other side of the gate. The moment Helen's story appears in the papers, Meadow Pines will come tumbling down. My home, the retreat—all of it will be gone."

"You don't know that," said Emily. "Oscar's suicide has nothing to do with the practices of Meadow Pines. People will understand."

Pamela surprised her by laughing. "Have you ever heard the phrase, mud sticks? I'm grateful for your optimism, I really am. But you know very well what happens when your reputation is dragged out in the open."

Emily's heart thumped in her chest as she stared at the woman's back. Did Pamela know who she was? Her paranoia was quickly met with relief.

"But that's the charms of the British tabloids for you," Pamela said. "Which is exactly why I stopped reading the newspapers years ago."

Emily peered down at her hands, which had clamped themselves to her knees. What the press had done to her following Phillip Gerard's suicide had been tantamount to a public flogging. A young boy had taken his own life, which was tragic and awful, but a dead child wouldn't sell as many copies as a child driven to suicide by his crazed teacher. The headlines had made the story front page news and suddenly everyone knew Emily Swanson's name.

She was the teacher accused of assaulting an already vulnerable child. The monster who'd reportedly attacked him after he'd turned to her for help, driving him to suicide. The truth —that Phillip had been saying terrible things about her recently deceased mother, that she had shouted at him, not hit him—had had little bearing.

Months later, as quickly as the tabloids had sought to destroy Emily, they had rallied around her, proclaiming her a hero for exposing the heinous crimes of Doctors Williams and Chelmsford. She had redeemed herself. All was forgiven.

The tabloids were as fickle as children, Emily thought; one minute they were your sworn enemy, the next your closest ally. She released her fingers from her knees and felt the tension sink into the floor. What people thought of her was none of her business, but it still didn't stop her from worrying.

"Are you all right?" Pamela was staring at her from the window. "You've lost a little colour."

Emily nodded. She hoped the headlines would be kind to Pamela and Meadow Pines, even if in her heart she knew it was a false hope. She turned her thoughts to the real reason she had knocked on Pamela's door.

"I keep thinking about Oscar. I wonder why he did it. I wonder why he chose Meadow Pines. Had he been here before?"

Moving away from the window, Pamela leaned against the wall. "No. I have a good memory for faces and I definitely hadn't seen his before. I have no idea why he chose this place. Tell me, Emily, what exactly did you see when you found Sam and Helen in the forest?

"Sam had already cut Oscar down," she said. "Helen talked him into it. She manipulated him."

Anger lit up Pamela's face. "Sam may not be the sharpest tool in the box but he's far from stupid. What he did, manipulated or not, will only make things worse for us."

Emily was quiet, observing the strain in Pamela's body.

"Did Sam tell you about the photograph?" she asked.

"Yes. A picture of a young man."

"Don't you think it's strange?"

"In what way?"

"Oscar didn't leave a suicide note, but he kept that photo in his pocket. It feels significant. I wonder who he is; the man in the picture."

Pamela's gaze flicked from Emily to the bookcase. "A family member, perhaps."

"They don't look related."

"A lover, then." The women's eyes met. Pamela clasped her hands together. "Regardless of who he is, these are matters for the police."

"Perhaps that man had visited Meadow Pines before," Emily said. "If you saw the picture you might recognise him."

"I think Oscar has been tampered with enough, don't you?"

Emily leaned forward on the couch. "You're right. Perhaps I could describe him to you instead."

Pamela sighed as her fingers intertwined. "Lots of people have passed through here, Emily. I highly doubt I'll be able to identify someone just from a description."

"But he was so distinctive. It was his eyes—they were deep and black, like staring into a void. And he had a scar just above his left eyebrow."

She watched as Pamela closed her eyes for a moment. When she opened them again, beads of perspiration had formed at her temples. "I'm sorry, I don't know what to tell you."

Leaning back, Emily eyed the shelves of books. "Well, I'm sure the police will have their ways and means of finding out who he is. It's just all very strange, isn't it? Oscar, the robbery, and now this photograph." She paused, watching Pamela closely. "There's something else. Something I haven't told anyone but Jerome."

Pamela returned to the armchair and sat down. "Do I want to hear this?"

Emily told her about the argument she'd heard coming from Oscar's room.

"An argument?" Pamela said, frowning. "With whom?"

"I'm not sure. But doesn't it suggest that someone here at Meadow Pines knew Oscar? Why else would they be in his room late at night?"

Pamela opened her mouth, then snapped it shut again. She shook her head. "But how could anyone know him? It was his first time at Meadow Pines. Unless one of the guests knew him from outside . . ."

"Whoever it is, they're keeping very quiet about it. Which makes me wonder what they're trying to hide." Emily hesitated, rubbing her chin with her thumb. "The more I think about it, the more questions appear, and they all keep coming back to how Oscar died."

Pamela stared at her with searching eyes. "Emily, what is it that you're trying to say?"

It was a good question, and one Emily thought about for a moment. "I'm having a hard time understanding how Oscar managed to hang himself without anything to stand on and with no way of climbing up to that branch."

Pamela's mouth moved silently up and down. Her eyes flicked from corner to corner. Then realisation punched her in the gut.

"You think someone murdered Oscar?" she gasped, sweat pouring from her brow. "I don't believe this! We'll never recover. It's all over. Meadow Pines is finished."

"I could be wrong," Emily said.

"And what if you're right?"

"If I'm right, if someone did kill Oscar, then there's a very good chance they're still here at Meadow Pines."

Pamela got to her feet. Her fingers twitched at her sides. Her eyes grew wide and glassy. "Where is my daughter? Why isn't she back with the police? What's happened to her?"

As Emily watched her return to the window and peer out, she felt a flutter of nerves in her chest. Was she right? Had someone murdered Oscar? She glanced over at Pamela and saw her shoulders trembling. Standing up, Emily went to go over to her.

Before she could move, the door flew open and Jerome burst into the room. He stared wide-eyed at Emily, then at Pamela.

"What is it?" Emily asked, her pulse racing.

When Jerome finally caught his breath, he said, "It's Ben and Sylvia! They're gone!"

CHAPTER 22

"I was heading up to my room when I saw the front door was open. I looked outside and there they were, making a run for it."

Emily, Jerome, and Pamela stood in the garden. In the northwest corner of the meadow, Ben and Sylvia were reaching the trail that would lead them from Meadow Pines back to civilisation. A second later, they were gone.

"They've cleared their rooms out," Daniel said, emerging from the house and joining the others at the garden gate. "If we hurry, we can catch up with them."

Pamela stopped him with a hand on his arm. "Let them go. We have more important things to worry about."

Janelle appeared, followed by Melody, who hung back in the doorway like a timid bird.

"Ben and Sylvia have done a runner," Jerome explained, pointing across the meadow. "Businesspeople, my ass—they're filthy, lying crooks!"

Janelle narrowed her eyes. "I knew those two were bad news! I could sense all that negative energy just oozing from them."

"What did I miss?" Helen's voice rang out behind them.

Jerome smiled smugly. "Your story. It would appear your pals Ben and Sylvia are our thieves."

Face flushing, Helen followed his gaze across the meadow. "But the room search was their idea."

"A clever cover which you unwittingly helped to orchestrate," Pamela said.

Helen fell silent, glowering at the ground.

"Earlier, you mentioned taking a booking over the phone," Emily said to Pamela. "That was before this morning's yoga session?"

Pamela nodded. "Yes, about half an hour before. I remember because I took the call, then went back to my quarters to change my clothes."

"Which would have given Ben and Sylvia thirty minutes to break into the office, steal everyone's belongings, then stash it out in the forest somewhere."

"They make a big fuss, suggest a room search to cover up their guilt, then make a run for it at the next available opportunity." Helen smiled. "Clever bastards."

Turning away from the group, Emily stared across the meadow. "What about Oscar? Are we saying that it's just coincidence?"

"Of course it's a coincidence," Janelle said. "Oscar committed suicide. Ben and Sylvia used everyone's panic as a distraction from what they'd done."

"But what about Marcia and the police?"

The words hung in the air between them.

"I'm going after them," Daniel said.

"And what will you do then?" Pamela called as Daniel headed for the gate. "Beat them into submission?"

He stopped, then turned back. "They have the keys to my bike. To your cars. How are we getting out of here if we don't get them back? We don't have time to wait for the police."

"I am not advocating violence," Janelle said, glancing around the group, "but Daniel's right. If we go after Ben and Sylvia, we get our keys back, and then we can drive to the police station at Lyndhurst and find out what on earth's going on. What's the time?"

Pamela dug a trembling hand into her pocket and pulled out her watch. Her complexion grew paler as she gazed across the meadow, towards the exit path. It's coming up to five."

"What if you don't catch up with them?" Emily said.

Daniel shrugged. "Unless we can hitch a ride, I suppose we walk to Lyndhurst. But that means we need to leave now before we're wandering around in the dark."

It was a solid plan, Emily thought, and one that would get the police here, even if it meant waiting for a few more hours.

"Sam should go with you," Pamela said. "If you can't catch up with Ben and Sylvia, he'll be able to show you the way to Lyndhurst. I'll go get him."

Daniel nodded. "We leave in two minutes."

An uncomfortable silence fell over the garden as they waited for Pamela to return. Still in the doorway, Melody shifted her weight from one foot to the other and glanced around the garden. Meeting Emily's gaze, she quickly looked away, shame painted on her face as bright as a rainbow.

"Don't feel so bad," Emily said, joining her on the doorstep. "You broke a rule not the law. Ben and Sylvia may have tried to use you to cover up their own crime, but Pamela knew you were no thief, didn't she?" Melody bowed her head. Her shoulders moved up to her ears, then back down again. "I mean it. Compared to everything else that's happened today, no one cares about the tablet."

"Pamela cares. She's always been so kind to me. I've let her down." Melody looked up to see Helen was watching her. "I don't like her."

"Come on." Taking Melody's hand, Emily led her towards the others. As they approached, Melody pulled back. Failing to hide her amusement, Helen turned away. A flame sparked in the pit of Emily's stomach.

"So what are you going to write in this so-called story of yours?" she said, releasing Melody's hand.

Helen arched an eyebrow. "I'll tell the facts as they happened."

"But that wouldn't be good journalism, would it? 'Man hangs himself at retreat' is just another suicide story."

"True."

"So, what will it be? 'Deadly Retreat—one dead as guests go on crime spree?'"

"You know, that's not bad," Helen said smiling, "It's a little clunky, but I could work with it."

Emily felt her face heating up, her shoulder muscles growing uncomfortably tight. "Pamela can't control the actions of her guests," she said. "This isn't her fault. Are you really prepared to ruin her business just to get a step up the ladder?"

All eyes were on Helen now. "I just report the news. What people make of it is their own business."

Emily felt Jerome's hand on her elbow. She shook it off. "So, you don't care? You journalists are all the same! It doesn't matter whose reputation you destroy, so long as you get paid."

"Sounds to me like you're talking from experience," said Helen, standing her ground. "Emily Swanson . . . You know, come to think of it, that's a familiar name. Why is that?"

The two women glared at each other, eyes burning.

Melody's quiet voice filled the silence. "Perhaps we could cook something nice for dinner. I expect everyone will be hungry later, and cooking is always a good way to pass the time."

Reaching out to touch Emily's arm, then thinking better of it, Jerome said, "I think that's a great idea, Melody. Em, are you in?"

Before either of them could speak, Pamela appeared in the doorway, her face deathly pale.

"What is it?" Emily asked.

"It's Sam," Pamela said, staring at the others with hollowed eyes. "He's gone. I can't find him anywhere."

Emily's heart skipped and jumped. "Perhaps he went for a walk to clear his head. He looked pretty annoyed earlier."

"He wouldn't disappear without saying anything, not with things how they are."

The others looked at each other uncertainly.

"Every minute we waste standing here is helping Ben and Sylvia to get away," Daniel said. "We need to leave now."

Pamela wrung her hands. "But without Sam how will you get to the deer sanctuary?"

"The same way as Ben and Sylvia—we follow the track."

"That only takes you part of the way."

"We'll follow the road. There'll be signs. We just have to hope those bastards don't flag down a ride." Daniel marched to the gate. Following behind, Janelle glanced back over her shoulder.

"We'll be as quick as we can," she said. "And try not to worry, Pamela. Your daughter may arrive with the cavalry before we catch up with those two."

The others watched Daniel and Janelle head out of the garden. Anxiety stirred in Emily's stomach as they crossed the meadow. Two minutes later they had disappeared into the trees. With just five of them now remaining in the garden, the surrounding forest felt suddenly infinite.

"We should look for Sam," Emily said. "I guess Pamela and I were the last to see him, but he didn't say anything about going anywhere."

"Maybe he went to look for Marcia," Helen interrupted. "Young love and all that."

Pamela shook her head. "He would have told me."

Emily stared up at the house. "Let's check inside."

The search didn't take long. Emily and Jerome took the upper floor while the others looked for Sam downstairs.

"I have a bad feeling," Jerome said, poking his head around the door of the guest bathroom. "Seriously, Em. What's going on here?"

"I honestly don't know, but my gut tells me it has everything to do with Oscar."

"I don't like the way your gut thinks."

With the rooms searched, they reconvened with the others on the back porch.

"Okay," Helen said, shooting Emily a challenging glance. "Sam's not in the house, which means we need to search the forest. It'll be faster if we split into two groups. Who wants to go with me?"

The ensuing silence was long and uncomfortable. Jerome sighed, and with his expression resembling that of a martyr facing his own demise, he raised his hand.

Emily stared at him. "Fine," she said. "Why don't you both take the west side? Melody and I can take the east. The lake is pretty central, so let's meet up there. If you move in a circle, you'll find it easily enough." She turned to Pamela. "Someone needs to stay at the house in case Marcia shows up."

Pamela nodded. "That'll be me."

"What if we find Sam?" Melody asked.

"Then we bring him to the lake. That way no one will be looking for him when he's already been found."

"Impressive organisational skills," Helen said, chewing her lip. "What did you say you do for a job?"

"Come on." Jerome tugged on her arm, pulling her away. "It'll be getting dark soon. See you at the lake, Emily."

"Be safe." Emily watched them leave, then placed a hand on Pamela's arm. "We won't be long. Try not to worry."

Together, she and Melody stepped off the porch and headed into the forest.

CHAPTER 23

An eerie quiet settled over Meadow Pines.
The sun drifted over the forest like a lost
balloon, dipping over the treetops. After the
noise and chaos of the day, the silence was a
welcome companion. But it was strange, Emily
thought, that the birds were not singing. In
fact, the only sounds she could hear were the
clomps of shoes as she and Melody made their
way through the forest, and the steady ins and
outs of their breaths.

As they walked, Emily stole glances at Melody.
Her pale skin seemed even whiter. Dark
shadows bruised the skin beneath her eyes.
Suddenly, she looked up.

"I can't believe this is all happening," she said. "First Oscar, now Sam. What's going on?"

"Sam's probably fine," Emily assured her, ignoring the niggling doubt in her mind. "Like Helen said, he's probably headed into Lyndhurst to find Marcia."

The path coiled around a collection of rocks that grew up from the ground like ancient monoliths.

"That's if she made it there in the first place," Melody said, ominously. "Meadow Pines used to be such a peaceful place. Now, all I want to do is to pick up Derek from the cattery and go home."

Streaks of dusky sunlight dripped through the canopies and burned circles into the growing shadows. Emily quickened her pace. Darkness could creep up in the forest like a venomous snake, and she had no intention of getting caught by it. Beside her, Melody peered into the surrounding vegetation.

"You've been here a few times," Emily said. "How well do you know the Hardys?"

Melody ducked beneath a low branch. "They've always been very kind to me. Why do you ask?"

"What about Marcia and Sam? How long have they been together?"

"A while, I think. I used to see them flirting with each other like school children. Then one time I visited, I saw them in the forest. They were . . ." Even in the waning light, Emily could see Melody's face blossom with embarrassment. "Anyway, I think it's very sweet. Even if some people don't approve."

"And by 'some people' you mean Pamela?"

"It's not that she doesn't like Sam. But he's her employee. I suppose she's worried if it doesn't work out between the two of them it could make things awkward. And then there's the—"

"The what?"

"Nothing."

"You can trust me," Emily said.

Melody glanced over her shoulder, then let out a heavy sigh. "Sam likes to smoke marijuana. Never around the guests, of course. But sometimes you can smell it on him, if you get close enough. Pamela knows about it for sure. I think she's worried Marcia will make some bad choices. But Marcia says she's old enough to make her own choices, good and bad."

The path turned. They passed by a dead tree, its bare branches reaching up to the sky like gnarled claws.

"How do you know all of this?" Emily asked, bewildered by Melody's knowledge of the Hardy family.

"Marcia talks to me sometimes. It must get lonely out here. Besides, sometimes you need someone to confide in who's not your mother or your boyfriend. Someone who's more like a sister."

"So, you're friends? Do you meet up outside of Meadow Pines and hang out?"

"Oh, no. Marcia rarely has a day to herself. And when she does, of course, it's only natural she would want to spend it with Sam."

The smile left Melody's lips. She stopped walking. "Do you think Pamela will forgive me? She looked so disappointed. But I didn't mean anything by it. It's just that I miss Derek when I'm away from him. Having all of my pictures of him nearby makes me feel better, that's all."

Emily linked arms with Melody and gently tugged her along the path. "I think Pamela's more worried about her daughter right now. And to be brutally honest, I'm not sure Meadow Pines will be around long enough for her to hit you with a lifetime ban."

Melody stopped again. "Why would you say that?"

"Because mud sticks. And so do newspaper headlines."

"Helen . . ." Melody clenched her jaw "I really don't like her."

The path grew wide and familiar. Emily felt her heart beating a little faster as they stepped into the clearing. Oscar's body lay wrapped in tarpaulin, half-covered by shadows.

Melody squeezed her eyes shut, her body growing rigid. "Sam shouldn't have cut him down."

"There's a photograph in Oscar's pocket. It's of a man," Emily said, an idea coming to her. "I think he might have something to do with Meadow Pines."

"Why would you think that?"

"Just a feeling." She moved closer to the tarpaulin. "Perhaps if you took a look you might recognise him."

"I don't want to look!" Melody still had her eyes closed, and now she covered her face with her hands.

Emily stepped towards Oscar's body. She froze. The tarpaulin had been pulled back to one side, exposing Oscar's arm and chest.

"Someone's been here," Emily said, spying the empty shirt pocket. "The photograph's gone."

CHAPTER 24

Jerome stumbled through the foliage, thorns and prickly leaves scratching his skin. He had insisted on taking the lead, determined to prove to himself—and to Helen—that he was unafraid of the natural world. But now that the light was beginning to fail, his survival instincts were kicking in.

"We should probably head back. It'll be dark soon." He slowed his pace until Helen caught up and was now by his side. She was proving to be equally inept at negotiating the forest paths.

"We've only been gone five minutes," she said, stopping to brush cobwebs from her face. "Besides, we have to meet your friend Emily Swanson by the lake."

She marched on, cursing as she stumbled over a fallen tree branch, and shooting a warning glance at Jerome when he failed to contain his laughter.

But Jerome's amusement was short-lived. He peered over his shoulder at the sea of tree trunks. It didn't matter that the house was just a few minutes away, it was beginning to feel as if they were lost in the wilderness, miles from civilisation.

Helen had gained some distance. Jerome quickened his pace and stumbled over an exposed tree root. "Damn it! Helen, wait up! It's not a race, you know."

"So, you and Emily have known each other for how long?" she asked once he'd caught up.

"About eight months."

"Is that all? You seem like old friends. How did you meet?"

"She moved into my building."

"I see." Helen walked on a little more. "And how come she's taking antidepressants?"

Jerome stopped in his tracks. "How did you know that?"

"A little bird may have flown by her room earlier and told me."

"Bloody hell! Don't you have any boundaries?" Jerome's nostrils flared as he ignored Helen's fluttering eyelashes. "Clearly not, seeing as how you convinced Sam to cut Oscar down! Well, you won't be getting anything else from me."

He raced ahead. Helen struggled to keep up.

"Come on, Jerome. What are you hiding? Emily Swanson—I know that name. I'm sure I've heard it before. Why won't you tell me?"

"Forget it!" Jerome quickened his pace, then ducked to avoid a low-hanging branch. "Emily's been through enough without some hack journalist wannabe digging things up all over again. Stay away from her."

"Hack journalist wannabe? And what do you do that makes you so much holier than me?"

"If you must know, I happen to be an actor."

Helen's laughter rang out through the forest.

Up ahead, Jerome slipped and struck his shoulder against a tree trunk. He twisted around, anger searing his insides.

"You think you're Barbara Walters," he growled, "but you write for some shitty magazine no one's ever heard of! Emily isn't part of the so-called story you're chasing. And speaking of your story, as much as I hate this hell hole, Meadow Pines is Pamela's business, her livelihood. I hope you bear that in mind when you're writing your snappy headline."

Helen closed the gap between them, then hurried alongside, trampling vegetation beneath her feet. "You know, you're pretty narrow-minded, Jerome. In the same way that not all actors are narcissistic, egotistical children, not all journalists are complete assholes."

"So, it's just you, then?"

Jerome froze, the fight instantly forgotten.

Up ahead, the trees parted. A wooden shack, which had seen better days, sat in the centre of a small glade. Tangerine light bounced off its mossy, corrugated roof. A dirt encrusted window stared back at them.

"Okay, Barbara, what do you think they keep in there?" Jerome said, pointing a finger.

Helen strode forward. "Shall we find out?"

"We're supposed to be looking for Sam."

"Maybe he's inside."

Jerome stared nervously at the ramshackle building. "What would he be doing hiding out in there?"

"Come on, pussy. I thought you men were supposed to be the tough ones."

"Your attempts to emasculate me using gender stereotypes is both outdated and frankly disappointing."

"Worked a charm, though," Helen said as Jerome jogged up beside her.

They moved closer, the wet smell of mould and rotting wood invading their nostrils. Standing on tiptoes, Helen cupped her hands to her face and peered through the window. Using her sleeve, she wiped dirt from the glass.

"I can't see anything," she said.

Jerome walked up to the door, which was secured with a bolt and a heavy looking padlock. "Well, we're not getting in there."

Taking a step back, Helen scanned the ground. Finding a rock the size of her fist, she lifted it with both hands, shouldered Jerome out of the way, and raised the rock above her head.

"Wait! What are you doing?" Jerome said, his jaw swinging open. "We're looking for Sam, not breaking and entering. And I think that huge padlock is a pretty good indicator he's not inside."

Helen's arms remained above her head, the rock swaying from side to side. With an exaggerated sigh, she turned and pitched the rock onto the ground.

"Well, you're no fun," she huffed.

"And you're not quite as monstrous as I thought you were."

They moved away from the shed and picked up the dusty path on the far side of the glade. Minutes later, the forest rolled out in every direction. The path veered to the left, taking them further into the trees and passing by a thick mire of bog water. A stench hung in the air, thick and putrid like sulphur.

Above them, the sun continued its descent. Shadows grew long and wide, moving through the forest like a black flood.

"So, Barbara Walters, what do you think's going on here?" Jerome asked, glancing up at the branches.

Helen chewed her lip. "As journalists, we're taught to differentiate between facts and opinions. The facts are that Oscar is dead— seemingly by his own hand, Marcia went for help but has yet to return with any, and now Sam appears to be missing."

"Don't forget the delightful Ben and Sylvia."

"I haven't, but I think we can eliminate them and the robbery from whatever's going on."

"So, if those are the facts, what are your opinions?"

Helen was quiet for a moment, thinking. "I think there are an awful lot of facts in this world that can't be put down to mere coincidence."

They emerged from the forest and stepped onto the path that connected Meadow Pines to the outside world. Jerome was suddenly tempted to break into a run, to reach the gate and vault right over it.

And then what?

It wasn't as if he had the car keys, anyway. Or a driving license. Or the ability to drive.

Instead, he crossed the path and continued into the forest. They found the trail a moment later, directed by a signpost pointing northeast towards the lake.

"You know, Emily doesn't think Oscar killed himself," he said, after a long spell of silence.

Helen wiped perspiration from her brow. "Regardless of the facts, I think Emily's right. But don't you dare tell her I said that."

All around them, insects clicked and chirruped. Up in the branches, a bird called out and was answered by another.

"Whatever's going on here, the quicker we get to the lake the better," Jerome said. "If Emily is right, then the last place I want to be right now is running around in the middle of the forest like some hapless idiot from a slasher movie. Let's pick up the pace."

Helen peered over her shoulder at the growing shadows. "I don't need to be told twice."

They fell into silence as they hurried along. More than once, they lost the trail in dense, overgrown thickets. As the treetops pierced the sun and molten lava spilled across the sky, the ground began to descend beneath their feet.

Jerome caught a glimpse of the lake's shimmering surface between the trees. Letting out a deep sigh, he stepped off the path, then looked back to make sure Helen was following.

Any relief he felt was instantly snatched away.

"What is it?" he whispered.

Helen was standing on the path, shoulders up to her ears, wide, frightened eyes staring off into the distance. She lifted a hand and pointed.

"There's something there."

Jerome stepped back onto the path. "Where? I don't see anything."

"Right in front of you, idiot!"

He squinted. It took a few more seconds to find what Helen was staring at. Then his heart slammed against his chest.

Slowly, Jerome backed away.

"We need to find Emily," he said. "We need to find her now."

CHAPTER 25

Emily leaned over Oscar's body, thankful that the tarpaulin was still covering his face. She searched the ground for the missing photograph. It wasn't there—which meant someone had taken it. In the middle of the clearing, Melody peered out from between her fingers.

"We shouldn't be here," she said. "We're meant to be looking for Sam."

"The man in the picture was white. Dark hair, dark eyes, a scar just here." Emily pointed to her eyebrow. "He looked around the same age as Marcia. Sound familiar?"

"That could be anybody."

Melody started to leave the clearing, but Emily stayed where she was, her eyes moving from Oscar's body to the tree.

Who else knew about the photograph? Sam and Emily had been there when Helen had pulled it from Oscar's pocket, and until now, Emily had only shared its existence with Jerome and Pamela. Following its discovery, they'd returned to the house, where Pamela had angrily pulled Sam into her living quarters, and Emily and Jerome had argued on the back porch—which would have given someone else time to run back, steal the photograph, then reappear just in time for Ben and Sylvia's grand escape.

Helen.

The photograph would have been her next big lead, and she'd been far from happy about returning it to Oscar's pocket. It had to have been her. Unless . . .

Emily looked over her shoulder into the forest. Sam had left Emily and Pamela in the Hardys' living room. And gone where?

"I don't understand. Why would someone steal that picture?" Melody said, rubbing her hands against her bare arms.

"It's a good question," Emily replied as she got to her feet. "Come on. It's getting dark."

They left the clearing, picking up the path and following it through the forest. As they continued, so did Melody's chatter.

"Poor Oscar. He must have felt very sad. I mean, we all feel sad sometimes, don't we? Miserable even, until you don't want to get out of bed. But you just have to bounce back, don't you? And come to places like Meadow Pines to make yourself feel better."

Oscar doesn't look like he's feeling better, Emily thought, but decided to keep that observation to herself.

"It's very worrying about Marcia, don't you think?" Melody continued. "She's been gone for hours. I'm sure there's a good explanation, and I'm sure she's fine, but it will certainly be a relief when she comes back with the police, won't it?"

The sun dipped an inch below the treeline as they reached the stream and made quick work of the steppingstones.

Melody sighed. "I suppose with everything that's happened and with the weekend finishing early, we won't get our group shot."

"What do you mean?" Emily asked.

"At the end of every weekend, Pamela gathers all the guests and takes a group photograph. She adds it to her Happiness Hall of Fame. Well, that's what she calls it, but it's really just a photo album." Melody's shoulders sagged. "I would have liked my picture taken with you and the others, but perhaps not with Ben and Sylvia. Or Helen."

They picked up the path again, the undergrowth growing thick and impassable in places. When Emily became unsure of the way, Melody took the lead.

"Who do you think that man is?" she asked, after a long bout of silence. Her expression had turned grave. "The one from the photograph."

"I don't know." A gentle lapping of water reached Emily's ears as the ground began to slope under her feet. "But I think somebody here does, and I think they're keeping quiet about it."

"Why would you think that?"

Spying the lake through the trees, Emily quickened her pace. "Because I don't believe Oscar killed himself."

Melody startled the air with a strange, frightened laugh. "You think someone . . . No, that's just silly! Why would anyone want to hurt Oscar? There's no one here capable of doing something like that."

"You don't know everyone here, Melody," Emily said. "Besides, you'd be surprised what people can be capable of."

They emerged from the trees and came upon the lake. Long, scarlet flames of sunset burned across its surface, setting fire to the forest's reflection. A few dark clouds were forming above them, suggesting a change in the weather was on its way.

Emily moved along the shore with Melody close behind. They reached the jetty and walked to the end. Melody sat down, legs dangling over the water. Beside them, the small boat tugged on its moorings.

"I wonder if they found Sam," Emily said. Knots of anxiety were knitting together in her stomach and twisting around her insides. She sat down beside Melody and drew in a deep breath.

A flock of birds sprang up from the lake and headed for the treetops. Staring into the water, Emily tried to forget the horrors of the day, and just for a moment, focus on the tranquil surroundings.

Melody began to hum under her breath. She swung her legs back and forth like a child.

"It's not fair," she said suddenly, her voice shaking with anger.

"What isn't?"

"That Meadow Pines could shut down."

Emily felt bad for having suggested it. Meadow Pines seemed to be Melody's only asylum from an unhappy and lonely existence.

"I was just thinking the worst. It might not happen," she said, hearing the doubt in her own voice.

"Nobody will want to come here anymore. That's what you said, isn't it? Well, I'll still want to come here. Even if what you say about Oscar is true. But what if you're right? What if Meadow Pines does close?"

Emily stared at the water, watching as a breeze rippled the surface. "There are other places, Melody."

"But I don't want other places. And what about Pamela and Marcia? This is their home."

"They'll find somewhere new."

Emily leaned forward. Something was floating in the water, bobbing up and down not far from the jetty.

"What's that?" she said, squinting at the object in the half light. It was small and black. She was surprised she'd noticed it at all.

"I don't see anything," Melody said.

The object moved closer, carried along by the breeze. Jumping to her feet, Emily jogged along the jetty, back towards the forest. Her gaze searched the ground, until she found a long, thin branch. Snatching it up, she hurried back to Melody.

It took her a moment to find the object again, which had floated off to the left of the jetty.

Sinking to her knees, Emily leaned over the water and reached out with the branch.

Melody watched with mounting curiosity as Emily lunged forward. The branch hit the object and dragged it under the water. It resurfaced a second later, bouncing up and down.

Her second attempt went wide.

She lunged for a third time and snagged the object on the end of the branch.

"What is it?" asked Melody. She pulled up her feet and watched as Emily freed the object and held it between finger and thumb, water raining down on the planks.

"It's a wallet."

Brushing pondweed and grit from the black leather, Emily unfolded it. There was no money inside, no coins weighing it down. But there were cards. Emily removed one—a credit card—and examined it. A surge of adrenaline shot through her veins as her eyes drifted down to the cardholder's name.

"This is Oscar's wallet!" she said.

She handed the card to Melody, who reacted as if she'd been given a spider to hold. The card dropped from her hand and landed face up on the jetty.

Emily studied the rest of the wallet's contents. A card holder with a clear plastic face sat in the centre. She cleaned off the dirt. Oscar's face stared back at her.

At first, Emily thought it was a driver's license. But as she inspected it closely, she drew in a sharp breath. Above Oscar's picture were the words: Oscar Jansen, Private Investigations.

Voices filled the air. At the west side of the lake, Jerome and Helen stepped out from the trees.

"Come on," Emily said. Folding the wallet, she got to her feet. Together, they walked the length of the jetty, back onto land.

Jerome wasn't smiling. Helen's usual smug expression was gone, replaced by a creased brow and troubled eyes.

Something was wrong.

"No sign of Sam, either?" Jerome asked as they approached. Now that they were closer, Emily could see Helen's pale complexion.

"No," she said, eyeing them both. "But we did find this."

She fished out the card from Oscar's wallet and handed it to Jerome, who held it up in the failing light.

"It was floating in the lake," Emily said.

Helen snatched the card from Jerome's fingers. "What the hell? Why would a P.I. be here at Meadow Pines?"

"I don't know. But it's strange, isn't it?" Emily took the card from her and slipped it back inside the wallet. "That a private investigator should come here, only to wind up dead."

"We found something, too," Jerome said, grimacing.

"What is it?"

"It's best you come and see for yourself."

Emily stared at him, frightened by his hardened expression.

"What is it?" she asked again.

CHAPTER 26

The Land Rover was parked beneath the thick, gnarled branches of an ancient yew tree, which curled and twisted like the tentacles of a Lovecraftian beast. The driver door was open, its window shattered. Shards of glass carpeted the earth.

Emily peered through the open door and saw splashes of blood on the steering wheel. A partial bloody handprint was pressed into the windscreen.

Her throat drying, she turned and examined the ground. The grass beneath the tree was flat, as if something had been dragged over it.

Stooping, Emily ran her hand through the blades, then recoiled as her fingertips came away wet and dark.

"I don't believe any of this," Melody said, her voice shattering the silence. She was crying. "Sam is a good person. He would never hurt anyone. Especially not Marcia. He loves Marcia."

Grimacing, Emily stood and wiped her fingers against her jeans. "No one's accusing Sam of anything. We have no idea what happened here, so let's not jump to conclusions, okay?"

"You don't need to say anything! I can see it on your faces," Melody said, glaring at them all. "But you're wrong. Sam is good and kind." Now she turned to Emily, her hands clenched into tight balls. "You think he murdered Oscar, don't you? And that he's run away. He doesn't even know Oscar!"

"You need to calm the hell down, Melody. Get a grip, for God's sake!" Helen snarled.

Emily glared at her. With the discovery of Oscar's wallet and now the blood-covered Land Rover, it was not the time for more ill-feeling.

"Someone's taken the picture from Oscar's body," she said. "I need to know if it was you."

"Me?" Helen pressed her hand against her chest. Her wounded façade lasted for about three seconds. "Look, I agree I may have overstepped the mark a little today, and I know I can sometimes be a little forthcoming with my opinions, but one thing I don't do is lie. And I'm telling you I've not been back to Oscar's body since we cut him down."

Emily nodded. "I believe you."

She did. There was an honesty in Helen's eyes that could not be faked. It didn't mean she was about to become friends with the woman, though. Or even polite acquaintances.

Emily glanced over at Jerome, who had been silent since leading them to the Land Rover.

He stood, watching the trees, his eyes darting back and forth.

"I have a theory," Emily said, returning her attention to Helen.

"Let's hear it."

Jerome moved in closer. Melody had stopped crying and was now crouched on her haunches, her back turned on the others.

Emily cleared her throat. "Oscar was a private investigator. Let's suppose the reason he was carrying the man's picture was because he was looking for him."

Helen chewed her lip. "Sounds reasonable. Often, families of missing relatives will turn to private investigators once the police have drawn a blank."

"If Oscar's search brought him here, it can only mean one thing," Emily continued. "The man from the photograph must have visited Meadow Pines."

"Go Miss Marple," Helen said.

Emily ignored her. "There's something else. Oscar's room is next to mine. Last night, I heard raised voices. He was arguing with someone. With a woman."

Melody looked back over her shoulder and saw Helen staring at her. "It wasn't me! I didn't even know him!" she cried, threatening to dissolve into hysterics again.

"Well, it certainly wasn't me, either," Helen said. "So that leaves Janelle, Sylvia, Pamela, or Marcia."

The bloody handprint on the Land Rover windscreen caught Emily's eye and a sliver of ice slipped between her shoulder blades. "Marcia wasn't here last night. I saw her walking in with Sam this morning. She'd spent the night at his place in Lyndhurst."

"Perhaps it was Sylvia," Jerome suggested. "After all, she and Ben robbed us. Perhaps they killed Oscar, too."

Melody stood up, freshly-picked bluebells in her hands.

"It crossed my mind. But that doesn't explain what's happened to Marcia. Or to Sam," Emily said.

They were quiet for a minute. Above them, a breeze rustled the canopies. Soon, it would be too dark to see.

"I think we should go back to the house," Jerome said. He looked tired, Emily thought. Tired and afraid. "Pamela needs to know what we've found."

Everyone agreed. As they turned to leave, Melody placed the bluebells on the front of the Land Rover, then caught up with the others. They moved quickly, negotiating their way through the forest. All around them, shadows lengthened and merged. As they reached the house, dusk snuffed out the last embers of sunset.

"Why don't you go ahead," Helen said, stopping in front of the garden gate. "There's something I want to check out."

Emily shook her head. It was a bad idea. "In another half an hour you won't be able to see your hands in front of your face."

"Jerome and I found something. An old shack."

"You mean a shack with a big padlock on the door," Jerome corrected.

"And who knows what inside. I'm going with my instincts on this one, and they're telling me that shack could be important."

"Your instincts or your ego? We have no idea what's going on here. People are missing and dead. It's not worth the risk."

"You won't come with me?" Helen said, disappointment dulling her eyes. "But it would be great research for that slasher movie role."

Jerome dug his hands into his pockets. "I'm sorry but Emily's right. It's nearly dark and we need to be inside, where it's safe."

"You're no fun," Helen said, then turned and tapped Melody's shoulder. "You'll do. But first we need to find a torch."

Before anyone could protest, she grabbed Melody's hand and pulled her through the garden gate. As they reached the front door of the house, Helen glanced over her shoulder.

"We'll be quick," she said. "And I promise to keep this one safe."

Melody shot a worried glance at Emily and Jerome, then she and Helen were gone, disappearing inside the house.

Emily stared at the empty doorway. "I can't decide if I really hate that woman or admire her tenacity."

"I'd say sixty-forty," Jerome said, his expression souring. "We'd better go see Pamela, give her the bad news."

Above their heads, rain clouds were rolling in. The temperature was plummeting fast. Emily squeezed Jerome's hand. She sucked in a breath and pushed down the anxiety blocking her throat.

"Don't worry, I'll do the talking," she said. They entered the house together.

CHAPTER 27

Pamela was waiting for them in her living room. She showed them to the couch, then perched on the edge of the armchair. Her skin had been drained of its vitality and was now the colour of spoiled milk. Her fingertips dug into her knees as Emily caught her up on the search.

"We've looked all over Meadow Pines but we can't find Sam. Perhaps Helen is right. Perhaps he did head off to go looking for . . ."

The words dried up in Emily's throat. She glanced sideways at Jerome, who was staring intensely at the rug.

"Where are Melody and Helen?" Pamela's voice was trembling.

"They're doing another quick sweep before it gets dark."

"I don't understand. How could Sam just disappear? Why would he go off without telling me? It's so irresponsible." Pamela brought her hands together and entwined her fingers.

"There's something else," Emily said. A wave of nausea washed over her as she struggled to assemble the right words. How did you share awful news? Did you soften it with kind words? Did you build a safety net of 'it's going to be alright' and 'I'm sure your daughter will come out of this alive'? Or did you plunge in headfirst? Rip out the heart, tear the last strands of hope like hair from the scalp?

No matter which way you chose to tell it, the end result would always be the same. Emily chose the quickest route.

"We found the Land Rover," she said, forcing the words from her mouth. As she described the broken window and the blood inside, she watched Pamela's face grow impossibly white. She decided to omit the drag marks she'd found in the grass—the image they conjured was worse than the blood.

Pamela grew very still.

"There's more," Emily said, hating herself as she pulled Oscar's wallet from her pocket. But it had to be done. Meadow Pines felt unsafe now. Dangerous. Which meant if Pamela was holding something back, everyone needed to know about it.

Emily held up the card. "Oscar was a private investigator. We think he was here looking for the man in the photograph. And now someone has stolen that photograph. It's gone."

Pamela sagged, the strength that had been keeping her upright suddenly spent.

Emily leaned in closer. "Who is he, Pamela? Why was Oscar looking for him?"

Slumped in the armchair, Pamela lifted her hands and covered her face. She was unmoving for the longest time, until finally she got to her feet. She stood still for a moment, swaying from side to side. Then she crossed the room and slipped through a door in the far wall.

Emily exchanged worried glances with Jerome.

"Do you think we should check on her?" he asked.

"Give her a minute."

Emily felt wretched. She shut her eyes, trying to conjure up Kirsten Dewar's soothing tones. "Imagine you are in a calm place. Somewhere you feel safe." She almost laughed. Meadow Pines was supposed to have been that calm place.

Drawing in a breath, Emily held it for a few seconds, then exhaled. She opened her eyes and found herself staring at Pamela's bookcase. Slowly, she reached out and squeezed Jerome's arm.

He frowned. "Um, that hurts."

In a flash, Emily was off the sofa and in front of the shelves.

"The Happiness Hall of Fame," she whispered, pulling a photograph album from the second shelf and setting it down on the coffee table. Sinking to her knees, she turned to the first page.

Jerome scooted closer. "What have you found?"

"Melody told me that at the end of every weekend, Pamela takes a photograph of her guests, like a kind of record of the happiness they find at Meadow Pines."

Emily scanned the photographs in front of her. Each one showed a different group of people. Some stood in the garden while others assembled in the dining hall. All had wide smiles, relaxed shoulders, and bright eyes.

Jerome glanced over at the door. "She'll be back soon," he said. "Let's not tip her over the edge."

Emily turned a few pages. She stopped.

"Look at this."

The group shot had been taken on the back porch. Melody stood at the centre of the back row, her face lit up with a smile.

Dates were handwritten beneath the photograph: 8-10 August.

Emily continued to flip through the pages, the memories of each weekend reflecting in her eyes. She froze, pressing her lips together until they were almost white.

He was standing at the end of the front row, a few noticeable inches separating him from the rest of the group. While his fellow guests flashed their teeth at the camera, his lips remained flat and still beneath unreadable, dark eyes.

Although the picture was slightly grainy, the scar above his left eyebrow was clearly visible. Emily caught her breath.

"It's him. It's the man from Oscar's picture."

"His name is Franklyn Hobbes."

She and Jerome looked up in unison to see Pamela standing in the doorway, a wad of tissues in her hand. She'd been crying and had done a poor job of covering it up.

For a few seconds, she hovered in the door, swaying back and forth. Then she drifted into the room and seated herself at the other side of the table. Taking the photograph album, she turned it around and pointed at the picture with a trembling finger.

"It was December. The year before last," she said. "We usually close for three months during winter. It's hard to heat this old house. Costly, too. But we were having such a mild start to the season that I decided to keep Meadow Pines open for an extra month. Marcia wasn't particularly happy about it.

Winter is our only real time off. But we'd had an unusually quiet summer, so any extra income was a blessing.

"That may sound very materialistic of me, but as much as I view Meadow Pines as a sanctuary, I have no illusions about it also being a business. Without money, Meadow Pines falls by the wayside. It's a sad fact, but such is the way of the world—even on its peripheries."

Emily stared at the man's picture, transfixed by his eyes. They were black and lifeless, like a doll's eyes.

"Back then, Meadow Pines was a different place," Pamela continued. "How much do you know about Vipassanā?"

Emily and Jerome shook their heads.

"Buddha discovered that we can remove suffering from our lives by understanding our true nature. Vipassanā means exactly that—to see things as they are. It helps us to step back from the situations we experience, to observe them unfolding rather than to react or attach to them. Because all forms of attachment, whether good or bad, lead to craving. And craving leads to misery."

Emily waited as Pamela considered her next words.

"A Vipassanā retreat isn't easy: ten days of Noble silence in which you cannot speak to or make eye contact with other participants; deep meditation sessions that begin at four-thirty in the morning and end at nine at night. There can be periods of intense highs, followed by intense lows. But it's all part of the path to the realisation of the true nature of things."

"And what is the true nature of things?" Emily asked.

"To truly understand the answer in its purest form, you must take the journey to awakening yourself. In its simplest form, the answer is this: Nothing is permanent. Our minds, our bodies—everyone and everything around us—

it's all in constant change. All our cravings, our aversions, our addictions, are borne from basing our happiness on things that change. You buy the latest TV and you feel great. Then a newer model comes along and suddenly your TV isn't good enough.

"Or you meet someone and you fall in love. You put your faith in the idea that you'll spend the rest of your lives together. But then the relationship suddenly ends, and it takes your happiness along with it—not because of the love you shared, but because of the attachment you developed to the idea of permanence."

Memories of Lewis flooded Emily's mind. She shoved them away. "As enlightening as this all is, what does any of it have to do with Franklyn Hobbes?"

Pamela ran her fingers over the photograph album. When she looked up again, the whites of her eyes were tinged with pink. "The first time Franklyn came to us, he was so quiet that taking a vow of silence didn't seem like anything out of the ordinary for him. He seemed pleasant enough. Harmless . . . but the type of person who'd spent his life being invisible. Anyway, he settled in quickly and he seemed to take to the Vipassanā technique easier than most, especially for someone who'd never been to a retreat.

"By the end of the ten days, I can always see a significant change in my students. Not just in the words they say or the thoughts they share, but in their physicality. It's as if they are seeing the world through new eyes. But with Franklyn, I saw nothing."

She pushed the album back to Emily and Jerome then glanced up at the window. Outside, darkness had almost settled. Rain clouds were fattening, threatening to burst.

"I don't doubt he underwent changes—it would go against Nature's Law for him not to —but his eyes were black and empty, as you've seen for yourself." Pamela pulled her knees up to her chest. "I didn't expect to see him at Meadow Pines again. But four months later, there he was. And the change in him was dramatic."

"What do you mean?" Emily asked. She tried to look away from Franklyn's picture, but those two black hollows were dangerously hypnotic.

"It was as if a different person had stepped into Franklyn's body," Pamela said. "Gone was the quiet young man who barely spoke a word, and in his place was a man filled with agitation and nervous energy." She paused, her shoulders heaving. "I should have put an end to it there. I should have stopped him from participating . . . but in my infinite wisdom, I thought the retreat would help him to work through whatever was troubling him. It wasn't until the second time he broke Noble silence that I learned what he'd been doing."

The air in the room grew heavy, pressing down on Emily's chest as she processed what she was hearing.

"As I said, the Vipassanā technique is not easy," Pamela said. "It requires extreme focus that comes from hours of practice. Ten days of intense, silent meditation is a revelatory experience, but also an exhausting one, which is why a period of at least three months between retreats is recommended. In the four months since we'd last seen him, Franklyn had attended six other Vipassanā retreats."

"Six?" Emily repeated. "Why would he do that?"

"As students of the Vipassanā technique begin to successfully detach from sensations, they can experience feelings of extreme peace. At first, this can feel like an intense high. But highs and lows are still sensations, and if we remain attached to them we only crave more.

"It's my belief that Franklyn Hobbes became addicted to those intense highs. I believe that because he was unable to detach from those cravings, he instead detached from the world."

"So he was like a junkie, but instead of drugs he was addicted to meditation?" Jerome said, looking from Pamela to the photo album.

Pamela nodded. "Franklyn moved from retreat to retreat, hoping to experience those peaceful feelings over and over; hoping each experience would cure him of the unbearable misery he believed was waiting for him outside. What he'd failed to realise was that his suffering was a trap of his own mind. By going from retreat to retreat without rest, the only thing he'd achieved was to push his mind to breaking point."

Pamela ran fingers through her hair and let out a trembling breath. "I believed I could help him. I believed I could guide him back onto the correct path. But I was nowhere near qualified."

The first drops of rain pattered against the window. Pamela gave Franklyn's photograph one last look, then closed the album.

"It was the ninth day of the retreat, the Saturday before Easter. We were five minutes into the final meditation, when I heard crying. I looked up and saw that it was Franklyn. Suddenly his tears turned to wailing, which of course broke the meditative state of every person in the room.

"I stood up. I gestured to Franklyn to join me outside. As I came closer, he screamed the words: 'I am nothing!' I removed him from the room as quickly as possible, and I took him to my office. He was inconsolable. His whole body trembled. The only words he would say, over and over like a mantra, were, 'I am nothing! I am nothing!' I tried to talk him down, but he jumped up and ran out of the house."

Pamela drew in a breath. As she exhaled, a tremor ran from her shoulders down to the tips of her fingers. "I didn't know what to do. I returned to the meditation room to reassure the other students. I told them that Franklyn was feeling unwell and that they should return to their rooms while I took care of him. I went to the kitchen. Sam was cleaning up. Marcia was outside, composting the day's food waste. Or so we'd thought." A look of horror washed over Pamela's face. "We heard her screams coming from the forest."

Goose pimples broke out on Emily's arms. Beside her, Jerome swallowed hard.

"Sam took off like a wild dog." Pamela's eyes were dull and lead-like. "As her mother, you'd think I'd answer my daughter's cry for help without hesitation. But I was paralysed. I stood and watched Sam disappear into the darkness. It felt like minutes until I could move again. I found Marcia just beyond the treeline. She was on the ground. Her clothes were torn. There was blood . . . I managed to get her to her feet. She wasn't crying. She wasn't anything. It was the shock, I suppose. I walked her back to the house. I ran her a bath and got her cleaned up. Sam returned soon after. He had cuts on his face and on his knuckles. He told me he'd wrestled Franklyn to the ground, and that Franklyn had managed to get away. Sam chased him into the forest, but he lost him."

Emily watched as Pamela shut her eyes and took in a deep breath. Her mind raced. What had happened to Marcia was truly horrifying. But how was it connected to what was happening at Meadow Pines now?

"I'm so sorry. I can't even begin to imagine what Marcia must have gone through," she said. "What about the police? Did they catch Franklyn?"

Pamela sat up. For the briefest of moments, anger lit up her eyes like lightning strikes. "I was going to call the police. I was. But you should understand the position we were in. We were struggling with filling the groups, and we were behind on the mortgage payments. Meadow Pines was dangerously close to shutting down for good."

Emily's eyes grew wide with disbelief. "You didn't call them?"

"We were all aware what would happen if I did," Pamela said. "Marcia, too. If word got out that one of our students had lost his mind and attacked a member of staff, Meadow Pines would have been finished. No one would want to come here. Everything Marcia and I had built up would be gone."

"What happened to having no attachments?" Jerome sat back, unable to hide his disgust.

"If you didn't call the police, what did you do?" Emily asked.

Pamela stared at the window, watching the rain grow heavier. "We locked the doors. Sam stayed on watch. I cleared Franklyn's room and packed his bag. We agreed that if he showed up again, Sam would drive him to the sanctuary, put him in his car, and warn him never to come back. But he didn't show. The next day was the last day of the retreat. I told the other guests that Franklyn had left in the night. When the time came for everyone else to leave, I drove them in the Land Rover back to the sanctuary car park.

"Before leaving, I checked Franklyn's registration number on his admissions form. His car was gone. After attacking Marcia, he must have somehow found his way back to the road. And that was that. We never heard from him again. Not until you found his picture in Oscar's pocket."

Exhausted, Pamela picked up the photograph album and replaced it on the shelf. She remained standing with her back turned to Emily and Jerome.

"I know what you're thinking." Her voice was quiet and low. "How could a mother do such a terrible thing? But my actions were based solely on the protection of my daughter. Marcia hasn't lived in the outside world since she was a child. If Meadow Pines was taken away, she wouldn't be able to cope."

She moved to the window, her body deflating with each step. "Where is she? What's happened to my Marcia?"

Jerome nervously chewed the inside of his mouth. "Do you think it's possible Oscar came to Meadow Pines because he followed Franklyn back here?" he said. "Do you think it's possible Franklyn Hobbes murdered Oscar, and that he's out there right now, hiding in the forest?"

An icy chill settled over the room. Before Emily could reply, a deafening crash rattled the living room door.

Jerome's eyes met hers. The next second, they were on their feet and racing from the room.

Quiet had resumed in the hallway. Emily looked both ways. The sound of rain on wood reached her ears. Moving quickly, she headed to the foyer with Jerome and Pamela close behind.

The front door was wide open. Rain was blowing in.

Helen was face down on the floor, sprawled next to a toppled side table. Dark blood oozed from her hair and pooled on the floor.

Emily raced to her side.

"A first aid kit!" she cried. "We need bandages. Now!"

At first, Pamela was paralysed. Then it was if she'd received an electric shock. She sprang to life, hurrying back towards her living quarters.

Pressing fingers into Helen's jugular, Emily felt a weak pulse. She shot a wild-eyed stare at Jerome. "Give me that tablecloth!"

Jerome moved quickly, snatching up the cloth from the fallen table and handing it to her.

"What the hell is going on?" he said, staring in horror at the widening pool of blood. "Where's Melody?"

A moan escaped Helen's lips. Her eyelids fluttered.

"Who did this to you?" Emily asked her.

"Sam," Helen croaked. "It's Sam."

She slipped into unconsciousness.

CHAPTER 28

Before Emily could register what she was doing, she darted through the open front door and into the falling rain. Shadows crawled over the house, the meadow and the trees, covering the land in a veil of darkness. She ran through the garden, cleared the gate, and turned the corner of the house. Then she was plunging into the forest, twigs and leaves crunching under her feet.

She stumbled blindly, breathless and panicked, disoriented by the darkness. Low-hanging branches whistled past her head. Rain lashed her skin.

A beam of light cut through the trees.

Emily slid to a halt then staggered back, shielding her eyes, her heart leaping into her throat.

"Are you trying to get yourself killed?" Jerome hurried towards her, a torch in one hand, a broken table leg in the other.

"You heard what Helen said!" she cried. "We have to find Melody!"

Jerome tightened his grip on the table leg as he nodded. "Then let's not die trying."

They found the shack minutes later, guided by the rain hammering on its corrugated roof. The door was wide open. A quick scan of the ground revealed the broken padlock and the rock Helen had used to gain access.

Impenetrable blackness filled the open doorway like a portal to an unknown realm. A rank, coppery odour choked the air.

"Melody?" Emily hovered on the threshold, suspended between curiosity and fear. "Are you in there?"

When no answer came, she shot a frightened glance at Jerome. Then she was stepping inside the shack.

The torch beam pushed back the darkness, making shadows dance over mouldy walls. Leaves and dirt carpeted the floor, as if the forest had claimed the shack as its own, while a tall shelving unit ran lengthways across the centre of the room, splitting it in two, its shelves filled with boxes, tools, glass jars of nails and screws. Gardening instruments hung from hooks on walls—a rake, a hoe, the curved blade of a scythe. A workbench sat in the left corner, metal scraps and wood shavings scattered on top.

Jerome swept the torch across the room. Light pierced through the junk on the shelves and hit the wall beyond, illuminating deep red splashes.

Emily's heart lurched in her chest. Her legs wouldn't move. One word played over and over in her head: Melody. Melody. Melody.

She could sense Jerome next to her, could almost feel the trembling of his skin. She reached out, found his hand. Then they were moving forward. She didn't want to see what lay beyond, but her limbs were betraying her, forcing one foot in front of the other, until she had moved past the shelves and was standing on the other side.

Emily saw the blood-spattered wall then quickly turned away, squeezing her eyes shut before she could see the body.

Jerome's voice trembled over the din of the rainfall.

"It's not Melody," he said.

Bile burning the back of her throat, Emily forced herself to look. The dead man sat in the corner with his head resting against the wall. His legs were folded at the knees, his hands placed neatly in his lap. Blood swamped the front of his T-shirt and smeared his neck and face, painting over skin that was as grey as wet cement.

"Oh God, it's Sam!"

He'd been stabbed multiple times. There were tears in his T-shirt where the blade had entered, each entry point caked with thick, black blood.

Helen hadn't been trying to tell them that Sam had attacked her, Emily realised. She'd been trying to tell them he was dead.

The torch wavered in Jerome's hand. "We need to go back to the house. We lock the doors. We all stay in the same room. We wait for Daniel and Janelle to return with the police."

"Melody is missing," Emily said.

"Maybe she got scared and ran off."

"Whoever did this, they attacked Helen. What if they've taken Melody? We can't just leave her."

Jerome swung the torch beam at the open door. The light cut through the rain, illuminating the forest beyond. "Do you think I'm right? Do you think it's Franklyn Hobbes? What if he's out there, right now, watching us."

Emily reached up and took the torch from Jerome's hand. As she directed it back to Sam's body, something flashed in the corner of her eye.

"What is that?"

Hidden in between the arterial splashes on the wall, a small symbol had been painted in blood. Four long arrows pointed north, east, south, and west, while four shorter arrows were carved at symmetrical angles in between.

"It's the same symbol," Emily gasped. "The same one I saw on the tree Oscar was hanged from."

Jerome's eyes grew round and wide.

"That's a chaos star," he said.

"A what?"

He rubbed his jaw. "Law is represented by a single upward arrow. Chaos by the symbol of eight—eight arrows pointing to all possibilities."

"What are you talking about?" Emily said, turning to face him.

"The chaos star originates from Michael Moorcock's The Eternal Champion, a fantasy novel from the early seventies," Jerome explained. "But pop culture ate it for breakfast and since then it's appeared in all kinds of places—modern-day occultism, heavy metal album covers, movies, TV, RPGs."

"RP-what?"

"You never played Warhammer? Dungeons and Dragons?"

Emily swung the torch back towards the symbol. "How do you know all this?"

"At school I was a not-so-secret fantasy geek."

Emily stared at the symbol, willing it to reveal its meaning. Why was it here? Why was it carved on Oscar's tree? It was pointing her to something. But what?

Her mind pulsed with a hundred thoughts, none of which formed a cohesive explanation for what was happening at Meadow Pines. For the briefest of moments, she had suspected Sam. But now Sam was dead; murdered alongside Oscar. Probably Marcia, too, she realised with sickening clarity.

Was Jerome right? Had Franklyn Hobbes returned to Meadow Pines in a dangerous and delusional state? Could his belief that he had become nothing led him to transcend moral beliefs of right and wrong?

Emily's skin crawled as she returned her gaze to Sam's body. If Franklyn Hobbes really had returned, how long did they have to find Melody before he claimed her as his next victim?

CHAPTER 29

They huddled together, eyes darting off to the sides, as they hurried back to the house. Safely back inside, they worked their way through the ground floor, locking every window and door, until they came to Pamela's living quarters. Helen was on the couch, still unconscious. Pamela was busy changing the soaked outer bandages of her head wound.

"How is she?" Emily asked.

"It's hard to tell. She's breathing. Her pulse seems a little slow. Beyond that, I have no idea what I'm doing." Pamela's gaze shifted between Emily and Jerome. "What is it?

Where's Melody?" she said, as if she'd somehow managed to catch a glimpse of their thoughts.

Emily bit down on her lip. She took a breath. "We found Sam. He's dead. Someone killed him."

Pamela stared at them, flinching at each word.

"Melody's gone," Emily continued, staring at the wall. "Either she ran off when Helen was attacked, or she's been taken by whoever killed Sam and Oscar. Either way, we can't leave her out there. We need to find her."

Pamela remained perched on the edge of the sofa, staring up at Emily as if she were waiting for the punchline of a cruel joke. When it didn't come, she got to her feet and moved noiselessly across the living room. Emily and Jerome watched her slip through the door that led to the rest of her quarters and close it behind her.

"Why does she keep doing that?" Jerome said.

Emily crossed the room. "Stay with Helen. I'll be back."

Following Pamela, she pushed open the door and entered a purple corridor with colourful rag rugs on the floor. The door at the end was ajar. Knocking softly, Emily stepped inside.

Except for a small Thai-style Buddha on the dresser, the rest of the bedroom showed no signs of the spiritualistic leanings of the rest of the house. Film posters from several years ago, aged and wrinkled, were tacked to the walls— King Kong. The Chronicles of Narnia. Happy Feet.

Pamela sat on the carpet, her back against the bed, one of Marcia's stuffed animals tucked under her arm. She looked up, her face stained with tears. Shadows circled her eyes.

"Tell me my daughter is fine," she said, lips trembling. "Tell me my Marcia is safe and well."

Emily moved further into the room, avoiding Pamela's gaze. Safety net or honest truth?

Nodding, she dug her hands into her pockets. "I really hope she is."

Photographs taped to the dresser mirror caught her eye. She leaned in to take a closer look. The first showed an adolescent Marcia and her long-haired mother, standing in the weed-choked garden of Meadow Pines, the house behind them in a ramshackle state. In the second, an even younger Marcia was puffing out her cheeks, ready to blow out the seven candles on her birthday cake.

The third photograph showed a handsome man in his mid-twenties with red hair and a full beard. Toddler Marcia sat aloft his broad shoulders, her eyes squeezed together with pure joy.

The final photograph was of Sam. It had been taken paparazzi style, as he'd emerged from the bathroom, a towel wrapped around his hips, wet hair flopping over his startled face.

Emily stared at the pictures, her heart aching in her chest. Marcia's room was a shrine to a childhood that had ended at twelve-years-old, when she'd been taken to live a friendless life in the middle of nowhere.

"Do you have children?" Pamela asked.

Emily shook her head.

"People always say being a mother comes naturally. That from the moment your child is born, you love her unconditionally, without question, without thought . . ." She paused, tears brimming. "Marcia's such a kind girl. She's so selfless, willing to help anyone in need. How am I going to tell her? When she comes back, how do I tell her that Sam is . . ."

Emily removed a fluffy white bear from a corner chair and sat down. She felt heavy, weighed down by anxiety. She longed to ask Pamela about the chaos star symbols, but now was not the time. A wave of helplessness washed over her. The longer they sat here doing nothing, the less chance they had of finding Melody alive. It was clear by now that Daniel and Janelle had failed to catch up with

Ben and Sylvia, that they'd been forced to head to Lyndhurst on foot. Until they returned with Sergeant Wells, the remaining residents of Meadow Pines were on their own.

Frightened and restless, Emily got to her feet. She couldn't just sit here, waiting for the police to arrive, hoping that Marcia and Melody were still alive.

"I'll check on Helen," she said. "Maybe she'll wake up and tell us what happened."

Across the room, Pamela pulled her knees up to her chin. She nodded without opening her eyes. "I'll be through in a minute."

"I don't think anyone should be left alone right now. Especially when—"

"A minute," Pamela repeated. "Please."

Emily moved over to the window, checked it was locked, then left the room, closing the door behind her. Returning to the living room, she found Jerome on the sofa with Helen's head in his lap. She was still unconscious. A pile of bloody bandages lay crumpled on the floor.

"Look at you Mr. Lifesaver," Emily said, the humour feeling at odds with the atmosphere in the room. "How's she doing?"

"Hard to tell. All I know is you can't mess around with a head injury. There could be swelling on the brain, who knows what else."

"That stint as a TV doctor came in handy after all." She moved to the window and checked the lock.

"How are you doing?" Jerome asked.

Emily hugged her ribs. "Can I get back to you on that? How about you?"

"Trying not to panic and failing miserably. This morning there were twelve of us. Now there's four. Meanwhile, Franklyn Hobbes is stalking the forest with murder on his mind." He glanced across the room. "Where's Pamela?"

"Having a moment."

Jerome frowned. Emily recognised his expression almost immediately. It said: You're hiding something.

She shook her head. "I don't think it's Franklyn Hobbes."

She'd been thinking it ever since Jerome had first made the suggestion.

"It's been over a year since he disappeared. Why would he come back here now?"

"Who knows how crazed psychopaths think? Perhaps he came back to finish what he started."

Emily's eyes roamed the room and landed on the photograph album—Pamela's Happiness Hall of Fame.

"Why was Oscar looking for Franklyn in the first place? Who hired him?"

"Concerned family?" Jerome said, staring down at Helen's unconscious form. "Franklyn had clearly come off the rails. Maybe he'd disappeared and they were worried about his safety."

"That would make sense. But if that's the case, why would Oscar be tracing him back to a place he visited over a year ago? And come to think of it, why didn't Oscar just come right out and ask Pamela if they'd seen him? Why go to the lengths of signing up for the retreat and pretending to be a guest?"

Jerome adjusted Helen's bandages. "Perhaps he already knew Franklyn was here, hiding out in the woods. Perhaps he thought he would try and track him down without causing a panic."

"But if he considered Franklyn to be a threat, keeping it to himself would put everyone in danger," Emily said, her brow creasing. "I don't know, Jerome. There's one thing that I keep coming back to that doesn't fit into this whole Franklyn Hobbes theory."

"Which is?"

"The argument I heard coming through his wall last night."

Emily picked up the photo album. On the sofa, Helen stirred a little, then was still.

"Someone's killing people," Jerome said, trying not to move. "If it's not Franklyn, who is it?"

Flipping through the pages, Emily examined each photograph. "I don't know. But while we sit here trying to figure it out, Melody is out there, either scared and hiding in the dark, or worse. We should be looking for her."

"You're right. But meanwhile, Pamela is having some sort of meltdown and Little Miss Head Injury here needs our help. We can't just leave them. Besides, Janelle and Daniel will be back with the cavalry soon."

Emily flipped through the pages until she found Franklyn's photograph. She read the dates below: 6-15th December. She skipped forward to the following April, when Franklyn had returned to Meadow Pines and lost his mind.

Her fingers hovered over the page. There was no group photo for the weekend before Easter. Which was understandable, she supposed, considering the horrors of the night before. Frustrated, Emily turned the page, then the next. Until her eyes landed on a different photograph that had been taken a month later.

Dressed in a salmon pink tracksuit, Melody stood front and centre of a group of nine. The ten-day retreats had come to an end, replaced by digital detox weekends. Emily turned to the next page. Melody was there again, just two weekends later, this time dressed in black leggings and a Bon Jovi T-shirt. She was waiting on the next page, too, in sweatpants and a white blouse.

Emily turned the pages and Melody's face continued to appear. Flipping back through the album, she checked the dates.

"What the hell?"

Hurrying over to the sofa, Emily pushed the photograph album in front of Jerome's face and turned the pages, until he made the connection—Melody had been attending the digital detox retreats every two weeks since they'd begun.

Jerome looked up, his mouth hanging open slightly. "That's weird. Maybe she's trying to detox from that tablet of hers."

"She doesn't come here to detox. She comes here because she's lonely." Emily closed the album, her mind trying to make sense of it all. "But this place isn't cheap."

"You're telling me. This weekend's cost me the first month's salary from the job I don't have."

Emily returned the album to the shelf, then stared at the door, her eyes narrowing. "If Pamela resurfaces, cover for me."

Jerome squirmed under Helen's weight. "Where are you going? It's not safe to be anywhere on your own."

"I'm just going upstairs. The house is all locked up. I'll be five minutes."

"Damn you, Emily Swanson—what are you up to?"

"Five minutes," Emily repeated.

Before Jerome could stop her, she opened the living room door and disappeared into the hall outside.

CHAPTER 30

The house was quiet. Emily stole through the hallway, conscious of the floorboards beneath her feet, the rustle of her clothes against her body. She passed the meditation room, the art room, Pamela's office. The table was still on its side where Helen had fallen. Her blood remained in a pool on the floor. Grimacing, Emily skirted around and rechecked the locks of the front door.

Shadows cloaked the top of the stairs. Rained drummed on the slate roof above. She climbed, one foot silently placed in front of the other. Reaching the top, she peered along the corridor, then turned and headed into

Melody's room. The tablet lay on the bed, the ceiling reflected on its glossy screen. Emily picked it up, circled the power button with a finger, then pressed it. The screen lit up. Seconds later, she was staring at the orange and charcoal face of a cat.

"Derek," she whispered.

Derek was grossly overweight and pissed off, his yellow-green eyes glaring at the camera, daring the viewer to come an inch closer, to feel the sharpness of his claws.

Emily scanned through the folders on the tablet's desktop, located the 'pictures' folder and opened it up. Melody had organised her photographs into folders for each year. Opening the current year revealed further sub-folders for individual months. Emily picked one at random—February—and scanned through the images. It didn't take long to build a picture of Melody's life.

Photograph after photograph, she posed for the camera; sometimes alone, pouting her lips or demonstrating a range of smiles, and sometimes with Derek; the cat pressed tightly against her cheek or held in the air for the world to see. Except the world wasn't watching.

There were no pictures of friends or family, no social gatherings or celebrations. There was only Melody, holed up in her small but meticulously-kept home, with the cat as her only company.

As Emily flipped through the images, she felt tendrils of loneliness reach out from the screen and pierce her chest. Melody's life was a solitary existence that reeked of unhappiness. It was no wonder she had so desperately attached herself to Meadow Pines. Emily's mind wandered back to yesterday evening, when Melody had arrived late to the dinner table, her eyes red from crying, then to the lake, where she had sat at the end of the jetty, looking sad and alone.

Exiting the February folder, Emily opened the most recent. There were more self-portraits.

More shots of Melody and Derek posing in their cramped living room or sharing a pillow in bed. But there were other photographs here, too—candid photographs taken here at Meadow Pines, this very weekend.

Her mind racing, Emily examined each one: a picture snapped from the front door of Janelle and Marcia toiling in the vegetable garden; another taken from the treeline of Jerome and Daniel sat on the back porch, their bodies turned to one another in an obvious display of attraction.

A series of shots had been captured through the kitchen window: Sam slicing onions with a sharp knife; Sam wiping sweat from his brow while hunched over a bubbling pot; Sam rolling a joint while sitting on the kitchen island. Then photographs snapped from a bedroom window: Sam smoking the joint at the edge of the forest; Sam staring into the trees.

Bringing the tablet with her, Emily moved over to the rain-covered window and stared out. The porch roof was directly below. Beyond, the forest was black and murky; a series of sharp points and angles in the shadows.

A thought struck Emily—if Melody had sneaked her tablet into Meadow Pines this weekend, it was more than likely she had done it before. Returning to sit on the bed, Emily worked her way back through the folders, finding countless pictures of past guests, each one secretly snapped from windows, doorways, and corners.

She moved on to the folders of the previous year, opening 'December', lingering over photographs of Christmas Day—of Melody and Derek wearing matching Christmas sweaters at a dinner table set for one.

'November' revealed yet more photographs taken at Meadow Pines: guests making sculptures in the art room; rusty leaves decaying on the forest floor while the pines stood bold and green.

Emily moved back through the months, her finger swiping again and again across the screen. She had no idea what she was doing, no idea why she was so wilfully invading Melody's privacy while she was out there in the forest, possibly enduring all kinds of horrors at the hands of a psychopath.

But instinct told her to keep searching.

There was something here, she was sure of it. The missing element that would connect what was happening right now to that terrible night of April last year, when Franklyn Hobbes had torn Marcia Hardy's world apart.

Emily found it minutes later in an unnamed folder. And what she saw made her eyes grow wide and round with horror.

CHAPTER 31

Jerome tried to temper the anger that was heating his skin. Why did Emily think it was fine to take off like that, knowing he couldn't go after her? He'd learned months ago that if Emily had set her mind on something, it was best to see how you could help rather than hinder her—no matter how much danger she was about to put herself in—but he'd hoped that after being abducted, put in a coma, experimented upon, and almost murdered, that she might have learned a thing or two about safety procedures in dangerous situations.

For a person who had once come across as quiet to the point of withdrawn, Emily could be surprisingly fearless. It was a quality that impressed and frustrated him in equal measures. Like now, for example—here they were, trapped inside a house in the middle of the New Forest with a maniac on the loose, and Emily Swanson had thought it acceptable to run off alone. It was obvious she was onto something, but couldn't she see how much she made him worry?

Did she even care?

He glanced down at Helen. Her chest rose and fell in slow bursts. The fresh bandages he'd applied were holding out but they would need changing soon.

What if it was Emily lying unconscious on the sofa right now, with a hole in her head the size of a marble? He doubted she would learn anything new from it—except to duck next time.

Pamela appeared in the doorway, staring at Helen.

"No change?" she asked.

Jerome shook his head.

"Here, I'll take over." She swapped positions with him, gently resting Helen's head in her lap. She nodded at a cherry wood cabinet in the corner. "There's whiskey."

Jerome took out glasses and a bottle of Glenfiddich single malt. He poured out two generous shots, handed one to Pamela, then held his glass up to the light. Tipping back his head, he drained it of its amber-coloured contents. A fire ignited in his belly, burning all the way up to his chest.

"We're almost out of bandages," he said.

"Well, we'll have to improvise. There are clean towels in the closet—through that door, then second on the left." Pamela grew still. She looked around the room as if she didn't recognise it. "Where's Emily?"

"Upstairs. She went to fetch something from her room," he said, annoyed by his loyalty.

"She shouldn't be wandering around alone. It's not safe."

"Yeah, good luck with that. I'll get those towels." Jerome made his way through the door and towards the hallway closet. Incense hung heavy in the air, making him nauseous. Taking a pile of towels from the shelf and carrying them under his arm, he took a slow walk back to the living room.

Pamela had propped Helen's head up with cushions and was now standing in front of the window. The rain continued to fall, clinging to the glass. The darkness beyond was infinite.

"I hope they're all right out there," Jerome said.

"I hope so, too." Pamela's eyes were red and sore-looking as she glanced past Jerome towards the living room door. "Emily has been a long time. What is she doing?"

Good question, Jerome thought. "Changing her clothes. There was blood on them from when we found . . ."

By the window, Pamela's shoulders tensed.

"I'm sorry about Sam," Jerome said. "I don't understand how anyone could do that—just take away someone's life as if it meant nothing. Is it really that easy?"

"The most awful things in this world are done at the hands of people," Pamela said, her gaze hardening. "You shouldn't be surprised by that. People kill people. It's been the same since we were given birth to on this planet and it will remain the same until we incinerate ourselves. Survival is our greatest instinct and our greatest downfall. We cling to the notion of our existence so desperately that we're prepared to destroy any threat to it, even if it means killing our own kind. Somewhere along the way, we seem to have misconstrued survival as control. To control the world and all that lives in it gives us a greater chance of survival. Isn't that what war is really about?"

Jerome shrugged as he stole nervous glances at Helen, then at the living room door.

"Yes, it's about money-making. Yes, it's about power, but doesn't that all translate as survival?" Pamela stared into her glass, swirling the whiskey around. "It's ironic. We care so much about survival, we fire missiles and shoot guns and detonate bombs, and in an instant, we steal the breath of anyone we perceive as a threat. That's the great tragedy about our survival instinct. Our survival really means my survival. Such is the way of people."

Jerome took a moment to absorb Pamela's words. It was an uncomfortable speech that filled him with deep-rooted anxiety.

"But what about all this?" he asked, waving a hand around the room. "If that's the case, why bother with Meadow Pines in the first place?"

"Because if I can help people to free themselves from suffering, doesn't that make the world an instantly better place? At least, for them."

"I like to think I have faith in the human race," Jerome said. "Yes, there are terrible people in the world. People who do awful things. But the majority of us are not monsters. The majority of us are good and kind."

"But selfish," Pamela said. "There is enough food and water to feed every single person on this planet, and yet children die in poverty every minute of every day. There's no need for it, and yet it happens relentlessly. Why? Because it means thinking about the survival of others, not just our own."

She paused, her gaze falling on Jerome's perplexed face. "I know what you're thinking. Why is she reacting so heatedly to the problems of the world when her whole ethos is not to react but to observe? I can meditate for twelve, thirteen hours a day, and during that time I can detach from my ego. But the rest of the time, I'm a human being living in the world, and that world doesn't give a damn if I'm enlightened or not."

She turned away from him to stare at the living room door. An uncomfortable silence filled the air. On the sofa, Helen groaned and turned her head. Her eyelids flickered.

Jerome rushed to her side. "Helen? Can you hear me?"

Just as quickly as her eyes had opened, they closed again. Hope sinking in his stomach, Jerome got to his feet.

"I'm going to check on Emily," he said. "She should have been back by now."

Pamela returned to the window and peered outside. "We live in a cruel, uncaring world. The best we can do is free ourselves from its grip, then help others do the same."

Jerome opened the door.

"Lock it behind me," he said.

CHAPTER 32

The rain hit the ground hard, tearing up loose soil. Emily cut through the dark, heading straight for the forest. She wore her raincoat, the hood pulled up. Her shoes and jeans were already wet, her skin damp beneath. A torch swung in her hands, switched off until she really needed it. Wandering around outside while a killer stalked through the trees wasn't the most sensible idea she'd had in her life, but what she'd discovered on Melody's tablet had left her startled and confused. Now she was determined to find out the truth—because people's lives were depending on it.

The forest came up to meet her. Glancing over her shoulder, she took a last look at the house and saw light pouring from Pamela's living room window. A pang of guilt prodded her in the chest as she thought of Jerome. No doubt he would be wondering what was taking her so long. He would be worrying about her. But Emily knew that if she had told him where she was going, he would have tried to stop her. And after realising he'd have a better chance of stopping the world from turning, he would have insisted on coming along. Emily didn't want to be responsible for putting him in more danger than he was already in. More than that, she didn't want him to die.

Switching on the torch, Emily squinted as trees were illuminated in cold light. By day, the forest was beautiful and serene, but now trees looked gnarled and twisted, their branches reaching down like skeletal hands to snatch her up. Steadying her trembling hand, Emily pointed the beam at the ground. The darkness swarmed around her as she crept forward.

She headed west, keeping the house lights on her right. With only the torch beam as her guide, it would be easy to become disoriented. One wrong turn would lead to another, and before she knew it, she'd be heading in the wrong direction, moving deeper into the forest.

The sound of rain splattering on the hood of her raincoat was deafening as she weaved between the trees, moving at a hurried pace, stopping when she thought she was heading off course, then ploughing forward once she'd regained her bearings.

Fear prickled the back of her neck. Her head swivelled from left to right as her eyes searched the darkness.

It didn't take long to find what she was looking for. She stumbled into the clearing. The torchlight fell upon the old shack, transforming it into a derelict haunted house. Rain hammered on its roof, sounding like a thousand drums.

Emily moved closer, her feet cautious and stiff. She froze in the doorway. The smell of blood was overpowering; a nauseating stench that was at once sickly sweet and horribly acerbic. Ignoring the fear pulling her back, Emily stepped inside.

The torchlight illuminated shelves and glinted off blades and sharp prongs. Sam remained in the corner, dead eyes staring into darkness. His blood had congealed, thick and reddish-black.

Emily turned away, overcome by a sudden urge to run. She couldn't breathe in here. The air was too rank and heavy. Now, a familiar tingling started at the top of her head and in the tips of her fingers, while panic flapped inside her chest like a trapped bird.

Her eyes moved back to Sam's body, lingering on the puncture wounds, the ragged gash in his neck. Whoever had killed him had done so in a panicked frenzy, plunging the blade into his flesh again and again, until he had lost too much blood to fight back.

Fear gripping her bones, Emily backed away. She hit the wall, sending a garden rake clattering to the floor. Shrieking, she spun on her heels, training the torch on the open door. The beam shot into the forest, lighting up nearby trees.

"Get a hold of yourself," she breathed. She hadn't felt this afraid since waking up at St. Dymphna's Private Hospital, a feeding tube rammed into her stomach, with no idea of where she was or what had happened to her.

Backing up into the far corner, Emily crouched down and closed her eyes.

In for four, hold for seven, out for eight.

She chanted the mantra that had always helped to control her breathing, over and over, until her heart slowed its beating to a steadier rhythm and the pressure on her chest grew lighter.

Opening her eyes again, she got to her feet. Turning away from Sam's body, she inspected the tools hanging on the wall and quickly located a shovel. Then she was out of the shack and hurrying from the glade, shovel gripped in one hand, torch in the other.

It took her a moment to orientate herself before she began retracing her steps. Glimmers of light appeared through the trees and Emily caught glimpses of the house.

Switching off the torch, she emerged from the forest and moved in a wide circle, keeping enough distance between herself and Pamela's living room window to pass by unnoticed.

She wondered what was happening inside. Had Jerome realised she was gone? Had Helen woken up and revealed the identity of her attacker? For a second, temptation drew Emily back to the house. Fighting it off, she ducked in between the greenhouse and the vegetable plot, and headed for the meadow.

The front of the house was pitched in darkness, leaving Emily blind. She switched the torch back on. Wildflowers glowed in the light, their petals shredded by the rain. Long grass swished against her jeans as she hurried eastward.

Emily's arm was already starting to ache with the weight of the shovel, so she swapped hands with the torch. Then she was heading back into the forest.

By the time she reached the clearing, the rain had become relentless, and even though her raincoat was keeping her upper body dry, her jeans and shoes were now drenched.

A gentle tapping directed her attention to Oscar's body. Pools of rainwater had formed in the dips and troughs of the tarpaulin. Emily circled him cautiously, half-expecting him to leap up and lurch zombie-like towards her. It was unnerving what horrors the imagination could produce in the dark; all those childhood terrors crawling out from under the bed in an instant.

Emily moved around the tree Oscar had been hanged from, until she stood on the other side. She pointed the torch at the chaos star carved into the trunk, then directed the light down at the ground.

The bouquet of rotting flowers lay at her feet, the rain turning it to mush. She had no idea if the conclusion she'd reached was right. If it even was a conclusion. But instinct had drawn her back to this clearing, back to the tree where Oscar had been strung up like an animal at a slaughterhouse.

And right now, as she pushed the dead flowers to one side to reveal soft, wet earth, that instinct grew white-hot in her belly.

Resting the torch against a tree root, Emily picked up the shovel. She tapped the ground at the base of the tree.

Moving a little further out, she tapped the ground again.

There was a difference.

The ground directly beneath the tree was looser, less compacted.

Emily lifted the shovel. Using both hands, she drove it into the earth. Pressing her foot down on the blade, she watched it sink into the soil. Then with her heart racing, Emily began to dig.

CHAPTER 33

The house ticked and creaked like the joints of an old man. Jerome hurried along the corridor, stopping at the dining hall and sticking his head through the doorway. It was dark and silent. Half-eaten food still sat on the table from an interrupted lunch. It seemed like days ago when they had all left the table in a panic.

A wave of claustrophobia passed through him as he made his way along the corridor. This house was beginning to feel like a tomb. He checked the art room, then the meditation room. Both were empty and silent.

Moving into the foyer, he saw the pool of Helen's blood. Stepping around it, he rattled the locked door to Pamela's office, then checked the front door. The bolts had been pulled back. Jerome swallowed down rising nausea. He'd locked that door himself. Now someone had unlocked it.

A sliver of fear slipped down the back of his T-shirt. He turned and faced the stairs.

"Emily? Are you up there?"

He already knew the answer. Cursing under his breath, he took two steps at a time, until he reached the landing.

Silence greeted him.

Jerome fumbled along the wall until he found the light switch. Orange ceiling lights flickered to life. Hurrying along the corridor, he knocked on Emily's door, then opened it without waiting for an answer.

As expected, the room was empty.

He made a quick search of the other rooms in the vain hope he'd find her snooping through someone else's possessions. But it was just that —a vain hope.

Standing in Melody's room, he reminded himself of all the foolish and dangerous things Emily had done in the past; albeit for the greater good. When he looked at it that way, heading outside to find Melody while a maniac was on the loose wasn't really anything out of the ordinary.

He would have to go after her, wouldn't he?

He would have to go out in the dark to find her. Not to rescue her—Emily Swanson would not tolerate being rescued—but to back her up. Jerome didn't know who he was angrier with—Emily for lying to him, for putting herself in danger yet again, or with himself for being so gullible.

"Damn you, Emily Swanson."

Wondering where he should look for her first, Jerome turned to leave the room. Something flashed in the darkness. Melody's tablet lay on the bed, the standby light pulsing like a winking eye. Curiosity momentarily getting the better of him, he picked it up and dragged a finger across the screen.

Light spilled out, illuminating the angles of his face, as he swiped through a series of photographs—images of wreaths and garlands, roughly fashioned together and placed at the base of a tree. Each picture had been taken in a different season. In one, the ground was covered in rusty autumn leaves, while in another, fresh grass sprouted between the tree roots. But one thing was consistent in every photograph—the flowers had all been placed in front of the same tree.

As Jerome used his finger and thumb to enlarge one of the images, his pulse quickened at an alarming rate. There, carved into the trunk, was the chaos star. This was the tree Oscar had been hanged from. But why had Melody been leaving flowers there for at least a year?

Anxiety knotting in his stomach, Jerome flicked past the photos, until he came upon a different set of images—secret pictures of Sam, Marcia, and Pamela, taken in and around the house.

And there was a photograph of someone else.

Jerome's jaw swung open, and his eyes grew round and wide. The photograph had been snapped from the upstairs corridor, a candid shot through the half-open door of one of the guest's bedrooms.

The man seemed unaware of the photographer's presence. He was shirtless, his body taut and lean, a mess of dark curls covering his head. Eyes as black as onyx stared into space. There were scars on his chest— thin, parallel lines of angry raised flesh that were clearly not the result of accident or surgery. But it wasn't the scars that had Jerome's attention in a stranglehold. There was something on the man's left forearm.

Jerome zoomed in on the image. It was a blemish of some kind. A birthmark, perhaps.

His pulse racing, he enlarged the image further and leaned in closer to the screen. His breath caught in his throat.

It was no blemish. It was a tattoo.

A chaos star.

It was the same symbol Emily had found carved into the tree. The same symbol painted in Sam's blood on the wall of the shack.

As for the man, Jerome recognised him instantly.

"Franklyn Hobbes," he whispered.

But why was there a photograph of him on Melody's tablet? She'd been nowhere near Meadow Pines the night Franklyn had attacked Marcia,

Had she?

A deep tremor of worry shuddered through Jerome's body. He stood and peered out the window, over the black trees.

Had she?

His thoughts tripped over each other as he glanced back at the tablet on the bed, at the image of Franklyn Hobbes.

Suddenly Jerome was no longer worried about Emily being out there alone and looking for Melody—he was worried about Emily finding her.

He needed to speak to Pamela. He needed Helen to wake up. Pulling himself from the window, he snatched Melody's tablet from the bed and turned to the open door, dimly aware that the corridor lights were now switched off.

Something stirred in the shadows just in front of him. Before he could react, hands slammed into his chest. Jerome stumbled back, almost losing his balance. Then the door slammed shut with a deafening bang that sent shockwaves through the walls. Stunned, he heard a key slide into the keyhole, then a crunch of gears as the lock snapped into place.

"Hey!" Throwing Melody's tablet on the bed, he ran to the door and pulled on the handle. He curled a fist and hammered on the wood. "Who's out there? Let me out!"

Then Jerome heard footsteps pounding downstairs and along the hall, heading straight for Pamela and Helen.

CHAPTER 34

Wet soil slurped around Emily's ankles. She pressed her weight on the shovel, scooping up dirt and flinging it onto a growing mound. The rain continued to fall, slapping against her raincoat and filling the deepening trench. The more Emily dug, the more her arms ached. She concentrated on the rhythm of her movements: the thrust of the blade into the earth, the force of her foot against metal, the pressure of gravity as she swung soil onto the mound.

She now stood in a hole that was approximately three feet deep. Brown, murky water splashed against her shins. The ground beneath was a thick sludge that sucked on her shoes and threatened to swallow her whole.

Above the rain, she heard a loud snap. Snatching up the torch, Emily pointed it at the trees. The noise came again. Someone was circling her, getting closer. Catching her breath, she tried to make her body still and quiet, but the thumping of her heart and the rushing of blood in her ears made it impossible.

At the peripheries of the light, something darted through the bushes. Emily snatched up the shovel and brandished it in front of her.

The bushes parted.

Two glittering black eyes stared at her.

Slowly, Emily lowered the shovel.

Frozen to the spot, its ears and snout twitching, was a deer.

Just for a moment, the horrors of the day were forgotten. Emily stared at the deer in wonder, as rain glanced off its svelte body. The creature stared back, regarding her warily. Then as Emily reached a gentle hand towards it, the deer lowered its head, turned, and bolted off into the darkness.

Relaxing her aching shoulders, Emily felt the sudden urge to laugh. Instead, she replaced the torch between the tree roots, took up the shovel in both hands, and resumed digging.

Minutes passed. The rain refused to ease. The more Emily dug, the more the deepening hole filled with muddy rainwater. It wasn't just spilling in from the surface, it was seeping through the earth itself.

Setting the shovel down, Emily began scooping up water and pitching it out, but it was a hopeless task; like Sisyphus from Greek mythology, doomed to an endless cycle of pushing a boulder uphill only to watch it roll back down.

Giving up, she grabbed the shovel and thrust it back into the mud. Her muscles complained as she dug faster.

It was the flowers that had brought her here. The flowers and the tattoo. But perhaps she had confused their meaning. Perhaps she was out here digging up nothing but dirt and rock while someone else was drawing their last breath. Had she been wrong to trust her instincts?

She had her answer a minute later.

The shovel struck something that didn't feel like earth or stone. A tree root, she wondered. But the sudden panic rising in her throat said no. Emily continued to poke the ground with the edge of the shovel. Then with a trembling hand, she snatched up the torch and pointed it at the dark pool of water sloshing around her knees. The water was too murky for the light to penetrate.

Repulsion crawled up Emily's spine as she realised what she needed to do. Tossing the shovel to one side, she balanced the torch on the edge of the pit, then sucked in a deep, calming breath.

Emily sank down into the icy water.

It rushed through her jeans, biting her legs, making her bones ache. She clenched her teeth as she peered into the murk. Then she thrust her hands under the water, clawing at the wet soil.

The earth was already taking back what the shovel had found, but Emily was determined, raking back the soil. Without warning, her fingers brushed against something soft and sinewy.

Horrified, she cried out, falling back against the side of the pit. Trembling with both cold and fear, she sucked in another breath, regained her balance, and plunged her hands back into the icy water.

Emily pulled back the earth and found what she'd been looking for. Ignoring the bile rising in her throat, she ran her fingers along its round contours, tracing the forehead, the nose, the hollows of the eyes. Her hand moved lower, scooping earth away from the neck, the shoulders, the left arm.

Her fingers moved down and rested upon the hand. Gently gripping the wrist, Emily freed the arm and lifted it out of the water. Nausea choked her as she stared at the limb in horror.

Without the protection of a coffin, nature had gonc to work on the body, sucking it dry of nutrients, withering it like a dead tree. But even though decomposition was occurring at an accelerated rate, the skin still clung to the bones like old leather.

Terror devoured Emily's insides. She fought it, pushing it to the corners of her mind. Scooping up a handful of water, she poured it over the arm, then gently wiped away the dirt.

The tattoo was faded, barely there, but she could see the arrows pointing outward in the shape of a star.

Horror swarmed like flies over Emily's body. She let go of the limb and watched it sink beneath the muddy pool.

Franklyn Hobbes had never left Meadow Pines.

He was dead.

Murdered. Buried in a shallow grave.

And Melody had been there the night he'd been killed.

Hoisting herself out of the pit, Emily pulled her knees up to her chest and shuffled back until she felt the tree pressing against her spine.

The cold dug into her ribs and nipped at her skin as she tried to make sense of it all. Either Pamela had been telling the truth—or what she believed to be the truth—or she had lied to cover up Franklyn's murder.

If she was being honest, how could Melody's presence be explained? Franklyn had visited Meadow Pines only twice, and Melody hadn't been in the group photo taken on his first visit. And yet there were images of Franklyn on Melody's tablet, as well as photographs of flowers left on his grave.

Emily's thoughts returned to Pamela, who had already admitted that Meadow Pines had been facing financial trouble, and that she'd covered up the attack on Marcia to save the business and their home. But what if she'd also covered up what had happened next?

Unearthing Franklyn's body had only resulted in unearthing more questions.

As Emily replayed the events of the last two days, her eyes wandered back to the shallow grave. Whatever had happened that night, it was now clear that Melody was at the centre of it all.

Why else would Pamela cover up her presence?

Why else would there be pictures of Franklyn and his grave stored on her tablet?

There was something else. Following Franklyn's disappearance, Melody had been attending weekend retreats at Meadow Pines with astonishing frequency—much more than she could possibly afford.

What did it all mean?

As much as she didn't want to believe it, Emily could only reach one conclusion: Melody had killed Franklyn Hobbes and Pamela had covered it up.

But why?

Had it been revenge for what he'd done to Marcia? Or was it because he represented a threat to Melody's only real escape from desperate loneliness?

Emily felt a deep ache in her heart. What had happened to Melody that she had ended up in the wastelands of society, unwanted and unloved? Sitting against the tree, the rain chilling her bones, she tried to think of an alternative explanation for the evidence she'd found, but no matter how many paths she followed, they all ended at the same place:

Somehow, Melody was responsible for the death of Franklyn Hobbes.

Did that mean she had killed the others, too?

Pushing up against the tree trunk, Emily got to her feet. She stared down at her soiled, wet clothing, and her trembling hands. Had Oscar shown Franklyn's picture to Melody? Had she flown into a blind panic and killed him before he could find out what she'd done? But what about Sam and Marcia? Why had she hurt the people she claimed were her friends?

Emily's head spun. She felt the beginnings of a headache at the top of her skull. Every question she asked was like a blooming flower, the petals unfurling to reveal yet more mysteries for which she didn't have the answers.

But she knew someone who might.

Picking up the torch, she cast one last look over Franklyn's grave. Then she pulled up the hood of her raincoat and started back towards the house.

She was halfway across the meadow when a blood-curdling scream echoed high above the treetops.

Emily stopped dead in her tracks. The scream had come from the direction of the lake.

Now it was quiet; the only sound was the gentle fizz of rain hitting the grass. Terrified, Emily turned her back on the house and broke into a run. She raced through the trees, heading for the lake, her arms pumping at her sides.

Minutes later, she slid to a halt behind a thick pine tree. Her lungs were on fire. The cold had got into her bones. But the rain had finally relented. Above the canopy, clouds were dispersing. In the near distance, Emily saw moonlight glancing off the lake like shattered shards of mirror.

Switching off the torch, she slipped it inside her coat pocket and moved up to the next tree. She cocked her head and listened. The lake lapped softly on the shore. Somewhere overhead, an owl let out a low hoot.

Emily moved closer. And saw yellow light glimmering through the trees.

Up ahead and to the left, she saw the jetty reaching out over the lake. A lantern sat at the end, illuminating the surrounding water and the small rowboat that jostled and pulled on its tethers.

Something else was on the jetty. Something long and crumpled like a pile of cloth.

Emily squinted in the dark. The pile of cloth moved. It moaned and squirmed.

"Marcia!"

She was still alive.

Adrenaline raced through Emily's veins as she dashed forward, keeping low and to the shadows, wincing at the crunches and snaps of the forest floor beneath her feet.

She edged closer, suddenly aware of the danger she was putting herself in—the only weapons she possessed were the torch and her bare hands.

Marcia lay on her side, her back turned to Emily, her clothing muddy and torn. Her wrists and ankles were tied together with thin coils of rope. Emily scanned the forest and the shore. Fear squeezing the air from her lungs, she stepped out from the trees and hurried along the jetty, stealing panicked glances over her shoulder.

At the sound of Emily's approach, Marcia began to thrash violently. Her moans became frightened sobs. She rolled onto her front and began choking on the gag in her mouth.

Emily rushed to her side. "It's going to be all right. You're safe now." She put her hand on Marcia's shoulder and felt her flinch. "I'm not going to hurt you. I need to turn you over so I can untie you."

With one hand on Marcia's shoulder and one on her hip, Emily rolled her over onto her back. Light from the lantern spilled across her face.

Emily stopped breathing.

She fell back on her haunches, confusion fogging her mind.

Lying on the jetty, tied and gagged, and peering up with terrified eyes, was Melody.

Emily blinked, coming to her senses. She sprang forward, pulling the gag from Melody's mouth.

"Help me!" Melody cried. "Please, help me!"

"What's going on here?" Emily said, tugging at the rope,

But then Melody was staring over Emily's shoulder, her eyes growing wide with horror.

Emily spun around in time to see a shadowy figure. And a thick chunk of wood swinging towards her head.

CHAPTER 35

Pain forced her awake. Her left eye was sealed shut. Her right eye stared up at a vast, black field of countless stars. She watched them sway from left to right, right to left, the motion repeating, over and over, until she felt sick.

Emily tried to sit up, but she was unable to move. The surface beneath her head was hard. She could smell damp wood, mould, spoiled water. She tried to move again, but it was as if her wrists and ankles were cemented together.

A second pulsating wave of pain swelled up from her temple. She wrenched her head to the side and vomited. When she was done, she returned her gaze to the sky. The stars wouldn't stop moving. The world turned yellow, then red, then black. She floated away once more.

When she next woke, she heard sounds: the rustle of leaves as a breeze shouldered its way through the forest; the rhythmic splashing of water followed by the soft patter of raining droplets.

Emily opened her good eye and looked around.

She was lying in a boat, trussed in ropes, her body trapped beneath the centre thwart.

Attempting to ignore the searing pain in her temple and the taste of blood in her mouth, she tilted her head. The boat was still moored to the jetty. She could hear Melody's muffled sobs coming from somewhere above.

Emily felt eyes upon her. A shadow sat at the edge of the jetty, legs dangling over the water.

"You're awake."

Emily thought she recognised the voice. The shadow moved into the light, peeling away layers of darkness.

Marcia peered down at Emily, then turned to look back at the jetty. Behind her, Melody's sobs grew even more pitiful.

"Sorry about your head. I didn't know what else to do."

Emily tried to move her hands and succeeded in wriggling her fingers. Attempting to rotate her wrists was rewarded by a stinging bite from tightly-coiled rope. She winced, then returned her one-eyed gaze to her captor.

"I don't understand," she croaked. "I saw the Land Rover. The blood."

Marcia's gaze returned to the jetty. "You saw what you were meant to see."

She picked up Emily's torch and flashed it at the trees. Then giving Melody one last glance, she slipped off the jetty and into the boat.

Nausea churned Emily's stomach as the boat rocked violently from side to side. Marcia untethered the tiny vessel from its moorings, then used an oar to push away from the jetty. Sitting down on the centre thwart, feet either side of Emily's body, she slotted both oars into the rowlocks. Marcia began to row, expertly cutting the oars through the water.

As the boat moved away from the jetty, Emily had a sudden and clear vision of what was about to happen to her, and a lightning bolt of panic shot through her chest and up to her head. She pulled frantically at the rope binding her wrists. The rope bit deeper, slicing through skin. Emily winced as her vision began to spiral.

Marcia rowed for a minute more, before pulling the oars from the water and resting them on her knees. She leaned back and picked up the torch. Blinding light flashed in Emily's face. She squeezed her eye shut and rested her head against the boat.

"I'm sorry this is happening to you," Marcia said, her voice flat and emotionless. "You seem like a nice person. If we'd had a chance to get to know each other a little better we might have become friends." She paused, staring down at her captive. "But you've brought this upon yourself. I hope you realise that."

Emily struggled to find her voice. Panic pressed down on her chest, squeezing the breath from her lungs. Lowering the torch, Marcia pointed it at the side of the boat. The light bounced back in a soft glow, allowing Emily to make out her features.

She was surprised by what she saw. Instead of the hardened face of a killer, she saw the pallid features of a terrified young woman.

Conscious of Emily's gaze, Marcia reached for the torch. A bloodstained bandage was wrapped tightly around her hand.

Emily found her voice at last. "Why are you doing this, Marcia? Why is Melody tied up? Is it because of Franklyn? Because of what he did to you?"

Switching off the torch, Marcia plunged the boat back into darkness. She picked up the oars again. "What would you know about that?"

"I know what your mother told me. That Franklyn attacked you. That Sam chased him away." Emily paused before she spoke again. "Why did you kill Sam? He loved you."

The oars hit the water and Marcia began to row.

"I didn't kill Sam," she said, her voice pushing through clenched teeth. "I didn't kill anyone."

Confused, Emily tried to sit up. Her neck hurt. Her heart throbbed. Her eye felt as if it had been scooped out and dumped in the water. Dizzy, she lay back down, forced to stare at the stars once more.

"If you didn't kill anyone, who did?" she asked, her voice sounding far away, like it was floating up to the stars. Marcia was silent as she rowed, a silhouette melding with the darkness. "Why won't you tell me what the hell is going on?"

Emily fell silent, the pain in her head growing unbearable. Above the slosh of water, she heard Melody's sobs, still audible but further away now.

"Tell me what you think you know," Marcia said.

Emily drew in a breath. Pain stabbed her lungs. "I know Oscar didn't hang himself. I know he was a private investigator who was searching for Franklyn. I know your mother lied to me. The night Franklyn attacked you, he didn't run away. Someone killed him."

"And how would you know that?"

"Because I just dug up his body."

Marcia lifted the oars. Water ran off the paddles and cascaded into the lake.

"Melody was there that night," Emily said. "Did she kill Franklyn? Did she kill the others?"

In the starlight, Marcia turned her head and stared over the lake. She was unmoving for a long time. At last, she spoke.

"I was happy before we came to Meadow Pines. I loved my friends, my school. Dance classes on a Tuesday evening, gym on Thursdays. Life was good. Then Pamela took it all away from me. She tried to convince me Meadow Pines was exactly what we needed. Of course, what she really meant was that Meadow Pines was exactly what she needed.

"I hated her for it. I wanted to run away, back to my home. Back to my friends. I was twelve years old. Who takes a child to the middle of nowhere and isolates her from the world? No TV, no phone. No one to talk to. How was that ever a good idea?"

The throbbing in Emily's head intensified, pulsating from her swollen eye and down to her jaw.

"It must have been hard," she gasped.

Marcia spoke through clenched teeth. "Like you can't imagine. Meadow Pines was a ruin when we found it. Even though I was just a child, I knew it would be a huge mistake to take it on. But Pamela was convinced it was meant to be. The setting, the house—it was all perfect in her eyes. Never mind the time and money it would take to make the place inhabitable before we could even think about receiving guests. But if you know anything about Pamela, it's this—she's stubborn as hell and she never gives up.

"So, regardless of what I wanted, off we went to live in the middle of the forest, without electricity or proper running water. She spent every penny we had and borrowed a whole lot more from the bank. I was already thirteen by the time Meadow Pines opened. Come opening day, Pamela was in so much debt even

I lost sleep over it. But I'd never seen her so happy. Especially when people finally started coming to the retreats."

"I've already heard this," Emily said, her patience fraying at the edges as she twisted her hands and wrists, trying to get free. "Fast forward a few years and Meadow Pines wasn't doing so well. You were in debt. One more knock and you stood to lose everything. What happened with Franklyn?"

Angry stars flashed in Marcia's eyes. One by one, they faded into darkness. "We were struggling with the competition. Thanks to a boom in mindfulness meditation other retreats were opening all over the place. We couldn't keep up with the mortgage payments and the bank was threatening to take Meadow Pines. Pamela was going to lose everything she'd built up.

"You see, regardless of my feelings, I knew she wouldn't be able to cope if we lost it all. Some people just aren't built for what our world has become. If Meadow Pines closed and Pamela had to return to society, she would have cracked. That's what we were facing when Franklyn came back."

On the floor of the boat, Emily had managed to wriggle her way along half an inch, so that her head was now resting against the inside bow. She still couldn't see over the edge but now she had a better view of Marcia.

"What happened that night?" she asked.

"What Pamela told you was true." Marcia's voice had turned to stone. "The first part, at least. It was day nine of the retreat. She and her guests were doing their meditation thing before calling it a night. I've never really shared her beliefs. I'm more of a humanist—be good to others and people will be good back to you. Pamela's experimented with most faiths, but she's never once forced anything upon me. All that she ever asked was I keep an open mind. And I have.

"Anyway, that night I was in the kitchen with Sam. We weren't seeing each other then, but I knew we liked each other." Grief filled the cracks in Marcia's voice. "He was cleaning up after the evening meal. I offered to take the food waste outside to the composter. It was already dark. I was about to head back to the house when I heard a noise. At first, I thought it was an animal moving through the foliage. Then I felt someone watching me. It's funny how you can feel that, isn't it? Like someone's touching you with their eyes."

She paused as she readjusted the oars resting across her lap. "I saw Franklyn crouched down behind a tree. At first, I was scared. But then he started to cry. I had no idea what had just happened to him in the meditation room. I came closer, wanting to help. That was when he started punching himself in the face. I tried to stop him and he screamed. Before I knew what was happening, he shoved me hard. I must have hit my head against a tree because the next thing I remember was waking up on the ground in the middle of the forest. Franklyn was on top of me, and he was . . ."

Marcia's voice trailed away. Her body grew stiff and still.

"I'm sorry," Emily said, horror stealing over her. "I'm so sorry he did that to you."

Marcia straightened, wiped her eyes on the back of her hand. She was quiet for a minute longer, her shoulders heaving up and down in the darkness, her breaths unsteady. "As soon as I realised what he was doing to me, I screamed as loud as I could. He put his hand over my mouth. But I kept fighting. The whole time he kept shouting, 'I am nothing! I am nothing!' He'd lost his mind. I felt around on the floor for a rock, a piece of branch, anything I could use. But he stopped me. He pinned my arms to the ground with his hands. I screamed again. And then I heard footsteps running towards me, and shouting . . . lots of shouting.

"And then I was free. Franklyn was on the ground beside me. It was dark and it was raining hard, but I knew it was Sam. I heard him beating Franklyn. Kicking him. Punching him. Stamping on him. Then somehow Franklyn managed to escape. I heard him run off. I thought that was the end of it. I tried to sit up. Everything hurt. I could taste blood. I called to Sam for help, but it was like he didn't hear me. He got to his feet and chased after Franklyn. He left me alone . . ."

"Then Pamela came and helped me to the house. The guests were already in their rooms. Pamela bathed me. She cleaned up the bruises, the bite marks. I fell into a dream. The next thing I knew, I was in bed, and I could hear Sam crying. I got up. Everything hurt. I went into the living room. Sam was covered with blood. It was on his face, his shirt. His hands. He looked at me and I knew instantly what he'd done."

"Sam killed Franklyn?" Of course he did, Emily thought. He'd just witnessed the woman he loved being beaten and raped.

Marcia nodded. "Sam chased Franklyn through the forest. He saw him run inside the tool shack. He followed him in, took a sickle from the wall, and . . . Sam said he didn't know what he was doing until it was too late. That it was like someone else had control of his body and was making him do all these terrible things. He didn't mean to hurt anybody. He was upset. He was trying to protect me."

"That's why you couldn't go to the police," Emily said. She had managed to shift the rope binding her wrists by half an inch. Now her fingers scrabbled with the knot.

In the darkness, Marcia let out a shuddering breath. "Pamela said if we called the police Sam would be charged with murder, that there was no way he could plead self-defence because he'd hacked Franklyn to pieces. She said if Sam went to prison, it would be because he'd been trying to protect me. Then she begged me, saying we'd lose everything we'd built together as mother and daughter; that Meadow Pines would be no more. It was the only time I'd seen her so helpless. I could see she was conflicted—I knew she wanted to do the right thing. But doing the right thing doesn't always get you what you need, does it?"

Emily ceased fumbling with the knot. "Your mother took advantage of you. She manipulated you to save herself."

Marcia shook her head. "At first, I thought my mother was the most uncaring, selfish human being on the planet. All those teachings she'd taken to heart—all gone the instant her livelihood was threatened. But do you know what I realised? In her own messed up way, Pamela wasn't just looking out for herself. She was looking out for all of us. We built that house together. We put blood, sweat, and tears into Meadow Pines. Sam, too."

"But what Franklyn did to you . . ." Emily said, shocked by what she was hearing. "Your mother wanted you to pretend it never happened—to ignore that Sam murdered someone, no matter how deserving it seemed. How could you go along with that?"

Marcia's voice was suddenly as cold as the surrounding water. "What choice did I have? I could call the police and destroy all our lives, or I could let that bastard get what he deserved. Any resentment I held towards Pamela, towards Sam, I told myself I'd have to keep it locked inside. That eventually it would disappear, just like Franklyn Hobbes."

"Those kinds of feelings don't just disappear," Emily said, fingers back to working at the knot. "Believe me, I know. If they did, we wouldn't be here right now in this boat."

Marcia shrugged. "Maybe. Maybe not. But back then, there was only one choice. We decided to make it look like Franklyn had left the retreat early. We would bury his body in the woods. Sam would take his car from the deer sanctuary, drive it far away somewhere and abandon it. It was simple, really. The other guests had witnessed his meltdown so they could easily corroborate our story if the police became involved. It would have all gone smoothly. Until Melody showed up."

The knot was too tight. Cramp stabbed at Emily's muscles. She tried to relax her body, but the bottom of the boat was hard and uncomfortable, the ropes rough and cruel.

"We decided to bury him in that clearing, underneath the big old oak," Marcia continued, her voice flat and emotionless once more. "I always thought it was a pretty spot. The light always falls so pleasantly. Perhaps burying Franklyn there was a way of bringing him some peace. Anyway, they carried him there, Sam and Pamela. I followed behind like a lost sheep. They laid him down. I held the torch while they both dug a hole. But then I heard a noise and I turned around. Melody was standing there, watching us.

"My heart stopped. Everything ran away from me. Melody had seen Franklyn's body. She'd seen what we were doing. I thought she was going to run, to call the police. But she just stood there, afraid and confused."

Emily's fingers pinched at the knot. "What happened?"

"Pamela told Melody everything. About what Franklyn had done to me, about Sam losing control when all he'd been trying to do was protect us all. She left nothing out. She knew we were the only friends Melody had. If she could get her to understand what we were about to lose—what she would lose in the process—then perhaps she would help us."

"So, she manipulated Melody, just like she manipulated you."

Marcia shook her head. The boat rocked slightly. "Melody Jackson is the girl at school that no one knows exists. She's not the smelly kid or the one from the wrong part of town. She's the invisible one. The one people don't even remember when they reminisce about their school days.

"Perhaps Melody thought adulthood would change things, that grownups were more mature. But Melody is still invisible. She has no friends. No family that cares about her. No social life. At work, she is a quiet voice on the telephone, a name signed at the bottom of an email. She has no face. No identity. Poor Melody Jackson—the girl the world forgot." Marcia paused, letting out a sad sigh. "Except for her cat, Meadow Pines is all she has. At Meadow Pines, she doesn't feel invisible. She understood what we all risked losing. She knew what had to be done.

"So, instead of running away, instead of calling the police, Melody took the shovel from Pamela's hand and she began to dig. Do you understand what she did? She incriminated herself without a moment's thought. She gave herself freely, willingly, to help protect the people she cared about."

"You all manipulated her into helping you cover up a murder," Emily said, anger rising in her throat. "Your mother took advantage, playing on her deepest fears."

"Pamela was protecting everyone, including Melody."

"And Melody was supposed to be grateful?"

"Why not? Without us she has nothing." Any trace of remorse in Marcia's voice was gone, replaced by iciness.

Emily's wrists were bleeding, the pain like razorblades dragging through her skin, but now the knot had loosened a little; the change barely noticeable to the human eye.

Marcia sat silently in the darkness, her body gently rocking in time with the boat.

The sound of water lapping on the hull reminded Emily why she'd been brought out here to the middle of the lake. Panic rising in her throat, she pulled at the knot with renewed fervour.

CHAPTER 36

Silence filled Melody's room like quicksand, slowly smothering its only occupant. Jerome sat on the edge of the bed, staring at the locked door. He wasn't sure how much time had passed. Definitely minutes. Maybe even half an hour. His attempts at escape had all failed. He'd tried throwing his weight at the door, but the door opened into the room rather than out, which meant there was no chance of him kicking it down. Next, he'd thought to remove the door hinges, but a search of Melody's possessions for some kind of tool had proven fruitless, with not even a pair of tweezers in sight. Jerome had then resorted to screaming for help until his throat was raw. But no one had answered.

Now he got up from the bed and paced to the window. The muscles in his neck and shoulders grew more knotted as he peered out at the darkness. The thought had already crossed his mind several times, but it presented itself again: there was only one way he was getting out of this room.

But he couldn't do it.

From the window, there was a ten foot drop to the porch roof. Even if he managed to land correctly, there would be the risk of slipping in the rain and breaking untold amounts of bones.

Then there was the risk of not landing correctly, of smashing straight through the porch roof.

Then there was his morbid terror of heights.

Frustration growing, Jerome returned to the bed and eyed Melody's tablet. She had been there the night of Franklyn's attack on Marcia —a fact Pamela had neglected to mention.

What did it mean? He wasn't sure he wanted to know.

Picking up the tablet, he sifted through Melody's photographs once more, coming to rest on Franklyn's haunted face.

What kind of a person went sneaking around, stealing pictures like that, anyway? It was creepy.

Jerome stared at the door. Was Melody really behind it all? Had she killed Franklyn? And what about Oscar and Sam? He didn't want to believe it, but if it was true it could only mean Pamela was involved, too.

A dragging unease clawed at his stomach. He couldn't sit here a minute longer. Helen was downstairs, slowly bleeding to death. Emily was out in the forest, getting herself into all sorts of trouble while a psychopath was stalking Meadow Pines.

Jumping to his feet, Jerome crossed the room and returned to the double-hung window. Unlocking the catch, he raised the lower sash, letting the night in. A cold mist drizzled over his skin, making him shiver. Crouching on his haunches, he stuck his head through the gap and peered out at the darkness of the forest.

Terror climbed his throat as he shifted his gaze downward. The world spun around him, leaving him sick and dizzy. Pulling himself back into the room, Jerome sucked in ragged breaths and willed his heart to stop pounding.

"You're in a movie," he told himself. "This is an action scene. There are crash mats right below."

Taking another deep breath, Jerome pushed up the window sash to its fullest extent.

He sucked in a final breath, held it, released it.

"Emily, I hate you!" he said between clenched teeth. Then he was climbing out the window.

CHAPTER 37

A muffled whimper echoed over the lake. Emily thought about what Marcia had just told her. If only Melody had called someone. If only she had stayed in her room and not followed them out to the forest.

But Emily understood what loneliness could do. She knew exactly what it was like to spend every night alone in an empty house, the silence crushing the breath from your lungs. But that was before she had moved to London, and regardless of all the terrible things that had happened since, her life no longer felt as lonely—because she had people in it now. People she cared about, and who cared about her in equal measures.

As Emily worked on unfastening the knot, she tried to imagine herself in Melody's position. The only people in her life were going to be taken away from her—and all because they had tried to protect each other from harm. They were going to be taken away, which meant Melody's life would become empty again, riddled with anguish and despair.

The knot loosened further.

Emily wondered whether she would have taken the same course of action if Jerome or Harriet had been in trouble. It was possible, she thought. In desperate times, people could go to extreme lengths to save the ones they loved. But were Marcia, Pamela, and Sam really Melody's friends? In her eyes, they probably were.

But what was Melody to them? Just another paying guest? Someone who they tolerated out of pity? Someone who, since that night, had burrowed into their lives like a parasitic worm?

Releasing her fingers from the knot, Emily tried to push herself up. She could just see over the edge of the boat. Melody was still at the end of the jetty, bound and gagged, whimpering and squirming on the planks.

"Tell me about Oscar," Emily said.

Marcia leaned forward. Moonlight glanced off her face, revealing drying streaks of tears.

"We thought he was just another guest, the same as the rest of you," she said. "It wasn't until Melody came to us late last night that we learned the real reason Oscar had come to Meadow Pines. Naturally, we all panicked. Pamela told us not to worry, that everything would be okay. She sent Melody back to her room, then told me and Sam to spend the night at his place in town. She said she was going to tell Oscar to leave. He was there under false pretences, so she had a right to get rid of him."

Emily looked up. "That was the argument I heard through the bedroom wall. Pamela confronting Oscar."

Marcia went on, desperate to confess it all. "Sam and I took the Land Rover and we drove to Lyndhurst. I started to panic. I was scared. Sam didn't want to hear it. He'd always smoked a lot of weed, but since that night, since what he did to Franklyn, he did nothing but smoke. We got to his place and he immediately started getting stoned. He kept telling me to forget about it, that come the morning Oscar would be gone and we could all carry on as normal. As if our lives had been normal before . . ."

Marcia laughed but there was no trace of humour in her voice. She stared across the water towards the jetty. "If you have an idea of what it's like to hold onto a secret, then you know how every day it becomes harder and harder. That it eats away at you like a disease. That night at Sam's, I felt as if my mind was imploding. It wasn't just the guilt getting to me. It was anger. I hated them all: Franklyn for what he did to me; Sam for causing this entire mess; Pamela . . . I know she was trying to protect us. I know there wasn't any choice, but sometimes I can't help thinking she chose her precious retreat over the well-being of her own daughter."

Emily sensed the conflict in Marcia's voice. Perhaps she could use it to change her mind. "Your mother left you to suffer for months," she said. "She pretended none of it ever happened. It's difficult to believe it was your future she was trying to protect."

"That night, with Oscar showing up, something in me snapped," Marcia continued, ignoring Emily's comment. "I was sick of the guilt. I was pissed off. Mostly I was just tired of it all. Sam smoked until he knocked himself out. I made sure he was asleep, left his place, and drove back to Meadow Pines.

"I told Oscar everything, said I'd show him where we'd buried Franklyn. He followed me to the clearing. We were about to head to the tool shack to fetch a shovel, when suddenly Oscar fell to the ground." Marcia wrapped her arms across her chest and stared up at the night sky. "Pamela had heard us coming down the stairs. She followed us into the forest, and when she saw what was happening, she hit Oscar over the head with a piece of wood."

Emily's fingers froze on the knot. Her mind spun, trying to process what Marcia was saying.

"Pamela was furious. She said after everything she'd done for me, I was behaving like a spoiled brat who was going to get us all sent to prison. Oscar was unconscious. Pamela dragged me to the shack. She grabbed some rope and we went back to the clearing." Marcia let out a trembling breath. "Oscar was sitting up. He was dazed, out of it. But he was awake."

The knot binding Emily's wrists loosened a little more. Strands of hemp sliced through her flesh. She bit down on her lip, attempting to mask the pain.

"Pamela blamed me. She said what she was about to do was all my fault," Marcia continued as fresh tears spilled down her face. "She made a noose, slipped it over Oscar's neck, and threw the rope over the branch. Then she pulled. I watched Oscar's hands fly to his throat, his legs kick out. He was heavy. Pamela couldn't get him fully off the ground. But it was just enough.

"It took him forever to die. But I stood and watched. When it was over, Pamela started crying. And then it hit me—she was right. This was all my doing. I ran to her, took the rope, and together we pulled. We lifted him off the ground and tied off the rope. His wallet had slipped from his pocket. We took it to the lake and threw it in."

"It didn't sink," Emily said. The knot loosened some more. "And you didn't make Pamela do anything."

Marcia's tears hung precariously from her chin, but she didn't wipe them away. Melody's sobs continued to echo over the lake. "It had all been so panicked, so spontaneous, that neither of us thought to search Oscar's pockets. We had no idea the photograph was there. Pamela told me to drive back to Sam's. The next morning, we would act like it was just an ordinary day. Then on my morning run, I would find Oscar's body. Everyone would assume he'd hanged himself. A telephone call to Sergeant Wells would take care of the rest."

"Except you couldn't make the call," Emily said.

"It was obvious come morning light that Oscar's death didn't look like a suicide. We'd been clumsy, thoughtless. Everything turned to chaos. Melody and I went back to the house to call the police. That's when we'd found out the place had been robbed and everything was thrown off-course. Sam started freaking out, accusing Melody and Pamela of killing Oscar while we were in Lyndhurst. Melody became hysterical. She had no idea what had happened the night before. It was a mess . . ."

"I knew if I drove to the police station it would all be over. And I wanted it to be over so badly. But this was my doing. If I had stayed at Sam's last night, then everyone would still be alive. Sam would . . ." Marcia was quiet, her breaths coming fast and shallow. "But then, when everyone had returned to their rooms, Pamela came up with an idea to make everything go away."

Straining her neck, Emily peered over the edge of the boat towards the jetty. "You're setting up Melody. You're making it look like she's responsible."

Marcia sighed. "Do you know how difficult she's made things? Turning up here all the time like she has a free pass, forcing her way into our lives, pretending we're all friends sharing a funny secret."

"She's lonely," Emily said, a flash of anger searing her skin. "She has no one else."

"She's trouble, that's all she is. Leaving flowers on Franklyn's grave, carving his tattoo on the damn tree—it's all just a game to her. It's all make believe. It doesn't matter how many times we warn her, she just won't listen." Marcia turned her head sharply in the direction of the jetty, a cruel smile on her lips. "But she'll listen now."

The rope was getting looser, the knot easier to manipulate. Emily stared at Marcia's shadow.

"No one's going to believe Melody's guilty," she said. "She's just a lonely girl desperate for friendship."

"That's exactly why people will believe it. Poor, lonely Melody. The girl with no friends, who finally snapped down in the woods. Who'd murdered Franklyn in a crazed fit of rage, then Oscar when his presence threatened to expose her crime."

"What about Sam?" Emily spat the words out. "How are you going to explain his murder?"

Marcia was silent. The boat swayed as she wept. "Sam wasn't part of the plan. He would have stayed quiet. He would have never said anything. But she wouldn't believe it. After he cut down the body, she said she knew he was going to ruin things, that it was only a matter of time. But she was wrong. He would never betray us."

Marcia's sobs echoed over the lake. A sickening wave of nausea threatened to spill from Emily's throat. It was suddenly clear. While they'd been searching Meadow Pines for Sam, Pamela had been busy killing him. Then she'd painted the chaos star on the wall with his blood, knowing it would incriminate Melody.

"Your mother murdered the man you love," Emily said, her fingers working faster, the rope cutting deeper. "She murdered him and you stood by and let her do it!"

Marcia slammed her fist against the side of the boat. "No! Melody killed him. She killed Franklyn and Oscar. She attacked me and crashed the Land Rover. When the police arrive, they'll find me tied up and badly beaten —a victim of Melody's crazed obsession."

"Your story's full of holes," Emily said, anger coursing through her body. "You really think people will believe someone like Melody is a killer?"

"They will when they find her suicide note, confessing to the deaths of five people. They'll find her hair in Sam's hand and Oscar's photo of Franklyn under her pillow. Helen will write all about it, as one of the few survivors of the Meadow Pines Massacre. Meadow Pines may not recover, but we'll be free. We'll find a new place and we'll start again—Pamela and me."

Emily stared at her in disbelief. Conflicting feelings of pity and disgust tore her mind in two. So many terrible things had happened to Marcia, and her own mother had forced her to internalise them all. But Marcia had buried her trauma so deep inside her mind, she had ruptured its very foundations.

"You already have blood on your hands," Emily said. "How will you live with more? How will you get through each day knowing you're responsible for the deaths of all these people? Including your boyfriend."

Fresh tears squeezed from Marcia's eyes.

The knot between Emily's fingers suddenly unravelled. Blood trickled into her palms. But her hands were free.

"Don't you see, Marcia? You were right all along," Emily said. "The only future Pamela is concerned about is her own. There's still time to put things right. When the police arrive, we can tell them the truth. We'll tell them what Franklyn did to you, and how your mother has been manipulating you all this time."

Slowly, sadly, Marcia shook her head then wiped away her tears with the back of her hand.

"It's too late," she said. "By the time the police get here, you'll be dead. Jerome, too."

A chill ran the length of Emily's body.

"I'm sorry," Marcia said.

Leaping up, she wrapped her arms around Emily's ribcage and hoisted her out from beneath the thwart.

The boat rocked dangerously.

Emily cried out. Her hands shot up to Marcia's throat.

For a second, Marcia stared in shock. Then she drove her knee into Emily's chest, slamming her against the bottom of the boat.

Emily's head hit the hull with a dull thud.

White sparks filled her vision. Blinding pain ricocheted from the back of her head to her swollen eye.

Marcia tugged on Emily's legs, twisting her around until her calves flopped over the side. The boat tipped violently to the right.

Marcia fell back.

Emily swung a fist, catching her in the stomach. Then as Marcia doubled over, Emily dragged her legs back in.

Before her fingers could reach the rope that was binding her ankles, Marcia flew at her, grabbing Emily's hair by the roots and yanking her head skyward.

Emily sank fingernails into the woman's face. Then with a shriek, Marcia slammed Emily's head into the side of the boat.

The night flashed in bright colours. Blood dripped down the back of Emily's throat. Dazed and groaning, she watched Marcia pull an oar from the rowlock.

She towered over Emily, panting and heaving.

"Stop fighting," she said. "It will be easier for both of us."

She swung the oar at Emily's head.

Emily kicked out, striking Marcia in the shins. The back of her legs hit the thwart, and for the briefest moment, with the stars behind her, she looked like she was floating through space.

Then Marcia fell, landing heavily on the edge of the boat, tipping it on its side.

Water rushed in.

Her ankles still tied together, Emily flipped over twice and struck her head again. Then the boat capsized, plunging her and Marcia into the icy waters of the lake.

CHAPTER 38

Slipping one leg through the window, Jerome straddled the sill. Swivelling himself up and around, he fed the other leg through, then slowly lowered his body, digging the tips of his shoes into the grooves of the stonework.

Now all he needed to do was let his feet hang and let go of the sill. It was easy enough—just as long as he didn't look down.

Behind him, treetops swayed in the night-time breeze. The space around him felt infinite. Shutting his eyes, Jerome let one foot slip, then the other. His hands now bore his full weight.

Cold fear hit him. He tried to return his feet to the wall, but his limbs had become paralysed. Panic swelled in his chest. His heart punched against his ribcage.

One by one, his fingers peeled away from the windowsill. Then with a startling cry, Jerome fell. Before he could catch another breath, he hit the porch roof, slipped in the rain, and tumbled over the edge.

One hand shot out and gripped the guttering. Jerome swung in a wide arc and slammed into a support beam. The ground came up to meet him with a bone-shaking thud.

When he could open his eyes again, he found himself sprawled at the foot of the porch steps, nursing bruised shins and a graze on his right cheekbone.

He stared up at the open window he'd just escaped through and let out a whooping cry.

He was on his feet again in seconds and staggering towards the back door. It was locked. Rounding the corner of the house, he headed towards the Hardys' living room window. Edging along the wall, he peered inside. Helen was sprawled on the couch, her head propped up with pillows. Her bandages had been changed again. In the opposite armchair, Pamela sat with her legs crossed and a book resting on her knee.

Jerome's eyes narrowed. Now it was obvious who'd locked him in Melody's room. But why?

Anger heating his insides, he headed to the front of the house, pushed open the gate, and entered the garden. The front door was still unlocked and he stole inside.

Sneaking along the hall, Jerome cut through the dining room, and ducked into the kitchen, re-emerging moments later with a large butcher's knife and a battery-powered storm lantern.

At the dining room door, he stopped and listened for signs of life. Satisfied that Pamela was still in her quarters, he pitched forward and raced out of the house.

He didn't know where he was going, and there were several acres of land to search. Pausing in the garden, Jerome cleared his mind and attempted to think like Emily.

Where had she headed? She'd been looking at Melody's tablet. She'd discovered Franklyn's picture. She'd realised Melody had been present the night Franklyn had died.

And there was something else—Franklyn's tattoo.

The chaos star that was carved on the tree.

Jerome raced through the garden and bolted across the meadow, crushing wildflowers beneath his feet. It took him a minute to locate the trail. Holding the storm lantern in front of him, he followed the muddy track into the forest.

The rain had eased off, sparing him a soaking in his T-shirt and jeans, but the cold was less forgiving, stinging his bare arms and travelling down his neck to the base of his spine.

The trail twisted and turned. At every corner, Jerome peered beyond the peripheries of the lantern light. Darkness circled him like a ravenous pack of dogs. He didn't care what nature lovers had to say about the great outdoors—when he finally got back to London, the first thing he planned to do was run out into the street and inhale big lungsful of traffic.

The trail reached the clearing, where Oscar's body still lay under the oak tree. Jerome turned away, taunted by images of the dead man's reanimated corpse crawling out from beneath the tarpaulin. Hurrying past, he vowed he would never watch another horror movie again.

Where was Emily?

He swung the lantern, catching a large mound of freshly dug soil in the light. Fear shivered through his body as he inched closer. Then his eyes fell upon the shallow grave and the shovel lying next to it.

"There's nothing there," he assured himself as he peered over the edge and into the muddy water below, half expecting a skeletal hand to reach up and drag him down.

Who or what had Emily found here?

Jerome didn't want to know. He spun on his heels, nausea and fear making him dizzy.

Where was she? Where else was there to go?

If you get lost in a forest, you stay in one place so people can find you. Emily had given him that little nugget of safety information on the drive down. He doubted she had taken her own advice. But he couldn't imagine her wandering aimlessly through the forest, either.

There were three possible locations where she might be: the tool shack, the lake, and the Land Rover crash site. He immediately crossed off the tool shack—she'd already been there to fetch the shovel. But the lake was closest to him, with the Land Rover beyond.

Tightening his grip on the knife, Jerome exited the clearing and continued along the trail. He would be at the lake in ten minutes.

He could only hope he'd find Emily waiting for him there, safe and sound.

CHAPTER 39

The first thing to hit Emily as she plunged sideways into the water was the biting cold. It was paralysing; as if her body had immediately turned to ice on impact. She went under, face slapping against the surface of the lake. Then she was sinking fast.

Above her, the capsized boat had made an umbrella of inky blackness that blotted out the moon and the stars.

Emily's lungs had sucked in a deep breath before hitting the water. But now pressure was beginning to build at the centre of her chest. As she sank deeper, she had the impression of falling in slow motion through a dream. None of this was real. She would wake up any moment now and realise she'd been in the grip of yet another nightmare.

But as her senses kicked in, as the icy water sank teeth into her limbs, she instantly became aware of where she was and what was happening to her.

Her first instinct was to kick her legs. But her legs wouldn't move. Her second instinct was to scream. But screaming beneath a lake would result in lungsful of water and certain death.

The pressure in Emily's chest grew, simmering like a pot on the stove. She felt the weight of the entire lake pressing down on her sternum. She tried to move her arms, to bend her knees, but the darkness had taken hold of her limbs and would not let go.

Emily sank further.

She heard pounding in her ears like a drum; an ominous, deep rumble that had started slow and deliberate, but was now increasing in speed and intensity.

The pressure on her chest grew unbearable, threatening to fracture her breastplate.

She needed to breathe.

To open her mouth and suck in lifesaving air.

The darkness around her began to change colour; from black to yellow to red. Shadows moved around her. And then a familiar face appeared.

Phillip Gerard.

What was he doing here at the bottom of the lake? Emily tried to reach out a hand. But his face had already vanished into the murk.

Her chest felt like an erupting volcano. Her lungs were going to explode. Desperate for air, Emily's mouth forced itself open.

The lake flooded in. Her body started to spasm. She felt life giving up on her.

Or was she giving up on life?

Months ago, she would have happily allowed the water to take her, for her body to rot away on the lakebed, until all that was left of her were algae-covered bones.

But things had changed. She had changed. She had made peace with Phillip Gerard's ghost. She had said a final goodbye to her mother. She had let the past die inside of her so that the present could live.

Was she really going to throw it all away now to be fish food at the bottom of a lake?

No. Emily Swanson wanted to live.

Regaining control of her body, Emily brought her knees up to her chest. She flapped her arms and kicked her legs, using her muscles to propel herself upward. She repeated the movements, arms flapping like an underwater bird, legs bucking like a mermaid.

Up she went, the last of her breath shooting from her nostrils in tiny bubbles, her clothes and shoes fighting against her, trying to drag her back down.

But Emily kicked and she flapped and she fought. Then she erupted on the surface in a froth of water, limbs, and painful gasps.

She went under again.

She pumped her arms, broke the surface once more, and spun around. The upturned boat was just in front of her. With a desperate cry, she lunged towards it.

Her palms slapped against fibreglass. Her fingers scrabbled against the round, slippery hull.

"No!"

There was nothing to grip. Nothing to hold onto.

Her strength gone, she went under again.

Her arms flailed above her head. Then they were still, trailing behind her like streamers.

Emily sank like a stone.

She was going to die down here, after all.

Water filled her insides until she became liquid, until she and the lake were one.

The pressure in her chest floated away.

Then there was darkness.

Darkness everywhere.

CHAPTER 40

And then there was light. And stars. Hundreds of thousands of them, all glinting and shimmering, filling her vision until there was nothing else. Voices echoed around her like memories. She floated through time and space, blissful and at peace. Then she felt hands on her chest and a cloying, building pressure in her lungs.

All around her, stars crumbled and fell. Voices came together and spoke in unison. The hands on her chest pressed down, over and over, crushing her.

She wanted them to stop. She tried to bat them away, but her body was cold and still.

She wasn't breathing.

She couldn't breathe!

"Come on!" she heard the voices say, the words soaring over her head. The pain in her chest became excruciating. Her lungs began to spasm uncontrollably. Her back arched.

Emily's eyes flew open.

She wrenched open her mouth and vomited a flood of dirty water, leaves and twigs. She drew in long, painful breaths that burned the inside of her throat. But the air was fresh and unadulterated and bursting with life.

She was lying by the edge of the lake, clothes swamped with water and lungs filled with fire. Jerome's stricken face appeared over her, raining droplets of water onto her skin.

"It's all right," he breathed, his teeth chattering. "You're okay. I got here just in time."

Emily tried to move.

"Just rest for a minute."

"But Marcia . . ." No more words would come. Emily rested her head on the ground, feeling wet earth and rock, grateful she could feel anything at all.

Jerome shuffled down to her feet and tugged at the rope still binding her legs. "I saw the boat go over. You both went into the water. I swam as fast as I could. It's a miracle I found you at all. Now stay very still."

Setting the storm lantern beside Emily's feet, he picked up a large kitchen knife and set to work on the rope.

Emily was in no mood to argue; her dalliance with death had left her disoriented and sore. As she lay there, she focused on her breathing —in for four, hold for seven, out for eight— until she heard a faint snap. Her ankles sprang away from each other.

"Thank you," she croaked. She sat up and the world rocked from side to side, as if she was still on the boat. The fog in her mind persisted.

"Where's Marcia?" she said, floundering as she grabbed the lantern and pointed it at the lake. The capsized boat floated halfway across like the hump of a whale.

Jerome shook his head. "I saw her fall in but I didn't see her get out. I can't believe it was her and Pamela. That crazy woman locked me in Melody's room. I had to jump out the damn window!"

Suddenly remembering Melody, Emily swung the lantern in the direction of the jetty, which was now empty.

"They were going to kill us both," she said.

"What the hell? I didn't even do anything!"

Emily quickly filled Jerome in on the reasons why, starting with the murder of Franklyn

Hobbes and ending with Pamela's plan to frame Melody. When she was done, Jerome sat back and let out an exasperated breath. Then he leaned forward again, eyes growing wide with panic in the dark.

"Helen's still in there."

"They won't hurt her," Emily said, her lungs still hurting. "Not when her story will vindicate them of all responsibility."

"But that was before I escaped. Before you didn't die. What if Marcia saw me pulling you from the lake? She'll be on her way back to the house right now to tell Pamela. Then the only way they'll get out of this is if all three of us are dead."

Emily hauled herself to her feet. Although her legs were shaky, she managed to stay upright.

"Come on," she said, tugging Jerome's arm.

He stared at her in horror. "We're going back to the house, aren't we?"

Clenching her jaw, Emily nodded.

"We don't have a choice," she said.

CHAPTER 41

They stumbled through the forest, almost losing their way, then hurried across the meadow. Emily clutched the knife in her hand, wondering if she would be able to use it if she had to.

The front door of the house was open. Light spilled out. Emily stumbled forward. Twice, she almost fell, but Jerome was there to hold her up. Passing through the garden, she saw two sets of muddy footprints trailing along the hallway towards the Hardys' living quarters.

Her chest rising and falling in quick succession, Emily nodded at Jerome.

Together, they stepped into the foyer.

"Wait!" Jerome tugged her back outside. In the northwest corner of the forest, a haze of blue and red lights flashed above the treetops. "They're here! The police are here!"

The lights were mesmerising, like the afterglow of fireworks. Emily blinked them away. Minutes would pass before the police would walk through the front door. Terrible things could happen in a matter of seconds. She stood, her senses pulling towards rescue and her conscience pulling towards the house.

No one else was going to die.

"Emily, no! What are you doing?" Jerome pulled her back. She tried to shake him off but his grip was firm.

"We have to go in there," she said.

Jerome stared at her with wild, disbelieving eyes, then jabbed a finger in the direction of the lights. "Are you out of your damn mind?

The police are right there! They'll be here any minute!"

"Melody doesn't have a minute!" she cried. "They're going to kill her, Jerome. Don't you see? They've played her all along. Used her loneliness to manipulate her into making a stupid, stupid mistake."

She stepped forward, but Jerome pulled her back again. "Even so, she should have known. There's this thing called right and wrong."

"So, we just let her die? You really think she deserves that?"

Their eyes burned into each other. Far behind them, the police lights inched closer. Jerome released his grip. His shoulders sagged.

"Fine," he said. "But this time, I'm coming with you."

They entered the foyer together, heading in silence towards the Hardys' living quarters. The door was ajar.

The knife wavering in front of her, Emily peered inside. Helen was alone, slumped on the sofa. They hurried forward. Jerome pressed two fingers into Helen's jugular.

"She's alive. Looks like the bleeding has stopped, too."

Emily glanced out the window. In the distance, she saw beams of torchlight emerge from the forest. She turned to face the door that led to the bedrooms. A smear of blood stained the jamb.

Trembling, Emily reached for the handle.

She glanced back at Jerome, who was propping Helen's head up with more pillows. Their eyes met. Jerome shook his head wildly.

Emily opened the door.

Pamela was standing in the centre of the corridor, hands pressed up against the bathroom door. As she turned around, Emily saw how old and weak she suddenly looked, all the vitality sucked from her bones.

"Please, help me!" Pamela sobbed, then turned back to the door, curled her hands into fists, and pounded the wood.

Emily pointed the knife in front of her. She looked uncertainly at Pamela, then at the door. Jerome appeared, breathing down her shoulder.

"Please!" Pamela screamed. "Stop her!"

Frightened now, Emily glanced back at Jerome then stepped to one side. He ran forward, pushing Pamela out of the way. Bracing himself against the wall, Jerome charged at the door.

The lock broke on the second kick, tearing away from the jamb. The door flew inward. The knife gripped in her hand, Emily entered the bathroom. And froze.

They were sitting in the bath, toe to toe.

Melody's hands were still tied, her knees pulled up to her chest. Her face was smeared with tears and dirt and splashes of blood. She turned to face Emily and sobbed into the gag.

Marcia sat across from her, unmoving.

She had made two deep incisions that began at the wrists and ran the length of her forearms. Blood poured and spurted from the wounds, effervescent against her cement-coloured skin and the white porcelain of the bathtub.

Emily was paralysed, watching scarlet rivulets run along the bottom of the tub and soak into Melody's sweatpants.

A bloody razorblade rested on the floor.

It took just a second to drink it all in, but that second seemed to last an hour.

Behind her, Pamela fell to her knees and wailed.

Springing to action, Emily pulled towels from the rail and hurried to the bathtub.

Marcia's eyes opened. She watched as Emily wrapped a towel around one of her forearms, then the other.

"I need more!" Emily cried.

Jerome dashed from the room.

Emily tightened the towels. Helpless, she glanced up and saw Marcia staring at her, the light draining from her irises.

"Why?" Emily choked. "Why didn't you just say no? Why didn't you just tell her to stop?"

Marcia swallowed. An exhausted smile found its way to her lips.

"Mother knows best," she whispered.

Melody continued to howl, squirming and thrashing in the bathtub. Pamela was crawling towards the tub on her hands and knees, her mouth hanging open in a silent scream.

Jerome returned with a large pile of towels. Emily snatched them from him.

"I'm not losing you!" she hissed, as she clamped them around Marcia's wounds. "I'm not!"

Somewhere behind her, voices and footsteps filled the air, followed by the crackle of police radios.

CHAPTER 42

The drone of a helicopter could be heard approaching the forest. Then a deafening roar shattered the quiet as the air ambulance descended, landing in the meadow. Paramedics jumped out and raced towards the house. Minutes later, Marcia was stretchered out, barely alive and semi-conscious. Her wounds had been sutured, but she'd lost a lot of blood. Getting her to the hospital was imperative.

Emily followed the medics out of the house, her clothes wet and stained deep red. She stood in the rose garden, watching them manoeuvre Marcia onto the helicopter. Jerome was near the gate, huddled with Daniel and

Janelle. They all shared the same shell-shocked expression.

"Ben and Sylvia were gone before we could catch up with them," Janelle explained when Emily joined them. "We had to walk all the way to Lyndhurst."

"Look at what you missed," Emily said. Her voicc sounded strange and distant. She glanced back at the house. Melody and Pamela were inside, handcuffed and separated, watched over by police constables. Sergeant Wells was inside Pamela's office, pacing up and down in front of the window as he radioed the station. Even from this distance, Emily could see his shocked expression.

Now Helen was being brought out on a second stretcher. She was awake, her headwound bandaged, but her gaze was unfocused and drifting. As she was carried through the garden, she suddenly reached out and grabbed Emily's arm. Startled, Emily bent down until her ear was by Helen's lips.

"I give Meadow Pines a big thumbs down," Helen croaked. "But I've remembered who you are now."

Before Emily could respond, Helen was whisked away towards the meadow and lifted into the waiting helicopter.

"What did she say?" Jerome asked, staring at Emily with haunted eyes.

The roar of the rotor blades grew louder. A second later, the helicopter lifted into the air. Wind battered Emily's hair and clothes as she watched the helicopter ascend into the night sky. Then she stared across the meadow and into the darkness of the trees, wanting nothing more than to go home.

CHAPTER 43

MEADOW PINES MASSACRE -

SEVERAL DEAD & INJURED AT WEEKEND RETREAT

By Jack Portland

The quiet communities of the New Forest were left reeling in shock last night following a spate of bizarre and gruesome murders at Meadow Pines, a local retreat specialising in digital detox. The retreat's owner, Pamela Hardy, 44, has been charged with the killings, while Melody Jackson, 25, a regular visitor to

Meadow Pines is also currently in police custody. Details of her involvement have not been released. Hardy's daughter, Marcia, 22, has also been implicated. She is currently in intensive care after reportedly attempting to take her own life.

The victims have been named as Oscar Jansen, 47, Samuel Turner, 26, and Franklyn Hobbes, 24. Turner, a chef at Meadow Pines, is thought to have been in a relationship with Marcia Hardy. Hobbes, who had a long history of mental health issues, disappeared in April of last year. Oscar Jansen, a private investigator, had been hired by the Hobbes family to find their son.

Although police have yet to issue an official statement, early reports indicate that a shallow grave containing the decomposed remains of Franklyn Hobbes was uncovered by Emily Swanson, a guest at Meadow Pines. Sergeant Wells of Lyndhurst constabulary has praised Swanson, a former teacher, and fellow guest Jerome Miller, for their help in uncovering what he described as, 'a tragic bloodbath that didn't need to happen.'

Police have also issued arrest warrants for known criminals Benjamin and Sylvia White, who are believed to have robbed fellow guests during the chaos.

Journalist Helen Carlson was reviewing the retreat for Modern Living magazine when the murders took place. Turn to pages 3&4 to read her exclusive eye-witness report, with details on how she narrowly escaped becoming Meadow Pines' next victim . . .

CHAPTER 44

Harriet Golding didn't look well. Perched on the sofa, Emily watched the old woman with concern. Beside her, Jerome munched on biscuits and drank tea. Harriet's middle-aged son, Andrew, sat in the armchair, adopting his usual pose, which involved a weighty-looking book pressed up to his face. Occasionally, he would glance over the top, his eyes widening as Emily and Jerome relayed the details of their weekend. Harriet had gasped and oohed and ahhed.

When the whole terrible story had been told, she sucked in a breath, then coughed and spluttered. Pulling a handkerchief from her cardigan sleeve, she dabbed the corners of her mouth.

"Well!" she said, when she'd recovered enough to speak. "Doesn't much sound like a relaxing weekend to me. And look at your eye!"

Emily touched her face. The swelling had decreased, but dark purple bruising now bloomed around her eye and temple.

Harriet shook her head. "What an awful thing to happen! I always had my suspicions about all those tree huggers. It ain't natural, is it? Flouncing around the woods, trying to float on clouds and what-not. They must all be on drugs!"

"Come on, Harriet. It's not exactly fair to tar everyone with the same brush now, is it?" Jerome said. "I happen to believe that meditation can do wonderful things for the mind. Even if it's just shutting your eyes for ten minutes and letting your thoughts go."

"Rubbish," said Harriet, dunking a chocolate chip cookie into her tea.

"You're a terrible cynic," Jerome protested. "As a matter of fact, I'm thinking about taking up yoga classes again. I think we'd all agree I could do with a little more focus in my life."

"And your own roof over your head," Harriet added. "And a job."

Emily arched an eyebrow at Jerome. "You've changed your tune. I would have thought that after this weekend the last thing you'd want is to delve back into the realms of the unconscious."

"What can I say? I'm a man of surprises. Besides, I spoke to Daniel this morning. We're meeting up next week. I've offered to show him some basic poses to get him started."

"I bet you have."

Harriet muttered something under breath, pulled her blanket from her knees, and draped it over the arm of the chair. "This place drives me insane. Too bloody cold in winter and too bloody hot in summer. I can't win. Andrew, can't you open a window or something?"

Andrew's voice floated over his book, flat and disinterested. "It's stuck."

Grumbling, Harriet returned her gaze to Emily, whose brow was pulled tightly over her eyes. "Are you all right, dear? Who's put a bee in your bonnet?"

"I'm fine," Emily said.

But it was a lie. She was far from fine. It had been two days since she and Jerome had been allowed to return to London, with an assurance from Sergeant Wells that CID would more than likely be in touch for further questioning. In that time, shock had turned to confusion, then exploded with anger.

Emily got up from the sofa and paced over to the window. She stared down at the alley far below, then across at the vista of tall buildings that sprawled into the distance as far as the eye could see. She turned back to the room. Harriet and Jerome were staring at her.

"It's just not right," she said, folding her arms across her chest. "A young girl like that, almost killing herself because of a ridiculous loyalty to her mother. That woman didn't give a damn about her."

"But she was her mother," Harriet said softly. "People will go to extraordinary lengths to protect their loved ones."

"Even if their loved ones don't deserve it?"

"People want to feel accepted. They want to feel loved. Even if that means giving up the things they believe in. It don't make it right. It's just how it is sometimes. Loneliness can make a person desperate."

Jerome nodded. "Just like Melody. But desperation has her on the way to prison as an accessory to murder. I suppose at least she won't be alone anymore."

Emily felt the weight in her chest grow heavier. It was all such a waste of life. Of time.

In some ways, she felt sorry for them all: For Franklyn, who she'd subsequently learned had suffered a long history of acute mental illness; for Oscar, who had just been doing the job he'd been paid to do by Franklyn's worried family; for Sam, who'd let his emotions get the better of him and instantly signed his own death warrant; for Melody, whose life had been so empty that she'd made serious errors of judgement.

Most of all, she felt sorry for Marcia, who had spent a lifetime under her mother's control, who had been left alone to deal with the traumas of sexual and physical assault, who had been isolated, manipulated, coerced, emotionally blackmailed, and who, riddled with guilt, had finally tried to take her own life. Emily hoped the courts would go easy on her when it all came to trial. She deserved that at least.

And what of Pamela? Should she be pitied when she was accountable for the shocking deaths at Meadow Pines? What had it all been for? To save a flagging business? To prevent bankruptcy? Emily suspected there was much more to Pamela's motivations than was apparent.

"What about the lady who got hurt? The writer?" Harriet asked, her limbs creaking as she reached for her cup of tea. "Is she all right?"

Emily nodded. "She was practically phoning in her story from the helicopter."

"You didn't see the newspapers?" Jerome asked Harriet. He bounced up and down like an excited puppy.

"All the newspapers are good for is lighting fires."

"Well, give credit where credit's due, Helen wrote a great story. She made us sound like real heroes, didn't she, Em? And after all that prying, trying to find out who you were—maybe she wasn't such a hack after all."

"I wouldn't go that far," Emily said.

"She could have written about Phi—" Emily's steely glare stopped him in his tracks. "But she didn't, is all I'm saying."

Harriet's eyes shifted curiously between them.

Jerome shrugged. "Well, who knows, maybe I can use this newfound fame to get a decent acting gig for once."

Emily shot him a glance as she moved away from the window and towards the door. "Having your name in the papers isn't necessarily a good thing, Jerome."

She said goodbye to Harriet and Andrew, then headed back to her apartment. Jerome followed soon after.

"What is it?" he asked, finding her in the living room in front of the centre window.

Emily turned away, shaking her head as she stared down at the city street below.

"I just can't stop thinking about how this all could have been avoided. Why couldn't Marcia have stood up to her mother? Why couldn't she have just said no? And Melody; what the bloody hell was she thinking? Those people didn't care about her. Not really. And now she's going to prison for them."

Jerome scuffed his shoe against the carpet. "Like we said, Melody was lonely. Maybe a little unstable, too. She must have been feeling pretty bad about life to go to such extremes, just to feel part of something. You can't blame someone for feeling alone."

"No, but you can blame them for covering up a murder. What Franklyn did to Marcia was unforgivable. One of the worst things a person can do. And yes, Sam lost control of his feelings, and yes, he made a terrible mistake, but it should have all ended that day. Three people are dead now. Pamela and Melody will go to prison. Probably Marcia too, even though she's one of the victims. Meadow Pines is finished. It was all for nothing."

She heaved her shoulders then felt a sudden surge of anger shoot through her body and into her fists. She wanted nothing more than to pound them against the wall.

But she didn't.

Instead, Emily pinched her fingers together and drew in a deep breath.

"I'm sure there's some sort of twisted loyalty in the middle of it all," Jerome said, slowly nodding. "But you're right. It has all the tones of a Shakespearean tragedy."

Emily's face softened. "How are you doing, anyway?"

"Oh, you know—traumatised, terrified. Nothing several months of therapy and a barrel of red wine won't cure. At least I got a date out of it. How about you?"

Emily flinched. Her mind had flashed back to the lake. To vanishing beneath its murky depths.

"I almost gave up," she said, staring at Jerome. "I was sinking deeper and deeper. The water was filling my lungs and everything began to turn a sort of yellow. For a moment, I stopped trying to get back to the surface. I could hear a voice saying: Don't bother. Just go with it. Close your eyes and sleep. And for a moment, I listened to it.

"I thought: what is waiting for me on the surface? What is better than being underneath in the darkness? It was peaceful down there. Calm. I didn't have to worry about the past or the future. I didn't have to think about Phillip Gerard, or my mother, or what people believed or didn't believe about me. I was nothing. I'd ceased to exist. And just for a minute, it felt like pure joy."

"But you came back up," Jerome said, his eyes glistening.

"I did, didn't I?"

"There must have been a reason for that."

"You mean apart from you saving my life? Again."

"Yeah, about that. Can you please stop putting yourself in harm's way? Or if you insist on repeatedly staring death in the face, could you at least do it in an official capacity? I don't know, join the police force like I keep telling you. Or get a private investigator license or something." He shook his head wearily. "All this fighting crime is doing nothing for my stress levels."

Emily glanced away. "I'm sorry. The last thing I want is for you to get hurt."

"And I don't want you to get hurt, either." They were quiet for a long while, the distant hum of the city below filling the silence. Then Jerome looked up. "So what was the reason?"

"Hmm?"

"Why did you change your mind about being fish food at the bottom of the lake?"

Emily glanced at him and shrugged a shoulder. "Just that in spite of all the mayhem, I decided I quite like my life after all."

"Glad to hear it," Jerome said, a devilish smile making his lips curl sharply. "Besides, drowning is never a good look. All that bloating . . ."

The sun was sinking over the cityscape, burning through the pollution and casting the sky in an unnatural shade of neon tangerine. Emily watched its descent, trying to stay in the present.

"The past is in the past," she said. "There's nothing we can do to change it. And who knows what's waiting for us in the future? So let's just live our lives one day at a time." She paused, mulling over her thoughts. "Perhaps I really did learn something at Meadow Pines."

"Me too," Jerome said.

"What's that?"

"That I'm never leaving this magnificent city again."

Emily rolled her eyes. Then she smiled. "Thank you. For everything."

Jerome shrugged and nudged her with his arm.

They stood at the window, watching the sunset. Eventually, Jerome's empty stomach lured him away to the nearest burger bar; a weekend of murder and mung beans had finally taken its toll.

Emily remained perfectly still, staying in the present, trying not to think about the future. But it was proving difficult. A spark of excitement had ignited her heart and she longed to know what tomorrow might bring.

DEAR READER

I have always been interested in meditation and have practiced light, daily sessions to help improve my focus before writing. I have never explored deep meditation such as Vipassanā. While most practitioners agree it is an intense yet rewarding experience, there are a number of recorded cases in which some people have experienced extreme anxiety, depression, and in rare cases, a complete emotional breakdown.

The character of Franklyn Hobbes was inspired by the real-life case of Aaron Alexis, who shot dead twelve people inside the Washington Navy Yard in 2013. Alexis suffered from severe mental illness, and it was alleged that he'd become addicted to transcendental meditation, pushing his already fractured mind to its limits.

It is not my intention with Mind For Murder to criticise the practice of Vipassanā, but rather to explore the strengths and limitations of our unconscious.

ABOUT THE AUTHOR

British writer Malcolm Richards crafts dark mystery & suspense thrillers to keep you guessing from the edge of your seat. He is the author of the Emily Swanson series, in which the titular sleuth tries to redeem her guilty past by helping others, and the Devil's Cove trilogy, which was a finalist in the 2018 Holyer an Gof Cornish book awards.

His first novel, The Hiding House, was published in 2012 and tells the story of two young siblings uncovering a dark web of family secrets after being left alone at their grandmother's isolated woodland home.

Previously, Malcolm worked for several years in the special education sector, teaching and supporting children with complex needs. Born and raised in Cornwall, he spent twenty-two years living in London before settling in the Somerset countryside.

For more information visit:

www.malcolmrichardsauthor.com

Printed in Great Britain
by Amazon

42492449R00281